Harry: to himself

K M Ballard

back
story
press

Published by Back Story Press

Printed and bound by CPI Group (UK) Ltd, Croydon, CR0 4YY

ISBN: 978-0-9928203-0-5

Harry: to himself

I
2008

I stand at the door, hesitate, then knock. For a few moments, silence. I hold my breath. Shortly, faint sounds of footsteps approach from within and the door is opened. A woman stands there, smiling. I like her immediately. 'I'm very sorry to disturb you,' I begin, not having thought about what to say, 'but some of my family used to live in this house.' Like a child with a flag at a victory parade, I wave a small faded photograph at her. 'Look, I have a picture.' I hand it over, my credential for being here.

While she inspects it, I glance back at my friend Clare, waiting patiently in the car with her children. We have been driving up the lane slowly, looking for the house, trying to match it with the photo. When we find it, we park at a discreet distance. There's no doubt that we're in the right place. I feel strangely excited, unsettled. Little seems to have changed about the dwelling, an end-of-terrace cottage. A plain wooden front door with an oval glass and the tiniest of porches over it. One upstairs and one downstairs sash window, each framed by some modest decorative brickwork. I can hardly believe how the house itself has materialised before me so similar to its earlier portrait, even after this much time.

Were it not for the front garden, I could almost believe that time moved imperceptibly backwards as we drove down the lane. In the photo, the cottage is half-hidden by an abundance of what look like wild roses, although they are reduced to smudges on the faded print. They almost fill the tiny patch. They have been trained up the side of the door and over the porch, and seem to have encroached on the narrow path. I can remember when I first examined the picture, thinking that all the smudges were bushes and flowers. I scanned the photograph and enlarged it to twice its size. Only then, zooming in, did I notice the figures standing in the garden, just to the right of the door, a woman, and two boys standing either side of her, her stance suggesting she has her arms around them. But they are only faintly visible among the foliage, hindering identification. The roses have been cleared now and replaced by a gravel driveway. The cottage is more readily accessible, although it's hard to guess what kind of person might live in it. There's a vehicle on the drive and the upstairs window is open. Someone is obviously at home. We sit in the car, considering what to do next.

'Why don't you go and knock?' says Clare. She can see I'm hesitant, although I can't fully explain why. 'You've nothing to lose. Go on,' she prompts again, lifting my handbag from my lap and giving me a gentle push. So I get out.

'I'm Jennie, by the way. Would you like to come in?' asks the woman. Already, it feels as if I know her. She's about my age, petite, casually dressed, unthreatened.

'I have my friend with me – and her three children.'

6

'You're more than welcome, all of you.'

I cannot refuse. She is eager for me to go in and see the house and I cannot deny myself this opportunity. I wave at Clare to get out of the car and the boys spill out behind her.

'Perhaps the children would like to go into the garden.'

They dart round the side and disappear. Jennie beckons us across the threshold and leads us into the kitchen at the back while I hurriedly tell her enough to make our connection clear. 'I'm researching my family history,' I explain. *I am searching for Harry and Ron.*

'That's fascinating. I want to hear all about it,' she says, genuinely interested.

In the kitchen, I tell her more about the photograph, retrieved from an attic to find its way into my possession. I show her how Harry, so meticulous, had written the address on the back with the simple statement 'We lived here more than 40 years', and provide her with the few details I know about Harry and Ron's upbringing. Jennie has brought up sons here too. She shows us a photograph of these two gangly lads building a giant snowman one winter. He seems half as tall as the house itself. She makes us tea while we sit at the kitchen table. I imagine Harry and Ron sitting beside us, writing and colouring.

'Go and have a look round upstairs if you'd like to,' she offers, sensing what it is I need from this house.

Clare stays in the kitchen to chat and I creep up the narrow stairs that turn at the top onto a tiny landing. There are three bedrooms. The biggest one, at the front, must be Jennie's. From the door, I glimpse a dress thrown over a chair, high-heeled shoes abandoned on the rug, beads and earrings scattered on the dressing table. The rooms at the back are the children's rooms. One of them has barely enough space for the single bed. But it is possible to lie in this bed and look out of the window. I am tempted to do so, but this would feel like taking a liberty. One of Jennie's sons has slept here. Maybe Harry or Ron has slept here (I wish I knew which one), and I imagine them alternately, lying in the narrow bed at dusk watching the light fade from the fields.

In the garden below, Clare's boys are rampaging around, loving the long charge from the kitchen door to the wire fence at the bottom which divides the back garden from the neighbouring farmland. I have read about these fields of childhood in Harry's letters to Fred, how he and Ron would dash across to the farm to get butter and milk for their mother, or how they would walk more sedately in their Sunday best to have tea with Mrs Buckley at Linden Hill. There are old trees too in the distance, beyond the farm, the ancient trees of Warren Woods, where they carved their initials in a trunk one hot summer when they were home from school. I have pictures of Harry and Ron in this garden, as adults, with their wives. I wonder, is there any place where they will seem more present than in this house?

Reluctantly, I go back downstairs, leaving Harry and Ron playing with the simple wooden toys their father has made for them. In the kitchen, I sit with Jennie and Clare while we drink tea. Jennie takes juice out to the garden for the boys. Clare and I exchange brief words. 'I'm so glad you made me knock,' I tell her.

Jennie invites us to stroll round the garden. It's simply laid out, and no longer like the garden Harry and Ron showed to Ella and Ivy the first time they brought them home. But the open fields beckon now as I imagine they once did to them. At the bottom of the garden, I turn to look back at the house, half expecting to see a child's hand waving at me from one of the upstairs windows.

Soon, we think we might have outstayed our welcome and suggest it could be time to go. Jennie is reluctant to release us. It seems to have engaged her, this quest of mine. She offers to show us the deeds of the house and back in the kitchen pulls a large folder of documents from a cupboard. She has a ground plan of the cottages, and the farm and the surrounding lanes. She smoothes it out on the table and spread before me is the little world that they inhabited. A square mile was their playground. A short distance further took them to the village shop and the church and Mrs Gertrude Buckley's. I have been to the church and the churchyard, although this is not where they are buried. What must it have been like, I wonder, living here, and leaving here? What did Harry and Ron feel when, as small boys, they had to go away to school? And for Harry, that second and final departure, what tumult of emotions must he have experienced then? I wonder again who took the photograph that has led me to this spot so many years later, how Harry came to keep it among his precious possessions, and when he inscribed on the back the clue I would need to find it.

II
1898 – 1918

Harry and Ron's parents had met just a few miles away from Bottle Green, at the public house in Warren Row. Harry never forgot the story, or the evening his mother related it, the last summer of the Great War when the two of them were sitting together in the back garden of what is now Jennie's cottage. He was eleven years old.

'I was working as a maid at The Old House at Home,' she told Harry. She liked the work and the atmosphere of the inn now that a new landlord and his wife had taken charge. They were kind to Violet, and treated her like a daughter. The landlord decided that a new sign was needed to commemorate his stewardship, and a local man was commissioned. Violet had first set eyes on Harry's father late one afternoon when he cycled into the yard, wobbling somewhat as he tried to steer with one hand and carry the half-completed sign with the other. Violet was dusting the sills in the saloon, and stepped back from the window to avoid being seen. The young man dismounted awkwardly, and Violet smiled to herself as she watched him and the signboard disentangle themselves from the bicycle. There was no one else about. Sign in hand, the man looked around the yard for a few moments and disappeared from view. Violet carried on dusting. Then he reappeared empty-handed, jumped back on his bicycle and sped down Warren Lane unencumbered.

Early the next morning he was back at the inn, this time with paint and varnish, ready to complete the commission. It was a fine day and he set up a makeshift easel in the yard. The landlord went out to speak to him about his work.

'Were you spying on him, Ma?' Harry wanted to know.

'Well, I liked looking out of the windows while I was doing my work. I wouldn't call it spying exactly.'

'What happened next? How did you get to speak to him?'

'At lunchtime the landlord asked me to take out some beer and sandwiches. Your father was working in the yard, cleaning his brushes. He must have heard me as I came down the steps, because he turned round and we smiled at each other.'

'What did he say?'

'He didn't say anything. Neither of us did. I think we both wanted to. I just put the tray down on an old crate and went back inside. Then all afternoon I was wondering whether I should go out and collect the tray but I left it where it was.'

'If you'd collected the tray you could have spoken to him,' said Harry with a redundant pang of anxiety. Supposing Violet had missed her opportunity? But she was determined that she would speak to him the following day when he came back to finish and hang the sign. So when, once again, the landlord asked Violet to take some lunch out for the worker, Violet was ready. She still remembered their first, unremarkable conversation:

'Is it nearly finished?'

'Just the border to do, and the varnish, and then I can hang it.'

'Will the varnish be dry?'

'Dry enough.'

'Can I watch you put it up?'

By late afternoon the sign was finished and ready to hang. Drinkers had started to arrive after their day's work. Harry's father had fetched a ladder and propped it precariously against the signpost. The landlord went out to hold the ladder steady for him. Some of the drinkers saw what was going on and went out to watch. Violet and the landlord's wife went out to join them. The hanging of the sign turned into a ceremony. The small crowd clapped when the young man let the sign hang free. It swung slightly as he let go, and the evening sun flashed on the newly painted 'House at Home'. As he was coming back down the ladder, it had wobbled slightly. He put out his arm to steady himself, and Violet reached up to assist him.

George and Violet were married a few months later. On her first morning as a married woman, Violet woke up in the cottage at Bottle Green and could have cried with joy. It was late autumn, there was an early frost on the trees and on the fields, but their home was snug and warm and Violet hoped she would live there for the rest of her life. Within a year, she gave birth to a son and they named him Frederick after his father, George Frederick Elston. On the eve of the new century, Violet and George sat in their armchairs by the fire, little Fred asleep in his mother's arms, as they contemplated with optimism the years that lay ahead.

Harry was born when Fred was nearly eight. The only concern in Violet's early years of happily married life had been the fear that she would not have another child. The April day of Harry's arrival was warm and sunny. Fred was sent off to play with some other boys in the village. When he came home, Violet was sitting up in bed holding his little brother. Fred came over, the first time he had been close to a new-born baby.

'What's his name?' asked Fred, taking the baby's tiny hand.

'We've named him Henry. Henry George,' said Violet, 'but we'll call him Harry.'

And when Fred had had time to marvel at Harry's delicate fingers and the sleepy, contented expression on his face, she sent him back out to find his friends. She could hear his excited shouts ringing down the lane, a perfect counterpoint to the calm happiness of her bedroom.

Harry was a placid baby. Unlike Fred, who, early on, wriggled to be free of any constraint, Harry was never more content than when his mother was holding him close. Only her voice could soothe him. When he fell and hurt himself, only her attentions could make the pain and the stinging stop. As he grew into a little boy, he became solicitous of his mother, and was fretful unless she was nearby. When Ron was born two years later, Harry, far from exhibiting

16

the jealousy which Violet had anticipated, was immediately protective of his younger brother, and would hush him if he started to cry. When Violet was cradling Ron in her lap, Harry would nestle up against her and she would put her free arm around him and hug them both together.

For several years, the pattern of family life at Bottle Green remained constant. Every weekday morning, George took his bicycle and set off to do his work as a carpenter and decorator. Fred had already left for school, but Violet, Harry and Ron would stand at the door and wave goodbye. George rang his bicycle bell as he turned into the lane and out of sight. Sometimes in the evening, if he wasn't too tired, he would take some off-cuts of wood, lay out his carpentry tools on the kitchen table, and make wooden toys for Harry and Ron. He made them a train and let them paint it with whatever paint he had left over from his work. It grew, section by section, starting with the engine, then a first class carriage and, over several weeks, second and third class carriages too. George made a second train, so the boys could have one each, and they pulled them round the garden on a string, imagining journeys to distant places of which they had no idea. He made boxes in which they could keep their treasures, carving their initials into the lids so there would be no confusion as to which was which. One particularly warm summer he made cricket bats, stumps and bails, and taught the boys the rudiments of the game. When Fred came home from school, the three brothers played a match of sorts in the garden, and when their father got home he was implored to join in. Violet

17

watched them from the kitchen window as she prepared the evening meal, her heart replete with love.

While Harry and Ron were close in years and content to play in each other's company, Fred was eager to look further afield for companionship. Even before he had started school, he had made friends with Robert Kenton, who lived further down the lane. Once they had become classmates, they were inseparable. As Fred and Robert grew older, their heads filled with relatively modest schemes for running away from home to see the world and more outrageous ones for building marvellous machines to take them to the moon or let them travel through time. Robert formulated the plans, and Fred elaborated them. Violet laughed when they showed her the sketches of their prototypes. She looked forward, she said, to seeing their names in the newspaper.

When Fred was nearly thirteen, a troop of boy scouts was formed in the village, and Robert announced to Fred that they were enrolling. Thoughts of their inventions were soon superseded by their obsession with scoutcraft. Two or three times a week, they would report for duty and in what seemed like no time at all they had both qualified as first class scouts. They were in the same patrol, the Ravens, and they would *kar-kaw* to each other in greeting when Robert knocked on the door for Fred. On summer evenings when the upstairs windows were wide open, Harry and Ron listened for them *kar-kaw*ing down the lane on their way to patrol meetings. In a meteoric rise, Robert, who was a few months older than Fred, was appointed as patrol leader.

Fred was overwhelmed with excitement when Robert asked him to be his corporal.

Over meals, Fred talked incessantly to his parents about what he was learning as a scout and his personal importance to the Great British Empire. He was expected to do a good turn every day, and Violet would send him on errands, make him hang out the washing, or scrape the mud off George's bike. Fred wasn't so keen on the good turns. It was the outdoor activities which he loved. Harry and Ron listened with open mouths as Fred, always keen to impress his younger brothers, related his scouting adventures. It was entirely thanks to Fred that the patrol had managed to light their campfire and hoist the Union Jack on a makeshift flagpole. If Fred had not had his wits about him, his patrol camp would undoubtedly have suffered a humiliating attack by the Owls or Kestrels. If his powers of observation had not been so acute, his patrol would have been utterly lost on a trail. Sometimes, Violet let Fred take Harry and Ron to Warren Woods to play. He showed them the secluded hollow where they had built their camp. He taught them to march, and to salute. He made Ron pretend to be injured or almost dead so he could show Harry the various ways to save a life. Harry enjoyed these first aid lessons, and the way they made him feel useful. Once, they took an old blanket to the woods and made a stretcher which was just strong enough for Fred and Harry to carry home the insensible Ron, much to the amusement of their parents. Fred could locate all the points of the compass and he showed his brothers how to keep watch on railway bridges and embankments, although never explaining who or what they were watching for. He told Harry and Ron he was going to be a soldier when he grew up and they stared at him in admiration. 'Country first, self second,' he taught them.

Of all the things she liked about family life, Violet was fondest of those days when her husband was at work and her eldest son at school, and she had Harry and Ron to herself. She took them for walks round the village, stopping for groceries or to talk to friends and neighbours. Once or twice a week, they cut across the fields to Westacotts Farm to buy milk and butter. In late summer, they collected blackberries in the lanes and took them home to make jam. In winter, they fed the birds on scraps and watched the clouds for signs of snow. Indoors, Violet worked in the kitchen, cooking and washing, while Harry and Ron sat at the table, learning to colour and to write their names. Sometimes, she taught them the songs she had known as a child and the three of them would sing together. When she was a girl, Violet had learned to play the piano, and she pretended to accompany them on an imaginary kitchen table keyboard. Harry and Ron laughed with delight at the muted clatter. Violet was making a rug from scraps of material, and when Harry was old enough she let him help her by choosing which coloured strip she should use next. Sometimes, she let him hold the hook and pull the rag gently through the stretched hessian. But he loved it most of all when she walked round the garden with him, teaching him the names of the plants, and sharing her plans for the flowers and vegetables she would grow. Her own father had been a gardener, and he had taught her the names which she now passed on to her son.

When Harry and Ron were old enough, Violet started taking them to church. They didn't mind this, even though it was a long time to sit still and listen. They set off early, while George and Fred, who were brisk walkers and always caught them up, would leave ten minutes later. Harry and Ron liked the walk to church and to hear the bells grow louder and clearer as they approached the churchyard. Sometimes, they could even hear the organ playing ready for the start of the service. Harry loved the music he heard in church. It was different from the songs his mother taught them. It thrilled him to hear the organ start the hymn and, with a held chord followed by a momentary pause, cue the appointed moment for the congregation to join in. He hardly understood the words they were singing, but the resonance of pipe and voice on stone echoed through him for many hours afterwards.

When they had been attending services for some months, their mother took them one day for a walk into the village, in the direction of the church. Harry was confused. It wasn't Sunday. It was mid-afternoon. No bells were ringing and not even the faintest trace of the organ could be heard. His mother was carrying a small bunch of flowers from their garden.

'Why are we going this way? Are we going to church, Mother?' Harry asked.

'Not today, not to church. But near the church. We're going to a special place I want to show you.'

'What's that?'

'You'll see.'

They turned into the lane that led to the church. A little way down, there was a gate on the opposite side. Harry had never noticed this before. It was almost hidden by the trees and bushes that crowded the lane. Violet unhooked the gate and ushered them into this unknown region. Harry stepped forward cautiously, Ron following behind him. It was a grassy area surrounded on all four sides by dark thick foliage. The only way in or out was the small gate they had entered by. The sun was bright, and casting distinct shadows from the many crosses and gravestones which stood before them. Birds were singing, gently, intermittently. The peacefulness made Harry feel he could only whisper. 'What's this place for, Ma? Why are we here?

'Let's go over there and I'll show you,' said Violet. She led them to the far corner where a dark damp mound of earth covered in fresh flowers marked a recent burial. 'Do you remember Mr Thompson, who worked in the village store? He's been very ill and you haven't seen him for a while, have you? When people are very ill, sometimes they don't get better and they die.'

'Has Mr Thompson died?'

'Yes, I'm afraid so. His wife is very sad, and so are his children, even though they are grown up.'

'Why are we here?'

22

'When people die we put them in special wooden boxes, and place the boxes in the ground so their bodies can go to sleep. We call this sleeping place their grave.'

'But don't they go to heaven?'

'Yes, their spirits go to heaven but their bodies stay here.'

Harry absorbed this information carefully. His mother placed her flowers down with the others.

'Why are there flowers?'

'We bring flowers to show we remember the person who has died, and that we miss them. In a little while, Mr Thompson will have a headstone or a cross on his grave and Mrs Thompson will ask the stonemason to carve his name on it so we always know which place is his.'

Harry stared at the grave. The flowers from their garden looked different here, sad as well as beautiful. Then he turned to see what Ron was doing and walked away in pursuit of his brother.

Violet left Harry and Ron to wander around by themselves. They seemed not to mind the presence of the dead, picking their way carefully among the graves like adventurers discovering a lost and unfamiliar world. Harry had started to read and he managed to make out some of the names on the headstones, which he then spoke out loud. He wondered if the dead people could hear him above the ground, enunciating them to his brother.

The following Sunday they went to church as usual. As they walked up the path, Harry suddenly realised something about the churchyard. 'Why are there graves

23

here, Ma? Why are there some here and some in the place you took us to?'

'When the churchyard was full, they made a new place for graves on the other side of the road.'

'Will we all be buried there when we die?'

'Yes, I expect so. I hope so. But that's a very very long time away. So long, you can't imagine it.'

She took Harry's hand and squeezed it reassuringly. He looked up at her and smiled, thinking, as they walked into church, of all the people he knew who would one day die and how they would all be gathered together, secluded, in the graveyard across the road, where the living would come, softly, and bring them flowers.

When Harry was seven, his older brother became obsessed with football and war broke out with Germany. Fred had learnt to play football at school and started going with his friends to Elm Park to watch the Reading team. Johnny Holt and Herbert Smith became his new idols. After matches, he always came home energised and talkative, entertaining his brothers by taking them into the garden to re-enact his interpretation of the tense moments which led up to the Reading goals, Harry and Ron positioned as defenders, and a bucket and a flowerpot marking the target. Even when his team had lost, Fred was able to draw something positive from their performance – the better side, who were unfortunate to be the victims of so many unnoticed fouls, or unlucky to have missed crucial chances to score by a whisker. Fred loved everything about football, not least the rough camaraderie of boys and men which had drawn him previously to the scouts. Violet saw how much this alliance mattered to her son and felt a twinge of anxiety. The rest of the family indulged Fred's latest obsession with mild amusement, and George encouraged it as a distraction for his younger brothers from the mounting concerns of the war.

For Fred, the issues of the war were inevitably articulated through his beloved game. Within a few months of Britain joining the conflict, he was frequently haranguing George with his views about the football league. Prominent public figures, authors and churchmen had been writing to the newspapers and making speeches about the professional players who had not responded to Kitchener's recruitment drive. Every week, the crowds at the matches were dwindling as more and more men joined up, and the irony of twenty-two able-bodied men kicking a ball around the pitch was evident to all the fans who had come to watch them. As much as Fred loved the matches on Saturday afternoons, he wanted his heroes to distinguish themselves on the battlefield rather than on the football pitch. With a surge of youthful patriotism, Fred attempted to convince his father that the players' contracts should be no obstacle if they were needed by their country. George was inclined to agree, although his was a somewhat broader perspective on what the footballers' absence would signify. In order to avoid questions he would rather not discuss with his son, he changed the subject. Fred had left school the previous year and was now working with George as an apprentice, and generally an enthusiastic one at that, so it was usually possible to turn his attention to the more immediate concerns of their daily undertakings.

One Saturday in early 1915, when many players had already joined the newly-formed 'football' battalion of the Middlesex Regiment, Fred came home in a different mood from his usual post-match ebullience. Instead of going upstairs to find Harry and Ron, he sat down at the kitchen table with his father and told him how a group of representatives from the Parliamentary Recruiting Committee had come onto the pitch at half time to call for more army volunteers. The mayor was there too and made a speech. A million men had already joined up, many more were needed. Hundreds of football players across the nation had responded to the campaign and now it was up to remaining fans to follow their example. A recruitment office had been set up in a nearby hotel, and a recruiting sergeant and medical officer would be waiting there over the coming weeks for those who came to enlist. The fans had cheered and waved their rattles, Fred told his father, but he said nothing of what he thought might be going through their minds.

Harry and Ron were to have an outing. On their walks about the village with their mother, she had occasionally pointed out to them a very fine house, set back from the road, and half hidden by trees. Harry had always longed to go inside. Even in its secluded position, he could see the house had many windows and he could only guess at the number of rooms they represented. His own house had seven windows, including the very small pantry window at the side. Just from looking at their position, it was easy to visualise the layout of the interior. Linden Hill, on the other hand, with its many intriguing windows, would be a wonderful place to explore. The house was owned by an army colonel and his wife. Colonel Buckley was away at war, but every Sunday morning Mrs Buckley attended church alone, sitting in a front pew with a space left beside her for her absent husband. This respectable lady was in charge of flower arrangements for the church and, for some months now, Violet had belonged to her little army of women who prepared the flowers on Saturday afternoon. Mrs Buckley had no children of her own, and started to take a great interest in Violet's. She liked Fred, but saw that he was frustrated by the confines of Bottle Green and just biding his time until life offered him a way of leaving the village. Harry was different. She'd noticed the way he stayed by his mother's side when they came to church. When Violet had first introduced Harry and Ron to Mrs Buckley she had been struck by his premature seriousness.

One Sunday morning, as Violet, Harry and Ron left church, George and Fred having already set off for home at a considerable pace, Mrs Buckley invited them to tea the following day at Linden Hill. Violet was flattered at the compliment to her well-behaved children. She liked Mrs Buckley, who showed no air of social superiority despite her husband's status and their evident wealth. Harry was beside himself with excitement. 'Do you think she'll let us explore all the rooms?' he said to Violet.

'I don't think so, Harry, and you mustn't ask.'

The tea was a great success. It was a cold day and when they arrived they were ushered into Mrs Buckley's corner sitting room where a fire was blazing. This room alone had three windows, and Harry managed to sneak a look at the garden before taking his seat. He could hardly believe how expansive it seemed when compared to his own. Mrs Buckley, glad of the boys' youthful company, asked them

28

lots of questions about their home life but particularly
about what they were learning at school. Listening
patiently, she nodded and smiled at their answers. Then, so
she could talk with Violet, she invited the boys to play by
themselves for a while. On a table in the corner of the room
were three wooden boxes, which contained some of the
Colonel's childhood toys. Mrs Buckley had had them
brought down especially. Standing among the boxes was a
model of Noah's ark, complete with little windows and a
working door, and in the largest of the boxes the boys
found all the painted animals and the figures of Noah, his
wife, his sons and their wives. They took all the figures out,
cleared the boxes from the table, and lined up the creatures
in pairs, the largest at one end and the little birds and the
mice at the other. The human guardians they arranged in a
family group, ready to oversee the boarding of the ark. In
the second box there were glass marbles of various sizes in
watery shades of blue and green. They left these, uncertain
where or how to play with these shiny, delicate baubles. In
the last box they found ranks of lead soldiers, which they
put into line along with the animals. While they played,
Mrs Buckley talked with Violet, in slightly hushed voices,
about the acquaintances they shared at church and then
about the progress of the war, and lads from the village
who had joined up. Violet told her about the recruitment
drive Fred had witnessed at the football match. Mrs
Buckley was thoughtful for a few moments, then she turned
to see what the boys were doing. When she saw how they
had put the painted figures in rows, soldiers lined up with

Noah's animals, she laughed heartily and the boys laughed with her.

The subdued mood in which Fred had come home after the football match did not lift. He got up early every morning, always ready to go to work with his father, but in the evenings he seemed distant and preoccupied. When George talked to him about the jobs they had to do that week, he showed none of his previous enthusiasm. Violet liked to chatter to him about the goings-on in the village. He listened out of politeness but his eyes gave away his lack of interest. He stopped playing games with Harry and Ron and instead walked down the lane to visit Robert Kenton. When she saw the abandoned looks on their faces, Violet got out the playing cards herself. George and Violet watched as Fred disengaged himself from his family, but neither of them knew exactly what was wrong or what to do.

By March, Fred seemed more remote than ever. Then one Saturday he came back from the football match buoyed up, nervous. He asked George and Violet to come into the sitting room. He had some news for them. He wanted his brothers to hear it too. They sat down, but Fred remained standing to announce to them that he had been to the recruitment office to enlist. He was going to be a soldier in the Middlesex Regiment.

Violet was disbelieving. 'But how can you be? You're not even sixteen yet. You're nowhere near old enough.'

'I'm not going to lie to you, Mother, but I told a lie to them. I told them I was nearly nineteen and they accepted

30

it. Robert was with me and he told them he was nineteen already.'

'You were both there? You've been planning this together? Surely they can see you're not old enough.'

'Well, whether they can see it or not, they've let us in and we have to report to barracks on Monday.'

'I don't believe this. There's been a huge mistake. You're not going.' She burst into tears.

George, more pragmatic, took over. 'Are you sure this is what you want, son?'

'I've been thinking about it for weeks. Everyone's joining up. They don't seem bothered if you're old enough or not as long as you're fit and strong. They liked it when we said we were in the scouts. They said scouts make good soldiers.'

'They don't make good liars though,' said Violet.

'I couldn't stop thinking about what they said at the football match. I want to take part. I want to do my duty. That's what we've been taught. That's what you've always told me.'

'You're too young. Your father and I can write to the regiment and tell them and they'll have to refuse to take you.'

'I know I'm under-age, Ma, but so are lots of recruits. Please let me go. I can take care of myself, I know I can.'

Violet was lost for words. Suddenly realising that Harry and Ron had been witnesses to this dreadful scene, she got up and ushered them out of the room. She put on their coats and boots and took them off for a walk down the lane.

'Is Fred going to be a soldier now, Ma?' asked Harry.

'Not if I have anything to do with it.'

They walked round the village until it started to get dark. They walked in silence, first at the brisk pace of Violet's anger, and then more slowly. By the time they got home, Violet seemed to have calmed down. Fred had gone out. She asked George to take the boys up to bed while she made herself some tea. When George came back down to the kitchen, they sat and talked and somehow, in the space of an hour, George convinced Violet to let Fred have his way. Then Violet wept once more for her son, and with a sense that the perfect happiness of her family life was somehow starting to disintegrate. Upstairs, Harry and Ron lay awake, bewildered, talking about Fred in whispers.

Their first letter from Fred after he left was written from his training barracks. He seemed in good spirits. He'd been issued with his equipment and was learning how to use a bayonet. He was getting used to the fifteen-mile training marches and the exhausting physical exercises. He and Robert were great companions and excited at being part of something on a grand scale. It was much better than the scouts, much better than football. As Violet read his letter, her anger with Fred abated. He had acted naively, thoughtlessly even, yet there was something honourable about his desire to do his duty. But nothing could convince her that there was anything honourable about the recruiting process which had wilfully ignored Fred and Robert's obvious youth.

All the time Fred was at training camp, Violet tried not to think about the possibility that he would be sent to the front. Surely his commanding officer had seen through Fred's lie and would make sure that he stayed in England. Much of the time she was more preoccupied with her husband. Although he had supported Fred's enlistment, George had not been the same since Fred had left. He was enervated, uncommunicative. His smiles were half-smiles, lacking warmth. Harry and Ron seemed to sense something was wrong and avoided their father by playing upstairs or in the garden. To Violet's mind, George looked washed out. She was sure he was losing weight. When Fred's letters came, he brightened up, but quickly relapsed into his more sombre mood once he had read them. Violet, Harry and Ron were left to write the replies.

Violet started to feel weighed down with worry, first about Fred, then about George. The happy early years of her marriage and their family life before the war seemed over and she felt helpless in the face of these new, possibly irreversible, circumstances. Letters of protest had started to appear in the newspaper from parents whose sons had also been allowed to join the army illegally, parents whose sons had not only lied about their ages but had given false names to prevent themselves being traced. At least Fred had been honest enough to tell his parents what he had done. When Violet's anxiety about her son or her husband overwhelmed her, she thought about writing to the war office to request Fred's immediate discharge. It was the only course of action she could think of which might turn back the clocks and make their family life perfect again.

Before Violet could make up her mind to disclose Fred's falsehood to the military authorities, another letter arrived which announced that he would be going to France in September. 'I know you will have been thinking all these months whether you should try to get me discharged but I have been happy here and I am looking forward to being part of the expeditionary force. Please don't try to stop me. If I am forced to come home I think I will just run away and join another regiment.' This time, Violet was too numb to cry over Fred's news. She sensed that he had become even more determined about his soldiering than when he first enlisted and she had little in reserve for a prolonged battle with her son. Besides, she knew what George would say about the matter, that he would take Fred's side whether he wanted him to go to France or not.

Fred was allowed to come home for a few days' leave before his departure. It was just like old times. Fred arrived in his uniform. There was no denying he looked the part, taller and stronger than when he had first gone away. They were all delighted to see each other. Harry and Ron made some flags to hang on the bushes that fronted the lane so that Fred would see them as he turned the bend. Every few minutes, they ran down to the gate to see if he was coming. Eventually, when he did arrive, they were in the back garden practising their cricket. He came straight out to find them, and they jumped up and down and cheered when they saw him. George and Violet followed Fred out and stood arm in arm watching their three sons celebrating their short-lived reunion.

With Fred in France, Violet grew more and more dependent on her younger sons. All day she worked mechanically at her tasks, becoming animated and more like her usual self only when Harry and Ron got home from school. Christmas approached. She sat them down at the kitchen table and asked them to write a long letter to Fred. Ron begged to be allowed to write it while Harry chipped in. It was the longest letter Ron had written:

'Dear Fred I hope you are well meny thanks for your nice letter what you sent ma. I hope your lads are well. Pa has got a cold and was sick. Harry is bisy at making his rug. I do like my watch for Sunday it is useful wen I want to now the time I honly have to get it out of my pocet and look at it. And evry night I always think of you and pray to God to bring you safe and well to us again. It has been a wet day for school. I am geting on alwrit at school and do you get very wet days were you are or frostee days I think I wood larf if I were to see you stamping about on the ice to get watter. I wish you were home I shood feele very happy if you can tell your ofisir if you kood have a weeks holiday. Pa is better now but he is not going to work yet. With love from all. A letter from your brothers Ron and Harry for Christmas time xxxxxxxxxxx.'

Harry watched Ron carefully as he wrote, sometimes helping him with the spellings. When Ron had finished, he asked Harry to read it aloud to Violet. She had already told

35

Harry it was unlikely that Fred would be home for Christmas, but he had kept this information to himself. He could remember Christmas the previous year, what fun he had had with Fred and Ron. The prospect of a depleted family group this year saddened Harry for Fred's sake, but at least Fred had Robert Kenton to talk to, and he still had Ron.

Robert Kenton had had a lot to do with Fred's enlistment. His older brother Albert had enlisted at the outbreak of war and had written to him from the front urging Robert to follow his example. 'Don't worry about your age,' the letter said. 'Lots of the lads here are not yet nineteen. And besides, what will you do if you stay at home?' Robert had been keen to join up, but knowing he was under-age he needed the moral support of having Fred with him. He had been with Fred at the football match and, seeing his friend's reaction to the recruitment campaigners, knew the time was right to broach the subject. But it had taken him several weeks to persuade Fred, those weeks when Fred was moody and remote, undecided whether he should bow to his friend's request or stay at home with the family who trusted him. Either step seemed like a betrayal. Eventually, and with some willingness, Fred had given way to Robert. Now, over a year later, he was writing home as he sat on an upturned crate in his billet a few miles from the River Somme, the distant sounds of the preliminary bombardment at the front line just enough to unsettle his concentration. It was the end of June, 1916.

Fred's mother and Robert's mother had been friends a long time. Shortly after Violet was married, she met Edith in the lane one morning on her way into the village. Edith lived a few hundred yards further down, beyond the next two bends, in a row of cottages that belonged to Westacotts Farm, where her husband William was a dairyman. Though she seemed barely older than Violet, Edith already had two children at school, and was evidently expecting another one very soon. Violet told Edith how she had met George in Warren Row, and how it had taken her a whole day and night to pluck up the courage to speak to him. In return, Edith told Violet how William had proposed to her one summer's morning just outside the cowshed when she had gone to the farm for milk. A few more such exchanges cemented their friendship. When Robert was born, Edith was very unwell and Violet had helped look after the older children, Jessie and Albert, until she had recovered, by which time Violet knew Fred was on the way. Over the years, they had watched each other's families grow and the friendship between Robert and Fred deepen.

When Fred enlisted, Violet suspected that he had done so under Robert's persuasion. As well as being angry with Fred and with the authorities, she was angry with Robert, but reluctant to voice her feelings and jeopardise her friendship with Edith. The day after Fred's announcement Violet had made her way down the lane to discuss the situation.

Edith broke the ice. 'I feel terrible about this. I'm afraid Robert may have talked Fred into it. I'm so sorry, Violet.'

'We've decided to let him go. If we don't, I think he'll just run away anyway. His mind seems made up.'

'Are you afraid?'

'Afraid of what? Fred leaving home? Learning to fight?'

'Of the war going on and on. Of them seeing action, being injured, being killed.'

'I can't bear to think of it like that.'

'I can't stop myself.' Edith pulled her shawl closer round her shoulders, twisting the edges together tightly, and for the first time it occurred to Violet that Edith might have taken the news even more badly than she had herself.

The Somme Offensive had already started when the letter Fred had written in the billet reached Bottle Green. 'My dear Mother and Father, we are just out for a bit of a spell and I have a little time to call my own. Your letter arrived today and many thanks for the photos of Harry and Ron which are jolly nice. I'm absolutely in the pink, couldn't be better so no need for you to worry. Robert is still with me and we are using Pears soap as you told us. We are resting here before we get ready to meet Old Fritzy...'

Harry wanted to know who Old Fritzy was. He sounded like the funny old man who lived in the village and always waved to Harry and Ron from his window as they walked past on their way to school.

George nodded to Violet to explain. 'Old Fritzy isn't just one person, Harry. He's lots of people. It's a name for all the German soldiers that Fred's army are fighting.'

'How many of them are there?'

'Well, lots of them, I expect. But there are lots of soldiers in Fred's battalion.'

'Fred's a good soldier, isn't he? He'll know what to do in the battle.'

'Yes, that's why he did lots of training before he went to France. So that he can be prepared for the battle.'

'That's like being in the scouts. Fred always said he had to be prepared.'

Violet doubted whether the preparations of the scout troop would be of much value to Fred in the coming onslaught. What use were observational skills in a barrage of smoke or in the confusing mud of no man's land? And what good was basic first aid when so many injured bodies were beyond repair? But she kept these thoughts to herself and assured Harry and Ron that Fred would indeed be prepared, at the same time as doubting her own readiness for the worst that the war could bring.

If any members of the Elston family had looked out of one of their two front windows early on the morning of July 21st, they might have seen a uniformed cyclist riding by, on his way to the Kentons' house with a telegram, bringing the news that their eldest son Albert, the admired older brother who had persuaded Robert to lie about his age and join up, had been killed in action some miles north of the line where Robert and Fred were serving.

A few hours later, Edith Kenton stood crying on Violet's doorstep. Violet took her into the kitchen and made her drink some tea. Not knowing what to say, she sat with her at the table, holding her hand and stroking her back while she sobbed. 'Tell me it's not true, that they've made a mistake,' Edith choked through her tears. 'Tell me Albert's not really dead.' She was inconsolable. Violet sent the boys down the lane to fetch Mr Kenton, who arrived looking as ghastly as death itself. George shook hands with him and led him into the kitchen where he sat weeping next to his wife, still clutching the telegram in his hand. Time passed. It was hard to tell how much. Harry and Ron crept upstairs to their bedroom and played quietly, mainly keeping their attention on their toys, but every now and then catching each other's eyes, awkwardly.

After the Kentons had gone, Harry ventured downstairs, where the lingering sense of grief made him feel like an intruder. His parents looked as bad as if it was their own son who had died. He had a pressing question he wanted to ask. 'Ma, will they bring Albert home and bury him in the graveyard next to Mr Johnson?'

Violet couldn't help the faintest of smiles. She thought about her answer. 'They may not be able to, Harry. It might be best if they bury him in France.'

'But who will put the flowers on his grave?'

'I'm sure one of the other soldiers will.'

'Fred's not going to die, is he?'

Harry saw his parents exchange glances.

'Fred can take care of himself,' said George. 'He'll be all right.'

The next morning, George didn't go to work. Mother said he was 'under the weather'. He stayed in bed and Violet took him his food there. But it remained untouched. Harry went up with the newspaper and talked to him for a

41

while but his father seemed listless, distant. After a while, George dozed off, and Harry went back down to his colouring at the kitchen table.

Throughout July, August, September, Violet watched the Kentons carefully. Inevitably, Albert had been buried in France, and his commanding officer had duly written to say what a brave soldier he had been, much respected by the men in his company. This was of no consolation to Mrs Kenton. Violet called on her every two or three days, more if she could find an excuse to do so, and endured the misery of watching her friend diminish week by week. Time is certainly not a healer, not in any true sense of the word, thought Violet, who could hardly remember what Edith looked like when she smiled. She took Edith bread when she had been baking, or some flowers from the garden, but these gifts were barely noticed. Sometimes, she made tea for Edith and Jessie, and tried to sustain a conversation about what was going on in the village. It was difficult, though, not to stumble upon a subject that would remind them of the war. Sometimes, Violet took Harry and Ron down the lane with her, but their cheerful presence seemed to do little other than bring back to Edith recollections of the son she had lost and the son she feared to lose.

One autumn evening, Violet went out yet again to visit Edith. Harry and Ron were sitting in the kitchen with their father. He was mending a clock and half watching the boys, who were playing with the painted metal soldiers Mrs Buckley had given them the previous Christmas.

'Do you have to go out, Ma?' asked Ron. 'I'm not feeling too bright.' He did look flushed. Violet felt his forehead. Maybe he was running a temperature, it was hard to tell.

'You'll be all right, Ron. Father and Harry can look after you. I won't be long.' She seemed anxious to go.

It occurred to Harry that this was a strange time for Violet to walk down to Mrs Kenton's. She normally visited her while he and Ron were at school or they all went together as soon as school was over. He wanted to ask why she was going now, when it was almost dusk and with Ron out of sorts, but something about her manner deterred him. Father didn't seem to mind so it was probably best to say nothing.

After she had gone, George abandoned the clock and settled down in the sitting room to read the newspaper. The boys decided to write a letter to Fred. They had written to him every week since he had been away. They didn't want him to feel homesick. And they both felt, without openly acknowledging it, that if they kept writing they could somehow keep Fred safe from what had happened to Albert.

When the boys went to bed, Violet had still not returned. George tucked them in.

'How are you feeling, Ron?'

'Not bad, Pa. Don't worry.'

'Goodnight then. Sleep well.'

But they didn't sleep. The blankets on Ron's bed became more and more crumpled as he fidgeted to get comfortable. Harry lay still, listening for when Violet would come home. She seemed to have been gone a long time, but it was hard to tell.

'Harry,' said Ron's voice after a little more time had passed, 'I'm so hot. I feel awful. When's Ma coming home? Can you tell Father I need her.'

He did sound feeble. Harry got out of bed and went downstairs to George.

'What's up, son?'

'Ron said he's very ill and needs Mother. He's very hot.'

George went upstairs and felt Ron's forehead as Violet had done earlier.

'Put your dressing gown on, Harry, and go and fetch Mother. She'll know what to do.'

Harry walked quickly down the lane, feeling rather strange to be out after dark in his pyjamas. But being a messenger gave him a sense of purpose. The lane was unlit apart from the soft glow coming from cottage windows. George had given Harry a torch so he could find his way but it was difficult to orientate himself when the beam reached hardly more than a couple of paces ahead and intensified the surrounding darkness. Harry had walked down the lane many times in daylight but it seemed so different in the dense gloom of the October night. Distances were lengthened and the curves of the bends were more obtuse.

He lost his bearings. Several times he thought he had arrived at the Kentons' when he still had some distance to go. Then, walking so quickly, he thought he had passed his destination and retraced his steps before realising his mistake. He had never seen the Kentons' cottage in the dark and wasn't really certain what signs to look out for. He wondered how Fred would use his scouting skills to locate his target. With the geography of the lane obscured, the nocturnal scents and sounds were accentuated. Only shadows kept him company.

By the time Harry found the right house, he was strangely disorientated. Fortunately, there was light emanating from the room at the front. The dwelling itself was set on a bank some feet above the lane and it was impossible to see in. Still not entirely sure that he was in the right place, Harry walked up the path and peered through the window. Much to his relief, there was Mother, sitting at a table with some other women. He was about to tap on the glass when his eyes adjusted to the light and something he saw made him hesitate. Violet sat between Edith and her daughter Jessie, but their faces were blank, distant, almost as if they were unaware of each other's presence. A fourth woman, whom Harry did not recognise, sat at the table with them. She had her palms flat on the table, her fingers spread. Her head was tipped slightly backwards and her eyes seemed to be closed. The impression of the scene was one of tension, expectancy.

Harry was unsure what to do. Then he remembered that it was important for Mother to come home quickly. It was probably best to knock on the door rather than tap on the window. There was no need, however, because he found the door slightly ajar. Pushing it gently, he stepped into the hallway and stood outside the door to the sitting room. A voice reached him from within, the voice of the unknown woman. He could barely make out what she was saying, but just caught fragments of her low mutterings: '...safe now, Mother... don't be afraid... not goodbye... not goodbye...'

'Oh Albert, Albert, my dear boy,' choked Mrs Kenton, 'we miss you so much.' Jessie started to cry.

Just then Violet gasped. She had suddenly seen the figure at the door. 'Oh Harry! What are you doing here?'

Harry sensed the mood of the room instantly change, like someone dropping a china plate on a stone floor. Uncomfortable, he avoided looking at the others and concentrated on his mother.

'Ron's unwell, Ma. He's burning hot. Father said to fetch you to come home at once.'

Violet glanced at her companions. 'I'm so sorry, Edith, Jessie. I have to go.'

Awkwardly, catching her skirt, she got up from the table, grabbed her shawl and Harry's hand, and drew him quickly out of the house. When they were back in the lane, she seemed to relax. 'Now tell me about Ron. Is he in bed?'

'What were you doing in there, Ma? Who was that strange woman? How did she know Albert?'

'Has he got a temperature? Has Father given him some water?

Returning home, the lane seemed familiar once again. Violet took the torch and they were back in a few minutes. Once indoors, Violet hurried upstairs to see Ron, ignoring Harry, who put himself straight back to bed.

Harry also had a temperature the next morning when he woke up so he and Ron both spent the day in bed, mainly dozing, sometimes quietly chatting to each other. Violet came upstairs to bring them drinks and soup and to check their temperatures. Ron complained that his throat was very sore. 'Try not to talk, then,' said Violet and she gave him a comic to read. By the evening, Ron was feeling a little better but Harry's temperature had soared. Violet sat by his bed, wiping his face every now and then with a damp flannel. She wondered whether she should call the doctor. She sent Ron next door to Fred's room, so she could sleep in Ron's bed. All night and all the next day, Harry was delirious. The doctor did come, but Harry knew nothing of it. For two more days, he lay in bed almost unaware of his mother's visits, or of Ron coming in from time to time to bring him a fresh glass of water. On the fourth day he woke early to find Violet asleep in his room.

'What are you doing sleeping there, Ma? Where's Ron?'

'You've been very ill, Harry. Ron's been sleeping in Fred's room so I could stay here with you. Don't you remember the doctor coming?'

But Harry could remember almost nothing of the last few days or the evening before he fell sick, at least not clearly. Had he really walked down the dark lane alone in his night clothes? He had never gone to the Kentons by himself, even in the daytime. The shadows in the lane, the scene he saw through the window, the strange lady sitting at the table and the words she spoke, Mother's gasp when she saw him – all this he must have imagined in a curious dream borne out of his illness.

Then Ron came in. 'You're better! You're better! Get up and come out to play. I've had no one to play with while you've been sick. But it's your own fault for going down the lane in your pyjamas.'

And then Harry knew that he hadn't dreamt the women at the table and that, however it had managed to reach them, the message from Albert was real.

Summer 1915 to Summer 1917

Mrs Buckley became an important figure in Harry and Ron's lives during those middle years of the war. It had been no surprise to her when Fred had enlisted, but she knew what it cost Violet to agree to let him go and saw how, with Fred away, she drew Harry and Ron closer to her. Tea at Linden Hill became a regular event. Gradually, as they came to know its layout and its routines, the house grew less daunting to the boys, as did its occupant, their initial shyness with her soon giving way to an open affection. Between visits, they would collect items to present to Mrs Buckley, a bird's feather, a pressed flower, a piece of pottery found in the field, and she accepted these gifts with unfeigned surprise and delight.

While the days were still cool, they had tea in Mrs Buckley's sitting room by the fire. As soon as the weather was milder, she opened the windows to air the room. When it became warmer still, they went outside and sat round a table in a shady corner of the garden beneath the oak trees. Harry liked this spot most of all, and this was where they were sitting one afternoon which Harry would remember over thirty years later in another place, and at the end of another war. The pleasant summer weather was soporific and the sounds of the garden filled the pauses in their conversation. The chinking of cups placed down on saucers made a sound as delicate as that of the twittering birds. Then from the other side of the high wall which divided the garden from the lane, the thinnest line of whistling could be heard. It seemed to move towards them, then grow faint again as the whistler passed on his way, leaving silence in his wake.

'I know what he was whistling,' Harry said. 'It was that song you like, Ma, you know, "just a song at twilight..."'

'"...when the lights are low", added Ron. That was all they could remember of the words.

'*Love's Old Sweet Song*,' said Mrs Buckley.

'Mother can play it on the piano. She learnt it when she was young,' Harry told her. 'She knows how to play lots of songs without the music.' He didn't mention the performances on the kitchen table.

'I didn't know you played, Violet. You'd be very welcome to play our piano.'

'Will you play it, Ma, on Mrs Buckley's piano? Can she really, Mrs Buckley? Do you mind?'

'Of course she may. If you'd like to, Violet?'

Violet said she'd be delighted. The piano was in the drawing room, Mrs Buckley told her. She pointed out an open French window not far from where they were sitting. Violet went indoors. A few moments later, she was seated at the instrument, her fingers hesitating above the keys. It was a long time since she'd played, since before she left home to go and work as a maid, long before she met George. But with her hands in the right position and the tune in her head, she soon found the notes and the music flowed for her once again.

Out in the garden, the others sat without speaking, waiting for Violet to begin. At first, the music came faintly, like the whistling they had heard from the lane, but the tune strengthened as the player's confidence returned. Mrs Buckley closed her eyes and hummed the chorus. Harry watched her, the trace of a smile forming the shape of her mouth. Maybe she was thinking about the colonel. When Violet reached the chorus for the second time, she sang, and the garden became rich with the scent of flowers mixed with that old sweet song of love, and Harry experienced for the first time the delight of hearing unexpected music from a nearby room.

When they got home that day, George had already finished work. Harry told him about their outing and how Violet had played Mrs Buckley's piano. When Ron came in, the two of them sang what they could remember of the refrain. George smiled, and put his arm round his wife. He looked happy, but thin and tired.

Harry and Ron were very fond of Mrs Buckley in the way they might have been fond of a grandmother. She was always interested in what they were doing and particularly in what they thought. She never talked down to them and they liked her all the more for that. One day in early autumn, they were invited to go to tea on their own, the first time the two of them had visited anywhere without Violet. It felt like a huge adventure as they walked through the village towards Linden Hill. It was too cold to sit outside that day, but Mrs Buckley had an indoor plan.

'You've got to earn your tea and cakes today, boys,' she told them, leading them into her sitting room. The little parade of Noah's animals which they had set up the last time in a new formation still wound its way across the table, but some of the animals had been removed. They were to go and find them in different parts of the house. 'You can go in any room you like,' said Mrs Buckley, 'as long as the door is open. Doors that are shut are out of bounds. There's one missing piece in every room but if you're looking for a pair of animals, they'll both be in the same room. None of the pieces are hidden but they might be hard to see. You can go upstairs but don't forget the kitchen and pantry.' Harry and Ron were about to charge off when she called them back. 'Haven't you forgotten something?' They looked puzzled. 'How will you know what to search for if you haven't looked to see what's missing?'

She watched them as they studied the line of animals. There were six animals without their pairs. The cats and the giraffes had disappeared altogether. One of Noah's sons had lost his wife. Harry counted on his fingers. 'Right-ho. We need to find ten animals and one lady. Got that, Ron?'

Off they went, shouting, 'We won't be long.' Mrs Buckley suspected otherwise, and sat down to write a letter to the colonel.

Harry and Ron thought this was the best game they had ever played. No one else they knew lived in a house as large as Mrs Buckley's and now they were to be allowed to explore it without the supervision of an adult. They decided to begin upstairs. There were two flights of stairs in Mrs Buckley's house, one narrow flight near the kitchen which led up to the servants' quarters, and a wider, grander staircase at the other end of the house which led to the main bedrooms. The Buckleys only kept one maid, and she slept in one of the little rooms above the kitchen. A couple who lived in the village came in most days to help with the garden and the meals. The boys decided to begin with the maid's staircase. When they got to the top, they were on a tiny landing, with three doors off it, all closed. Two further steps took them up to a broad passageway. At the far end they could see where the other staircase, lit by a long, high window, reached the upper landing. More doors invited them. They walked along the passageway and picked one of the rooms. It was a bedroom, but without any signs of habitation although the bed was made up and there was a small pile of books on the bedside table. They looked around the room and quickly found one of the giraffes tucked up in bed as if taking a nap. Harry remembered Mrs Buckley's instructions. 'The other one must be in here somewhere, Ron.' It took them some time to find the giraffe, which had been propped on a tiny shelf in the corner behind a vase and cleverly positioned so it was camouflaged against the floral wallpaper.

When they came out of the first room, each carrying a giraffe in his pocket, they couldn't decide which room to explore next. There were three more open doors. Each one looked like a bedroom. Then they noticed that halfway down the passage was a recess which led to another small flight of stairs. 'Come on, Ron, let's see what's up here.'

The stairs led them into a huge lumber room, which had the most wonderful smell of dusty books and old leather. Standing on a suitcase in the middle of the floor was an errant cat. They hunted high and low for its companion, which they eventually found in a thick woollen sock inside an old boot. The attic had two windows. One of them looked out onto the front courtyard, and the other towards the garden where they had sat that afternoon of Violet's piano playing. Harry looked down. Mr Jennings was dead-heading the roses. A wheelbarrow stood on the lawn. A bird flew from the roof into one of the elm trees. Suddenly, the attic felt stifling.

It didn't take them too long to find the creatures hidden in the other bedrooms. When they got back down to the ground floor, they had three creatures and Noah's son's wife still to find. Ron's stomach rumbled. 'How long before tea, Harry?'

'Not long now. Why don't we split up like Fred showed us in the woods? I'll do the rooms at this end and you go back down the other end and do the kitchen and dining room.'

When Ron had run off, Harry decided to start with what he discovered to be the colonel's study. He had never been in a room like this before, and was surprised to find it open now. It was a complete contrast to Mrs Buckley's sitting room, which was cluttered and friendly. The colonel's domain was frighteningly neat and tidy. On the shelves, the books were lined up like so many ranks of soldiers. Harry imagined the colonel at his desk, a vast expanse of rich mahogany, flawlessly polished. It was empty apart from a wooden tray, which held the colonel's writing equipment, and a small wooden horse which stood beside it, as if drinking from a trough.

Almost stealthily, Harry took the horse, then moved on quickly to the adjacent drawing room. Eager to get to know the layout of the house better, he had worked out which room this was the day of *Love's Old Sweet Song*. Besides, he wanted to look at the piano for himself. It was a beautiful room. Light flooded in through the south facing windows, and made the rich crimson glass of the lustres on the sideboard sparkle. The piano was positioned so that someone sitting at it would have the garden window on their left-hand side. Harry imagined his mother as she sat playing. The lid of the piano was closed now as if the music was trapped within. Harry couldn't resist. He pulled back the piano stool and sat down. Only his toes touched the floor. He wriggled his bottom and wiped his hands on his trousers. Then he lifted the lid with both hands and sat looking at the silent keys. What would it be like to press one down? He had to know. He was afraid to make a loud noise so he pushed down very gently. He was surprised at the resistance of the key to his finger but he kept pushing and suddenly there came the *ting* of his first note. He tried it again to learn how much he should push. Then he played three notes in a row, still trying to be very quiet. He was just about to try something more adventurous by stretching out his arms to play a high note and a low note together, when he heard Ron's cough. He turned to see Ron standing in the doorway with Mrs Buckley behind him.

'There's only one thing for you, young man,' said Mrs Buckley. Harry swallowed and put his hands in his lap. 'Piano lessons.' Harry grinned at Mrs Buckley, and she smiled. He hadn't noticed Noah's son's wife looking down at him from the top of the piano until Ron came in and pointed her out.

Mrs Buckley arranged for Harry to have piano lessons at her house once a week, and to practise there as often as he liked. Violet was overwhelmed at her kindness. Time passed, another Christmas came and went without Fred, and while Harry was preoccupied with his scales and arpeggios, George was becoming preoccupied with his health, a concern he tried to keep to himself. He hadn't felt the same since Fred went away and had felt worse since the news of Albert Kenton's death, but it was hard to convince himself that pining for his son was the only cause of his weight loss and frequent bouts of illness. Eventually, he asked Violet to come with him to consult the doctor, who prescribed a series of tests. As they had feared, the prognosis was not good.

They decided to keep as much as possible from the boys. When they asked why he was at home and not going to work, Violet told them Father had worked so hard he had run out of decorating to do for local people. And besides, the war had affected business. George made a half-hearted attempt to do some carpentry but the little oak table he designed for Violet was never finished. He struggled on through autumn and into Advent, which he mainly spent in bed dosed up with morphine. On Christmas morning, he rallied a little and made it to church with Violet and the boys. He pecked at his Christmas lunch, played some games with Harry and Ron, and was then forced to go back to bed. Violet, Harry and Ron felt forlorn, sitting downstairs without him, trying to be cheerful. By the start of the new year, it was clear he would have to be admitted to hospital. Violet faced facts and realised she would have to tell all her sons the seriousness of the situation. First, she wrote a letter to Fred. She had no idea whether he could be granted compassionate leave but asked him to try. Then she called Harry and Ron into the kitchen and explained to them that Father was very poorly indeed and would have to be looked after properly at the hospital in Reading.

Harry found the courage to ask the question which had been on his mind for weeks. 'He's not going to die, is he?'

'I don't know, Harry. The doctors and nurses will do their best to make him better, but it may not be possible. We must all be brave and try to be cheerful for Father's sake.'

She reached out and took their hands and they wept for the loss that they knew would come.

On the afternoon George died, Harry and Ron were at Mrs Buckley's. Fred was still in northern France. Violet was sitting at George's hospital bedside holding his hand.

A numbness crept over her as she walked away from him. She had no idea what would happen now. When she got back to Bottle Green she went straight home. She lay on the bed they had shared for so many years and gathered together all her memories of George. Only when dusk came and she opened her eyes to a changed quality of light in the bedroom, did she rally enough to get up, wash her face and set off to collect the boys.

Mrs Buckley opened the door to Violet and knew at once what had happened. She took her hand and squeezed it, and led Violet into her sitting room where Harry and Ron were playing by the fire. They looked up when Violet came in, and their faces fell. Mrs Buckley left the three of them together, closing the door behind her. Respecting the vastness of their grief, she went and sat in the kitchen with the maid.

Fred managed to get home in time for the funeral. It was a dismal January morning, snow on the ground and more snow falling. In the church, he and Violet sat with Harry and Ron between them. When they followed the coffin to the graveyard, the path was too narrow for the four of them, so Harry went first with Violet. He was quite tall now, and he put his arm around her waist as they walked. In the far corner, not far from Mr Thompson's grave, a place had been prepared for George. Harry was determined to be brave when the moment came to lower the coffin into the ground but the dread of that committal had been with him for days and the tears flowed. He bowed his head but he knew the others were sobbing too. Behind him, he was vaguely aware of the village folk, Mrs Buckley, the Kentons, and others whose presence he felt but did not see.

Fred was allowed two days' leave in England. He had to return to France the day after the funeral. That evening, when Harry and Ron were in bed and fast asleep from the exhaustion of sadness, he discussed with Violet what would happen. There was little money to spare, especially since George had hardly worked for months. Violet assured Fred she would manage somehow. Maybe she would be able to find work. Fred promised that she would have his army wages of a few shillings a week. Whatever happened, he would see that she stayed in Bottle Green. Elsewhere in the village, Mrs Buckley was sitting in her armchair by the fire, making her own plans.

It was some months before she acted. As the weeks passed after George's funeral, she continued to see Violet and the boys but said nothing about what she had in mind. When at last Violet seemed to be emerging from that first dark stage of mourning, Mrs Buckley sent a note round saying she had a new school in mind for the boys. When she felt ready, would Violet like to call and talk this over? What was not mentioned in the letter was that the school was in Kent, a charity home for boys who were orphaned or in straitened circumstances. With Harry and Ron away at school, Mrs Buckley's intention was to employ Violet as her housekeeper. Mr and Mrs Jennings were getting old and frail, the housemaid was sweet but her head was full of nonsense, and she needed someone she could trust to manage her domestic concerns.

Violet duly called on Mrs Buckley and heard her proposal. At first, she could not begin to entertain the prospect of sending Harry and Ron away, but, kindly, tactfully, Mrs Buckley made her see sense. The boys would be well provided for and well educated. They could stay on at school and learn a trade when they were older. The school had an excellent reputation. One of the colonel's former superiors was on the executive committee. Violet started to see that resistance was pointless. As she listened to Mrs Buckley, a scene some years earlier flashed into her mind, and she saw George sitting there beside her, convincing her that Fred should be allowed to stay in the army, a decision she regretted more bitterly now her own circumstances had changed. This time, there was nothing else to be done. And so, once more, she put her compunctions aside, and braced herself for further regret in the future.

Looking back, Violet could not decide which was worse: telling Harry and Ron of their father's death, or telling them they were to go away to school that September. Every week since her husband's burial, she had walked with them to the graveyard, taking what greenery they could find for a wreath. The three of them would sit by the grave when the ground was dry and relate to George what had been happening at home, or in the village. If there was a letter from Fred, Violet would read it to him. She chose this weekly visit to break the news to Harry and Ron about their new school. Before they set off, when she had gathered some early flowers from the garden, she sat them down in the kitchen and explained how kind Mrs Buckley had been to help them and to find such a special school for Harry and Ron where they would thrive and be very happy. They listened in silence, not knowing how to react to something of which they had no real comprehension. 'Come on, boys,' said Violet after she had told them, 'let's go and tell Father all about it.'

August 1917

Very early on the day the boys were leaving for their new school, while Violet was helping Ron to pack, Harry made his way to the graveyard at Bottle Green, proud in his new school uniform. The shadows were still long and the ground lacked warmth. He knelt by his father's grave to say goodbye. He promised he would do his best at school, look after Ron, and try to make his parents proud. The prospect of leaving his mother was painful to him, and he was fearful of that lurching moment of separation which would take place on the railway platform. With Fred away, he felt the son's burden of responsibility for his mother, but he was determined to pray for her every day and to write to her at least once a week. When the time came to leave the graveside, he touched the headstone with the tips of his fingers. 'Goodbye, Father. I don't know when I'll be back.'

At Reading station, the boys put on a brave face for their mother, who hugged them and told them to be good. They bit their lips and nodded compliantly. As the train pulled away, Violet kept her eyes on their carriage window until she could see nothing more of them than their pale hands, waving goodbye. For the first part of the journey the boys sat in silence, bewildered by this unlooked for experience of travelling away from home. Harry pictured his desolate mother, sitting at the kitchen table, crying over her tea for three absent sons and a dead husband. He imagined Father coming in, as if just home from work, and placing a comforting hand on her shoulder.

The train rolled on. Eventually, Ron broke his silence. 'Who's going to look after us instead of Mother, Harry?' Ron already knew the answer to this question, but Harry understood why he was asking, and did his best to reassure him.

It was to be many months before Violet and the boys would see each other again and Harry was anxious about who they would find in her place when they reached the school. They were to live in a house with a matron, Mrs Shepherd, in charge. They knew nothing about her except that she was a widow who had worked at the school for many years. She had written to Violet to introduce herself and the boys had been allowed to read the letter. But it was impossible to tell from that whether she would be kind or severe, a half-acceptable substitute for their mother or a harsh, unfeeling woman who would make their young lives a misery. Harry thought about how he would look after Ron. What would he say to Violet if Ron was unhappy? He didn't want to let her down.

At Paddington, they were met by a senior boy whose job it was to accompany them to Kent. They had been told to look for a lad in scout uniform. They spotted him at the end of the platform. He smiled as they approached. 'Hello there. You must be the boys for Farningham. Jolly good! I'm Atkins, by the way,' and he shook their hands. He helped them with their luggage and chatted enthusiastically as he directed them to the bus stop. When the bus arrived, Atkins jumped on first so Harry and Ron could pass their cases to him. The conductress helped, and said she would watch their luggage if they wanted to sit upstairs. It was the first time the boys had been to London, and Atkins laughed as they gawped around, and pointed out some of the landmarks to them, Marble Arch, Hyde Park Corner, Buckingham Palace. The boys could barely take it all in, hardly noticing that they had shivered all the way to Victoria. But every now and then, as Harry changed his gaze from one monument or street to another, he saw a momentary image of Violet, standing bereft on the platform at Reading as their train pulled away, diminished by her separation from them.

The last part of the long journey took them out of London by train again and down into Kent. Atkins told them about the school. He had been there since he was five years old, and was now in the senior house and training to be a printer when he left. The teachers were pretty decent. Some of the matrons were dragons. There was always plenty to do and this term there was harvest festival followed by spud-picking if you were over eleven and then Guy Fawkes. The war hadn't bothered them too much but last year a Zeppelin had dropped a bomb on Swanley. After a while, Atkins ran out of things to say and rummaged in his backpack for three apples and a book. He settled down to his reading. Harry and Ron crunched their apples as they stared out of the window and watched the shadows lengthen once more on the fields. Bottle Green receded further into the distance.

As they approached Farningham, Atkins leaned forward. 'We're nearly there, you know. Look out for the viaduct as we come round this bend. The school's just beyond that. You might be able to see some of the buildings. The chapel spire – that's the best landmark.'

Harry and Ron sat up and waited to catch sight of their new home.

The scout explained how the school had its own platform on the down side of the track so there was no need to go all the way to the local station. Harry absorbed this piece of information. It made the school feel special that the railway authorities had gone out of their way to do something for the convenience of its pupils. It was late afternoon when they disembarked on West Hill. Once more, the scout helped them with their luggage. 'You're in Moore House. I'll take you there.' He led the way past the lodge and the chapel and along a wide avenue where the gardens seemed to take up more space than the school buildings themselves, which seemed friendly, comfortable. And beyond, there were fields which sloped away into the valley. In all his imaginings about the school, Harry had not anticipated it would be set on a hill for all to see. He breathed a sigh of relief. 'Looks quite all right, Ron, doesn't it?'

The gardens were planted with vegetables and fruit bushes, and Harry breathed in the late summer aroma as they walked past, catching scents that reminded him of home. Ron stared about him. Moore House was the third building they came to on their left.

Mrs Shepherd, a small, neat woman whose wispy white hair made her look older than her years, greeted them warmly. 'Come in, boys, come in. How was your journey? Did Atkins look after you? Have you got all your luggage? That's it, come and make yourselves comfortable.'

Harry glanced at Ron, who was almost smiling now, and decided the day wasn't going at all badly. Standing in the entrance hall with his brother, he felt the significance of the moment, the start of this next phase in his young life. Mrs Shepherd shooed away some of the boys who had come into the hall to inspect the new arrivals, preferring to fuss over these additions to her large surrogate family by herself. She took Harry and Ron into her own sitting room at the front of the house and installed them on the sofa.

'Now you must be very tired and hungry after your journey. The other boys have already eaten but you're going to have tea in here with me, and then I'll show you your bedrooms.'

She disappeared, leaving the door ajar. Down the corridor, Harry and Ron could just hear the gentle chink of china being set out. Afraid to talk to each other, they glanced round the room, absorbing some of its details but noticing especially the many photographs which adorned the walls and the sideboard. Apart from one portrait of a younger Mrs Shepherd with a man who was presumably her late husband, the photographs were exclusively of her many charges over the years. These were mainly formal photographs of the members of Moore House, arranged in rows with the smallest boys sitting cross-legged at the front. In one of the pictures, a shield almost as big as they were took pride of place in the centre of the row. In addition to these archives of schooldays and school friends, there were several portraits of soldiers in uniform. They reminded Harry of Fred.

Mrs Shepherd soon returned with the tea tray. There were delicate white cups and a teapot decorated with green ivy. She placed the tray on a small table in front of the sofa. Harry liked this sign of confidence that they were to be trusted with her good china – it reminded him of Mrs Buckley - and hoped Ron was up to the occasion. Mrs Shepherd disappeared again and came back with a plate of bread and jam, and another plate of rock cakes.

'Come on, boys, don't stand on ceremony.' She passed them each a napkin and poured three cups of strong tea. Ravenous, they tucked in as politely as they could, while she told them more about the house. 'Now you two have arrived, that makes twenty-eight boys altogether. Don't be afraid of the oldest boys. Just be polite to them and say good morning or good afternoon. Harry, you'll be sleeping in a room with four other lads. Ron, you'll be just down the corridor in the junior dormitory. You'll soon learn the rules. Tomorrow it's Sunday so we all go to chapel as soon as we've had breakfast. Wear your uniform and don't forget your handkerchiefs. Then after lunch if the weather's nice we'll go for a walk and I can show you round. Mr Jackson will be here in the morning before we go to church. He's the housemaster and he teaches music and coaches the first eleven cricket team. He has a wife and children of his own so he lives in the village. But some of the masters live here in school. Lessons begin on Monday and the other boys will show you where to go. Meals take place three times a day...' She rattled on cheerfully while Harry and Ron did their best to absorb all the information. Eventually she paused. 'Well, you're both looking rather tired so I'll take you upstairs now. Is there anything you'd like to ask me? Harry?'

'Yes please. May I write to Mother tonight and how will I post my letter please?'

A short while later, the boys found themselves in their sleeping quarters. The other boys in the house were now allowed to inspect the newcomers at close range. Mrs Shepherd was helping Ron to unpack, leaving Harry to his own devices. The boys who shared his bedroom came in, said 'hello there' and left him to it, carrying on with their chatter about the football matches that afternoon. Harry was happy to be virtually ignored. Each boy had a small desk near his bed, and when he had hung up his clothes and set out his writing materials, he sat down and started his letter: 'Dear Mother, Ron and I have arrived safely. Ron is in his dormitory unpacking. I have unpacked my things and am sitting at my own desk writing to you. We had a comfortable journey on the train. Mrs Shepherd is very nice and gave us tea. I think we will like it here. Your loving son, Harry.' And in the bottom right-hand corner he drew a small picture of a grave with a cross on its headstone and wrote underneath 'Father is watching over us all'.

The next morning, the boys were woken by the ringing of a handbell. Mrs Shepherd did a round of the bedrooms, knocking on the doors to make sure everyone was getting up. When Harry came downstairs, he saw Ron with another boy in tow. 'Hello, Harry. This is Walter. Walter, this is my older brother Harry.'

Ron had already made a friend: this was a good start to the day. Harry wondered whether to dash back upstairs, peel open Mother's letter, and add a PS. But then he would need something else to tell her in the next letter and decided against it.

When all the boys had assembled in the common room, Mrs Shepherd came in. Immediately they started to form up in pairs. A boy from Harry's bedroom was told to accompany Harry. Mrs Shepherd led the boys out of the house and down the main avenue, younger ones at the front, and the seniors following up the rear, their voices loud and deep over the heads of the juniors. In the dining hall, they sat in house groups and were joined by their housemasters. Mr Jackson made a point of shaking first Harry's hand, and then Ron's, which was rather awkward while they were sitting on long benches and had their hands full of bread and margarine. Breakfast finished, they were led off again, back up the avenue to the chapel, where services were held morning and evening on Sundays. On the way, Harry and his assigned companion had just long enough to exchange a few preliminary details about themselves. The boy was called Cyril and he pointed out his older brother, Ernest, a few yards behind them. Their father, a captain in the army, had been killed early in the war, and some months later their mother had died too, seemingly of grief, whatever that entailed. With no one else to look after them, they had been sent to Farningham, an arrangement made by a distant and elderly relative. Harry wondered whether to tell Cyril about Fred, who had survived the Somme, even though he didn't fully understand what that meant. Instead, he told him that his father was dead too.

'Was he a soldier?' asked Cyril.

'No, but my older brother is. He's still in France. I don't really know where.'

Cyril nodded, but made no further response to this information. Now they were almost at the chapel, the boys in the group had fallen quiet. Supervised by some of the teachers, others were already filing in, doffing their caps as they did so. The organ could be heard faintly. The chapel was another aspect of the school that Harry had not anticipated. It was smaller than the church at Bottle Green, and plainer, with no intricate tracery or stained glass. The small spire over the crossing had clocks on each face of its square base. There was no excuse for being late.

Inside, the boys were directed to their pews, where they sat in silence listening to the music until the service began. The officiating teacher announced: 'Hymn number 533, "Now Thank We All Our God".' Harry glanced at Ron, at the other end of the pew. They exchanged silent relief at knowing the first hymn, one of their father's favourites. Harry had known the words almost by heart for some time now and found them reassuring. He liked the idea of being *blessed on our way*. Maybe he had been blessed on his way to school on the train. He thought of Fred, and hoped he was being blessed on his way in the war. And then he thought again of his father, his body asleep in the graveyard, his spirit safe in the next world, freed from the anxieties and fears that made him grow ill and die.

After the hymn, the teacher sat down, and another man appeared in the pulpit. Mrs Shepherd had explained that there would be a sermon for the boys given by the Reverend Arthur Bell, the school's superintendent. She had also said that he would want to meet Harry and Ron after the service, so it was best to pay attention to everything he said in case they were asked questions.

'Boys,' he began in a sonorous voice, 'this is the start of a new year at Farningham and I hope you will all work hard and be a credit to your parents, whether they be living or have entered already the glorious Kingdom of Heaven. I should like to welcome the new boys to the school. I wish you many happy years with us.' After a few more such introductory comments, he moved on to his central theme. 'As we sit here in the calm and beauty of the Kent countryside, we must not forget that a fearful war is being fought for our freedom less than two hundred miles from this place. You boys are too young to fight but you are not too young to be mindful of your duty to God, to your country, and to the Empire. Many of our Old Boys are in France and Belgium. Theirs is the enduring honour of fighting the battle for freedom. Your duty is to carry the torch of freedom when the fighting is over, as we trust in God it will be one day soon. Boys, I say again it is your duty, here in our little colony, to make yourselves men before your time. Those of you in the scout troop will know this as the bidding of the Chief Scout. You must pray to God for the health and strength to take the place of those who are away, to be willing to work to do whatever is needful in these dark times.' So the sermon went on, the tone becoming sterner and the message more compelling than anything Harry had heard in Bottle Green. He resolved to do his best to become a man as a matter of urgency. It was his duty to his mother, his father, to Ron and to Fred.

After the Reverend Arthur Bell had finished, the boys knelt down to pray for their school and for absent loved ones and for an end to the war in the name of the Father, and the Son, and the Holy Ghost. At the end of the service, the organist, one of the seniors from another house, did his best to deliver a stirring voluntary while the school filed out. It was strange for Harry at that moment not to have his mother nearby, or to see Mrs Buckley coming towards them.

Reverend Bell intercepted Harry and Ron by the church porch. 'You must be the Elston boys. Good morning. How are you settling in?' He shook their hands.

'Very well, sir, thank you.' Harry spoke for Ron too.

'And you are, what, eleven years old. Is that correct?'

'I'm only ten, sir. And Ron was eight this summer.'

'I see. And what have you learnt this morning, young man?'

'We've learnt that we must do our duty, sir.'

'That's right. Very good. Hurry along then or you'll be separated from the others.'

That evening Harry wrote another letter home: 'Dear Mother, I hope you are well. Today we have been to church and we sang father's favourite hymn. I am going to become a man as quickly as possible so do not worry. All the adults here are kind to us. Ron has made a friend called Walter. The food is not bad. Your loving son, Harry.'

Harry and Ron's first Saturday and Sunday at their new
school had not gone at all badly, nor did the following
months bring them any unbearable shocks. They settled
into the Home for Little Boys and learned its ways,
sometimes conscious of the war being waged in Europe,
sometimes not. But Harry did not forget for a single day
that he was trying to become a man. He worked hard at his
lessons, watched to see that his brother was happy, and
wrote regularly to his mother and to Fred and to Mrs
Buckley. Along with the other boys in Moore House, he
helped Mrs Shepherd by distributing the post and running
errands for her. He tried not to mind that his father had
died. His notions of what manliness was exactly remained
cloudy and half-formed but he hoped his goal would
become clearer to him as time went on.

Within a couple of weeks Harry had familiarised
himself with the school grounds. That first Sunday he had
acquired at once the routes to the chapel and the dining
hall, and from then on he began to feel at home. For the
chapel, you came out of Moore House and turned right
towards the school entrance. Other direction for the dining
hall and, beyond that, as he discovered on Monday
morning, the schoolhouse itself. Next, he identified the
other buildings on Top Road, as it was nicknamed, most of

them boarding houses. Then he ventured away from Top Road to the workshops where the older boys were learning the trades that would later earn them a living. These little industries were distinguished by the sounds which emanated from them during the school day – the rhythmic clatter of the printing presses, the tap-tapping of shoe-making, or the rough swish of a plane on wood. There was a bakery from which delicious yeasty scents of fresh bread drifted out to the hills beyond, and even a small farm where more earthy smells were generated by pigs, hens and cows.

But what Harry liked most were the gardens which had been cultivated between the boys' houses, and the pathways that led behind some of the buildings to allotments or orchards. Not a square yard was wasted. Sometimes he would explore these places with Ron in tow, but he preferred to wander them alone, noticing the signs of the changing season, watching the subtle shifts in the colours of the foliage. When the leaves fell, they made vast crackling carpets through which the boys scrunched their way, ankle-deep, kicking up the leaves as they went. Mrs Shepherd asked Harry if he and two other boys in his room would collect up the leaves which were steadily filling the garden of Moore House. She supplied them with a wheelbarrow and they gathered the dead leaves and twigs into a huge pile in the centre of the lawn. Later, Mrs Shepherd came out and lit the bonfire, and they watched the gentle twist of smoke rise and disappear, as they inhaled the breaths of autumn. Harry stood quietly apart from his workmates, enjoying the faint warmth, aware for the first time of a not unpleasant feeling of happiness and sadness mingled.

As Atkins had promised on that first train journey, the long stretch of the autumn term was punctuated by some important events in the school calendar. The first of these was Harvest Festival, when the chapel was decorated with home-grown produce, giant turnips and onions, oddly shaped parsnips and mangel-wurzels. Curious, but not unattractive adornments, Harry thought, as they belted out the harvest hymns. The harvest was completed a few weeks later when the older boys were sent out to the fields to gather the potato crop, exhausting work which was considered too strenuous for the younger pupils. Classes continued for Harry and Ron, and the schoolhouse felt strangely empty for days on end. With the potatoes safely gathered in, it was time to begin preparations for Guy Fawkes night. Every house designed and made a guy. In Harry's house, the older boys were put in charge. Ron and his friends were given the job of collecting stuffing for the guy wherever they could find it. Harry and Cyril were given some rags and asked to turn them into a pair of patchwork trousers. While work went on in the houses, a huge bonfire mysteriously arose on Forty Acre Field, some distance from the school buildings. On Guy Fawkes night, dusk was the signal for the festivities to commence. The boys left their houses, parading to Forty Acre in tight-knit house groups, their guys displayed proudly aloft. Eleven effigies were lined up before the bonfire and the Reverend Bell picked the winner with an exaggerated display of solemnity. Then the bonfire was lit and the boys watched with fascination as their handiwork vanished in the flames.

Christmas was celebrated at school. As the days grew shorter, the boys would go back to their houses after lessons and sit in their common rooms making paper decorations and painting cards to send to friends and relatives. As he wrote messages for his mother and for Fred, Harry became increasingly homesick. Bottle Green was often in his thoughts, the multifarious images of times spent with his family, with his brothers in the woods, with Ma and Pa at the kitchen table, attending church, the teas and piano lessons at Linden Hill. Sometimes, he thought about the scene he had witnessed that night at Mrs Kenton's, the disorientation, the bewilderment, the illness which had followed. Knowing he was unable to find the words to describe that episode or to explain – even tentatively - his understanding of it, he had not mentioned it to anyone. But he had not wavered from the conclusions he had drawn about what he had observed, even now he was older and away from home. If anything, his sense that there was a world beyond his daily experience of which he sometimes had intimations had strengthened, and, in a way he only half acknowledged, he had come to believe that, like music heard from a nearby room, he might experience it more fully if he could only find the door.

Sitting now at the large table in Moore House common room, he pined for the accustomed Christmas festivities of Bottle Green, when he and Ron would wake to find stockings at the ends of their beds filled with nice things to eat and useful items like pencils and string. He felt his eyes fill with tears, but conscious of Ron sitting across the table from him, he bit his lip and tried to think of something else. Still, it was hard to do this when so many of his conscious and involuntary thoughts ran upon the members of his family, and inevitably filled him with a deep longing for Christmas at home.

In the end, Christmas at Farningham wasn't so bad. On Christmas Eve, there was a visit from Father Christmas himself, although most of the boys realised it was the Reverend Bell who delivered a huge slab of iced cake and some other mystery items which he gave directly to Mrs Shepherd. When the boys went to their rooms, they were told to hang stockings at the ends of their beds, making sure they were clean ones. And just like home, the following morning Harry found his stocking filled with fruit and sweets. There was a special service for Christmas morning, with carols instead of hymns, and the chapel twinkling with candles. In his sermon, Reverend Bell asked the boys to remember their brothers and former pupils of the school who were spending Christmas on the western front, cold and far from home. Harry did not need to be reminded about Fred. He had been thinking of him since he had tipped the contents of his stocking onto his bed and been treated to a cheering array of apples, nuts and toffees. Then they sang 'O Come All Ye Faithful' and when they left chapel it was time for lunch. The dining hall had been decorated with holly and ivy which some of the boys had collected in the grounds. A Christmas tree stood in the corner, and Father Christmas made a second appearance, this time to deliver the plum pudding, welcomed by cheers from the whole school. Back in their houses, there were presents for everyone. In the weeks preceding Christmas, parcels containing gifts had been arriving regularly and Mrs Shepherd had hidden them away ready for this afternoon. Harry and Ron had parcels from Mother and from Mrs Buckley, and even a small present each from Mrs Kenton. No boy went without and every boy enjoyed this communal ritual of unwrapping and comparing their gifts.

But how different last Christmas had been, Harry kept thinking. A visit to church, the decorations, the giving of presents, that was the same, but how strange to be in this other place, familiar now but also unfamiliar, as if he had woken into a dream. How glad he was to have Ron here so they could talk about home. Mother was spending Christmas at Linden Hill and Harry supposed that must be even stranger for her, with none of her family there. This time last year, Father was still alive. If only he could have got better then Harry would be at home now. If the war had not begun, or if it had already reached its conclusion, Fred would be at home with them. If only the act of wishing hard enough had the power to bring wishes about. But he was already old enough to know that this was impossible.

At least Harry was doing well at most of his lessons. 'Fairly good' for Mathematics but 'very good' for Scripture and Reading, said his report. Ron liked measuring things and seeing how they worked, but Harry was drawn again and again to stories. He loved the poems that Mr Chandler read to the class, mainly tales of the heroic past. But Mr Chandler also told them how soldiers were writing poems about the present war and selected one or two to read to them. It seemed a surprising thing to do. Harry couldn't imagine Fred sitting in his trench writing a poem. When he was in the scouts there had been no mention of poetry. Nowadays, Fred hardly had time to write letters home and that was far more important, he was sure.

One spring morning in the English lesson, Mr Chandler read out a poem by a writer whose unusual name Harry, sitting near the back of the class, did not catch. But the poem itself, with its cumulative list of conditions for achieving the very goal his heart was set on, struck him deeply. At the end of the lesson, Harry gathered all his boyish courage to stay behind and talk to Mr Chandler.

'Well, Henry, how are you getting on?

'I'm getting on nicely, thank you, Sir. I liked the poem you read today.'

'Ah yes. Would you like to read it again?

'Yes, please, sir. Very much.' He hoped he would not be asked the particular reason for this request.

Mr Chandler paused for a moment. 'Why don't you borrow my book for this evening and return it tomorrow?'

This was the first time an adult had offered to lend Harry an item as expensive as a book. He wondered whether he should refuse, but the desire to read the poem in private was too strong. 'If you're sure you don't mind, sir.'

'You're very welcome. Look after it carefully.'

That evening after supper, when his room-mates were outside playing football before dusk, Harry sat down at his desk, checked his hands were clean, and took Mr Chandler's book from his satchel. He set it before him gently. There was gilt lettering on the spine and a gilt elephant stamped into the front cover which hinted at something exotic within. Tentatively, Harry opened the book at the flyleaf and saw his teacher's writing: 'F S Chandler: to himself. Christmas 1910.' '*To himself.*' How strange that seemed. Harry had some books he had bought with his pocket money. Mother had told him what to put inside and he had written simply his name and the date of acquisition. Some of his books were gifts and said things like: 'To Henry, with best wishes from Mrs G Buckley. Christmas 1915.' '*To himself.*' It made it sound like a gift. Mr Chandler had given it to himself as a gift. And this simple dedication spoke to Harry of something he had only vaguely sensed about Mr Chandler until now.

Inside the book, which contained stories as well as poems, the page Harry was searching for was indicated with a bookmark. Slowly, almost reverently, trying to imitate his teacher's rhythms, Harry read the poem in his quietest voice. He wondered if he could memorise it but it was too long. So he took a clean sheet of paper and his best fountain pen and spent the next hour or more laboriously copying the poem. So many *if*s. Each one he inscribed in large letters which he adorned with hooks and curlicues. When he was finished, he blew vigorously on the sheet to make sure the ink was dry and, feeling he had taken possession of something very significant and precious, put it away carefully in the drawer of his desk. The book he slipped back into his satchel ready to return to its owner.

The following day, Mr Chandler was absent from the English lesson and the class was taken by Mr Matthews, the history teacher. Harry asked him where Mr Chandler was, so he could return his book. The English teacher had been called away on a personal matter and would not be back until that evening. After supper, Harry asked Mrs Shepherd if he could walk down to Mr Chandler's house to return a book. He explained about him being absent from the lesson. Mrs Shepherd hesitated. 'Well, yes, Harry, because he'll be pleased you took the trouble, but he'll be tired after his journey so just return the book and come straight back.' She didn't explain her apparent knowledge about the teacher's absence or the mention of a journey, and he didn't like to ask.

Mr Chandler's house, East Lodge, was only a few minutes' walk away, at the other end of the school grounds, just within the school boundary. This was the first time Harry had been to one of the masters' houses and he felt a little unsure of himself. When Mr Chandler answered the door, Harry wondered if he had made a mistake calling that evening instead of waiting until class the next day. Mr Chandler normally made a passable effort to look smart but now he looked like a tramp Harry had once seen in the churchyard at home. Harry had no idea how old Mr Chandler was but suddenly he seemed tired, feeble, not someone who could read poetry in a stirring way to a class of boys.

For a moment, Mr Chandler appeared somewhat bewildered to see a young boy standing on his doorstep but then he seemed to gather himself. 'Ah, Henry. What brings you here at this time of the evening?'

'I'm sorry to disturb you, sir, but you asked me to return your book and then you weren't in class and I didn't want you to think I'd forgotten.' He offered the book to Mr Chandler and the blue volume suddenly prompted his memory.

'Yes, of course. The poem. How did you get on?' Then, becoming more animated, 'In fact, why don't you come in and tell me about it?'

'Well, Mrs Shepherd said not to stay because you'd be tired. Are you tired, sir?'

'I am a little. But come in anyway and tell me about the poem. It'll cheer me up to have some company.'

Harry followed his teacher into his study, proud to have been the recipient of such an invitation. It was very different from the colonel's study at Linden Hill. Books and newspapers were piled messily on every surface. Dust was everywhere. Mr Chandler indicated which chair he should sit in of the two worn armchairs either side of the hearth.

'How was your journey today, sir?' Harry felt he should try to make polite conversation as his mother and Mrs Buckley had taught him.

'Have you ever been to a funeral, Henry?'

'Yes, sir, my father's. Is that where you've been? To a funeral?'

'I'm afraid so. Will it upset you if I tell you about it?' He seemed to want to.

'I don't think so, sir. Whose funeral was it?'

'My nephew's. My brother's eldest son. It wasn't unexpected, not really. He was a soldier, you see, in France. But he didn't die in France, he was very badly wounded there. They brought him back to a hospital in London. My brother and sister-in-law visited him every week. I used to visit him too when I could. We were very close. I thought for a while he was getting better but then...'

He looked down. Unused to receiving such confidences from adults, Harry could find no words of his own to say. Instead he asked, 'Is that why you read us the poem?'

When Harry got back to Moore House, he went to say goodnight to Mrs Shepherd. She didn't seem cross about him being so long at Mr Chandler's house. Upstairs, his roommates were getting ready for bed by having a pillow fight. They invited him to join in, which he obligingly did, though the enthusiasm for battle was somehow lacking. After lights out, Harry lay awake, thinking about Mr Chandler's nephew, wondering what wounds he had sustained in that terrible battle and imagining the long months when the soldier had languished in hospital not knowing whether he would live or die. His anxiety for Fred, still serving somewhere in France, quickened, and he resolved to write to him the very next morning. He thought of Mr Chandler sitting alone in his armchair by the fire, staring across at its vacant companion. When he slept, the words of the poem came back to him over and over in an almost senseless jumble: *if you can if you can you can be can be a man*. Then when the words subsided, he was standing once more outside Mrs Kenton's house, peering through the window at the four women communing with the dead, and there among them sat Mr Chandler, the saddest and most desperate of them all.

Spring 1918

The following week was a happy one when the days seemed full of promise and the fearful image of Mr Chandler's wounded nephew faded from Harry's thoughts with the tell-tale signs and airy scents of spring. To celebrate the better weather, one of the teachers organised a tug-of-war competition, every house and every boy to take part. The pupils, dressed in their sports kit, duly assembled on Forty Acre Field at the appointed time one mild sunny afternoon, ready to dig in. They stood around in their house groups waiting for instructions. Harry was overawed at the sight of his three hundred or so fellow pupils on the vast playing field, the first time he had seen the whole school together in the open air and in daylight. It exhilarated him and, small though he was in comparison to many of the boys, he was determined to do his bit. He and Ron had played tug-of-war in their village but never on this scale. Anchors had been done away with. The biggest boys in the house were to stand firm at the head of the rope while the smallest and youngest boys would do their best at the back. Their first pull was against Finlay House. They lined up dutifully, waiting for the signal to take the strain. Tension mounted as they held their positions, and an eerie quietness engulfed them. As if from a distance, they heard the next instruction: 'Steady.' They braced themselves. Then a pause before 'Pull!'

A burst of activity and noise. At the back of the rope, Harry and Ron and the other junior boys dug their heels in, gritted their teeth and pulled with all their might. For what seemed like a very long time, they just kept pulling, each in his own little world of exertion, oblivious to the grimaces on the faces of the other pullers. If any of the senior boys were shouting them instructions, it was impossible to hear amid the din. This distance from the marker, they had no idea what ground was being gained, if any. But gradually, and still straining hard, they started to move backwards, inch by inch, the boys at the rear having no way of judging how much more there was to do. Then, after more long moments of tugging and heaving, the judge gave his signal and Moore House had won their first pull. The boys collapsed on the ground where they were, panting to regain their breath. Harry looked round to see Ron and Walter laughing with delight, then he let his head fall again on the soft grass, staring at the blue sky and relishing his own small part in the victory.

The fair weather continued and the boys in Harry's class were sent on a cross country run. From the chapel, they jogged as a pack over the railway and ran down towards the village past the huge chimney of a paper mill. This in turn was dwarfed by the arches of the railway viaduct which carried the stretch of track between Farningham station and the school. It was wonderful to stop at the foot of the viaduct and look up and up. They followed the river under one of the arches and along the valley towards the church, the pack now elongated into a straggling line. Harry found himself at the back and running out of steam. But being a poor runner was a fine excuse for enjoying the run and looking for the signs of spring on the riverbank. The muffled footfalls of his fellow pupils receded and Harry heard someone call to him to hurry up. On he went, trying to keep the other boys in sight, for nearly a mile along the path of the river until they reached a tiny bridge where they crossed back over the water and came up along the edge of the churchyard. Harry was just tall enough now to look over the hedge and see how, with the trees barely in leaf, the spring sunshine fell generously on the graves. From the church they headed uphill again, across the fields and towards home.

By the time the boys arrived at the east entrance of the school, Harry was at least a hundred yards behind the rest, exhilarated but out of breath. He paused for a moment for some large gulps of air. Coming in the opposite direction towards his house was Mr Chandler, who stopped and asked him if he was alright and had he sixty *minutes* worth of distance run? For a moment, Harry was puzzled and then the joke struck him.

'Well, you'd better try to catch up, young Henry. By the way, if you want to come back after you've changed, I've another book you might like to borrow.'

'Thank you, sir. See you later then.'

'Tell Mrs Shepherd where you are. And bring a friend if you want.' The kindness of Mr Chandler's offer to lend

Harry another book was somewhat diluted by this second offer, which threw Harry into confusion. Did that actually mean he *should* bring a friend, and who would he ask? The boys in his bedroom were pleasant and he liked them, especially Cyril, but he wasn't sure if they were friends yet, or at least the kind of friends for this occasion. Then he had a better idea.

Back at Moore House he went to look for Ron, who was in the common room oiling his cricket bat in readiness for the new season. 'Come on, Ron, put that down. We've been invited to Mr Chandler's,' and he explained about the books.

There was a reassuring sense of familiarity about visiting Mr Chandler's home for a second time. Its location at the edge of the school grounds gave it an air of secluded independence. It was impossible to see the cottage until you passed the school house, when it appeared on a gentle rise a hundred yards or so further on. Harry noticed that there was a chimney at each end of the building, and he deduced from this which room was the study where he had sat on his first visit.

This time, Mr Chandler was prepared for visitors and looked more like the man Harry was used to seeing at the front of the classroom.

'Hello, Sir. I hope you don't mind but I've brought my brother Ron with me.'

Mr Chandler, who didn't teach the younger boys, shook hands encouragingly with Ron and led them both into his study where an additional chair had been placed between the two usual incumbents.

'Sit down,' said Mr Chandler. 'I'll be back in a moment.'

Harry took what he already regarded as his seat by the fireplace and pointed to Ron to sit in the new chair. After a few moments, Mr Chandler came in with biscuits and lemonade for the boys.

'So I have the pleasure of two new boys for company. Mrs Shepherd tells me you have an older brother too, is that correct?'

'Yes that's right, sir. Our brother Fred. He's a soldier.'

And with considerable pride and with Ron chipping in, Harry told Mr Chandler all about Fred, how he had joined up before he was old enough, but it was quite alright because their parents had agreed to let him go. He thought it better not to mention his mother's tears when Fred had first made his announcement. He told him how Fred had been posted to France and survived the Somme, and how smart he looked in the uniform of the Middlesex Regiment. Only then did it occur to Harry that this enthusiasm for his living brother might be somewhat painful to Mr Chandler, still grieving for his nephew. He fell silent.

The book which Harry was to borrow had been written by the author of the poem Harry had copied the week before and whose curious name was now starting to become familiar.

'I bought this for my nephew when he was your age, Henry, and it was a great favourite with him, so I thought you might like to give it a try.'

Harry wiped his hands on his trousers and took the book as if handling something very delicate indeed. The cover of this volume was embossed not with one small gilt elephant but with three huge beasts, each with its own driver on its back, and together they were being led by a guide, as if through a jungle. Harry turned the spine towards him and read the title. A snake undulated menacingly up the spine as if hoping to pounce on the snarling creature that appeared to float above its attacker. Although itching to look inside to see if there was another inscription in Mr Chandler's writing, Harry thought it best to wait until later.

'It's a collection of stories set in India. Some of them are about a young boy who grows up in the jungle. It was written for children. My nephew read those stories over and over again, and knew the names of all the animals. Perhaps when he's finished, your brother will tell you the stories,' Mr Chandler said, turning to Ron. Harry noted this as an obligation. He couldn't wait to get back to Moore House with the book. 'When would you like it back, sir?'

'When you've finished with it, Henry. I've plenty of other books to read.' And he gestured vaguely at the many books untidily crowding his bookcases.

Having thanked Mr Chandler for the refreshments, the brothers made their way back to Moore House, falling together into a jogging rhythm as Harry chanted *Rudyard*

Kipling's Jungle Book, Rudyard Kipling's Jungle Book all
the way through the school grounds.

When the boys got back, Mrs Shepherd's door was ajar,
a sign that it was acceptable to knock and go in. Sitting on
the sofa was a young man, about Fred's age, or maybe a
little older, dressed in army uniform. Harry immediately
recognised him as one of the soldiers in Mrs Shepherd's
gallery, which he had now had several opportunities to
scrutinise. In the flesh, however, the soldier looked tired
and gaunt.

'Hello there. You must be new. Mrs Shepherd's gone
upstairs to see to something. Do you want me to give her a
message?'

Harry hesitated, wondering what the soldier was doing
there. Before he could respond, Mrs Shepherd herself
appeared. 'Henry and Ronald, come and meet Lieutenant
Holloway. He left school last year and is back for a few
days on leave so he's come to pay me a visit. Isn't that
thoughtful of him?'

'Well, I couldn't leave without coming to see dear Mrs
Shepherd who looked after me for so many years, could I?'
The boys stepped further into the room. 'So how are you
both getting on here? Everyone being kind to you?' And
Holloway proceeded to ask them in detail about their
experiences of the last few months. They were pleased to
answer his questions as if to confirm that the soldier's
memories of schooldays really were memories of happier
times.

When he seemed satisfied with what he had heard, Holloway turned his attention to Mr Chandler's book, which Harry was still holding. 'What's that book you've got there, then, Henry?' Harry handed it over for inspection. 'Ah, Kipling. Dreadful business about his son.' He addressed this remark to Mrs Shepherd. Then, turning back to Harry, 'You'll enjoy that,' he said.

Harry had no idea what Holloway meant by his remark to Mrs Shepherd. Mr Chandler hadn't mentioned a son. Perhaps he didn't know about the dreadful business, whatever it was. Mrs Shepherd seemed to know, though, in the way she nodded her head and looked at the floor. But this was not the moment to ask. He liked the young soldier he had only just met, although he wished he looked as happy and healthy as he did in his photograph. He liked the way Holloway had taken the trouble to talk to him and Ron and ask how they were settling in at school. Then the bell went for tea and the boys said their goodbyes to Mrs Shepherd and her guest.

The next morning, letters arrived for the boys from their mother, except Harry's was more of a package. He took it off to his room to open. It contained a letter for him and a smaller package addressed: 'To Harry and Ron. Open it together!' Harry decided to read his letter before going to find his brother. There was some very good news. Fred had been home on leave, wrote Mother, and what a wonderful time they had spent together. Mrs Buckley had been sure she could manage without Violet for a few days and insisted she spent them with her son. They had been out for a walk and picked primroses in Warren Woods, which they had taken to put on Father's grave. Another day they had walked to the inn where Violet had first met her husband and Fred had treated her to lunch. The sign George had painted so many years before was gone now and had been replaced by a new one in a very different style. Harry realised he had never heard the full account of this first meeting and resolved to ask Mother about it when he and Ron went home for the summer holiday.

When he had finished his own letter, Harry ran down the passageway with the package to find Ron. He showed him Mother's instruction. The brothers sat side by side on Ron's bed.

'Go on, Ron, you open it.'

Inside was a photograph, which Ron held on to, and a short note, which he gave to Harry to read aloud: 'We had this taken while Fred was on leave. As you can see, I am sitting in front of father's portrait. Fred said he didn't mind carrying it so we took it with us to the photographer's studio! Father would have been so proud of Fred.' When the letter was finished, Ron handed the photograph to Harry. Mother, seated with her hands crossed on her lap, was smiling gently at the camera. Fred, in full uniform, was standing at her side, his left hand loosely holding the back of her chair. He looked more serious, but there was a glimmer of a smile on his face. Behind them, Father, looking incongruously youthful, stared out from his portrait on the wall. This was a little less than life-size and its frame was barely visible, so in the faded vignette he seemed to be emerging from the shadowy near-distance, as if coming from another room in the house to join them.

In his letter home that evening, Harry wrote: 'Dear Mother, thank you for your letter. It must have been nice having Fred at home. Ron and I hope we will see him too when the summer holiday comes. We have been playing tug-of-war and today I have been on a long cross-country run. I am going to read *The Jungle Book* by Rudyard Kipling. Thank you for sending the photograph. It was comforting to see Father with you and Fred. Your loving son, Harry.'

When he next bumped into Mr Chandler, Harry had decided, he would ask him about Kipling's son. He saw him most days in class, but he wanted to speak to him privately. He suspected there might be more to say on the subject than could be managed in the few minutes of changeover time between lessons. Besides, he liked talking to Mr Chandler, and didn't feel entirely comfortable about doing so in front of his classmates.

His opportunity came the following Saturday when he was returning from the village after running an errand for Mrs Shepherd. As he came through the school gates, he saw Mr Chandler walking in his direction. The teacher spotted Harry and waved.

'Henry! Not been on another cross-country run, I hope?'

'Hello, sir. No, I've been to the village for Mrs Shepherd.'

'Doing a good turn. Well done. In fact, if you've a bit more spare time, you can do one for me. I've got to get the chapel ready for the service tomorrow. Would you come and help me?'

Inside the chapel, Mr Chandler asked Harry if he would tidy the hymn books and pick up any rubbish on the floor. While Harry did this, Mr Chandler put up the numbers of the hymns for the next day, tidied the music on the organ console, and replaced the burnt-down candles of the previous week with some new ones. When everything was done, he sat down on the front pew and stared up at a point above the altar as if contemplating a world less visible. Harry came over and joined him.

'So how are you getting on with *The Jungle Book*? Are you enjoying it?'

'I am, sir...'

'What about the animals?'

'I think I like Baloo the bear best, sir. Who was your nephew's favourite?'

'Do you know, I'm not sure, but he was a very big fan of Kipling's stories.'

'Mrs Holloway had a visitor last week, a soldier, and I heard him say something about Mr Kipling's son and a dreadful business. Do you know what he was talking about?'

'I think I do, Henry.'

'Are you allowed to tell me? Did his son do something wrong or did something happen to him?'

'No, he did nothing wrong. Quite the opposite. He was a soldier. His name was John and he was Kipling's eldest

96

child and his only son. He died fighting in France - over two years ago now, I believe.'

'Is he buried in England, like your nephew?' Even as he spoke, Harry realised that this was an impossibility.

'Sadly not. He died on the battlefield and after the battle they couldn't find his body. That's made things much worse for his poor parents.'

'So doesn't he have a grave with his name on it?'

'No, he doesn't.'

Harry thought about this. He couldn't imagine not knowing where his father was buried, not being able to visit the grave and tell him what had been happening. Surely a body wasn't that hard to find, even if it was in France. The other soldiers must have helped look for him. Perhaps they didn't look hard enough. Then his thoughts took another turn.

'Sir, do you believe dead soldiers can send messages to their families?'

Mr Chandler turned to face him.

'Well, that's a very difficult question. What do you mean exactly? Why do you ask?'

Harry was reluctant to mention the night his mother had visited the Kentons. Instead he said, 'Well, if they were, then maybe Mr Kipling's son could tell his father where his body is.'

By now the setting sun was turning the western windows of the chapel to a faint pink.

'Goodness, look at the time. You ought to be getting back, Henry, or Mrs Shepherd will be worried about you. Thank you for helping me. Off you go. Better hurry.'

Harry was old enough now to realise that adults were not always prepared to tell you the full story and made up excuses sometimes to avoid doing so. He sensed Mr Chandler was holding something back. He hadn't said it was impossible for the dead soldiers to communicate with the living. But nor had he offered any guidance as to how such a communication could take place. With so little to go on, Harry had to draw his own conclusions. The soldiers could send messages, he decided as he walked back up Top Road to Moore House in the glow of the setting sun, but maybe you had to take the trouble to *ask* them.

The long school year at last came to an end and Harry and Ron were to go home for their first summer holiday. Not all pupils were as fortunate, with some facing the prospect of dull, uncomfortable weeks with distant relatives they hardly knew. Others were looking forward to seeing grandparents or cousins. Boys who had nowhere to go were being taken on school camp, which was generally reckoned to be a good thing. A few days before the holiday began, every boy was given a haircut and seen by the doctor. On the final night at school, a bath was obligatory, after which the boys were presented with clean clothes for their various journeys, these simple preparations adding to a rising sense of anticipation. As they packed their suitcases, Harry and Ron could barely contain their excitement, which was considerably increased by the news from their mother that Fred might also be home on leave.

Violet was there to meet them at Reading station. The boys spotted her as the train slowed, and it had barely stopped before they were on the platform with their belongings. None of them could contain their delight at this long-awaited reunion and other travellers turned to watch them laughing and hugging each other. Harry presented Violet with a small bouquet, and Ron handed her a lettuce, school-grown gifts that the boys had been given that morning. Violet almost cried as she accepted them.

It was a warm summer's evening by the time they arrived back in Bottle Green. The front garden was luxuriant with wild roses and other summer flowers. 'We're home, we're home,' they shouted as they ran up the path. Violet unlocked the front door and they burst through, down the short passage and into the kitchen, fumbling excitedly with the back door key, then straight into the garden for a celebratory lap while Violet was still in the hallway managing their luggage.

Over tea, they poured out everything they could think of to tell their mother, whether they had already written it in a letter or not. Harry let Ron do most of the talking while he sat quietly, adjusting to the feeling of being home. Then Violet told them more about her work at Mrs Buckley's, about Fred's visit a few months earlier, and how she visited Father's grave every Sunday after church to tell him how proud she was of their three dutiful sons.

There was a surprise for them in the sitting room. Mrs Buckley had recently acquired a new piano and had sent her old one over to Bottle Green as a gift and as a way of thanking Violet for all her kindness. That evening before the boys went to bed, Violet played them a song they had not heard before, one taught to her by her Irish grandmother. The boys sat on the sofa, captivated. Ron gazed proudly at his still beautiful mother. The exquisite lilt of the song and its rising cadences sank down into

Harry's heart as if concentrating there all the sadness he had known in his life so far.

Later, as Harry lay in bed, enjoying the comforting familiarity of home, he heard his mother playing the piano again. She was singing too, very softly. He wondered what story could possibly be told to such a haunting tune and fell asleep straining to make out the words. The bedroom window was open and he imagined the music drifting across the fields, a woman calling for an absent loved one, perhaps a soldier gone away to war.

The boys had arrived home on a Saturday, and the next day they attended church. Violet felt proud as a bride as she took her place with Harry on one side and Ron on the other. Joy flooded through her when she heard their voices piping the hymns. How good it was to be back, Harry thought as he sang, and nothing changed too badly. But of course there were many small changes, if you looked closely enough. The Kentons were in church. Mrs Kenton looked pinched round the mouth now, tense from sustained grief. Jessie seemed somehow abandoned, no longer like a young woman waiting confidently to meet her future husband. And the cares that had weighed so heavily on Mr Kenton since Albert's death now appeared to have taken full possession of him. The churchyard was somehow shabbier, untidy. But at Father's grave, it was more evident that time had passed. The conifer which Violet had planted by the plot was taller now than the headstone. The ground around the grave had resettled after its disturbance, and was once more grassed over. The headstone itself had started to weather and the lettering no longer had that awful starkness of the newly-prepared epitaph.

Violet bent to clear away some dead roses. 'Look who's come to see you,' she whispered.

The rhythms of home quickly replaced the rhythms of school. Mornings were spent at Mrs Buckley's house. She had been almost as excited as Violet at the prospect of seeing the boys again and welcomed them with huge hugs. Her questions about school seemed endless. She had kept all their letters in a box and read them over and over. Now she wanted to fill in missing details. Did Mrs Shepherd have any children of her own? Why wasn't Mr Chandler married? What about that nice young soldier, Lieutenant Holloway? Harry did his best to answer her questions. The ones about their lessons and their daily routines were straightforward. For the rest, the answers seemed unsatisfactory.

There was plenty to do at Linden Hill. Often, Mrs Buckley would ask the boys to help Violet in the house, where there were jobs like dusting and polishing. There was a lot of rain that July, but when the showers had passed, she sent them outside to sweep the yard or wipe the cobwebs from the windows. Harry liked it most when he was allowed to help Mr Jennings in the garden, deadheading the roses, trimming the hedges, weeding the beds. Taking Harry under his wing, Mr Jennings supplemented the knowledge of plants which Harry had already acquired from Violet, teaching him their growing habits and the secrets of helping them to thrive.

Most mornings, Mrs Buckley sent Harry into the parlour for half an hour to practise the piano. Ron was allowed to go with him and read or colour while Harry played. Mrs Buckley would often come and listen once Harry had finished the exercises and moved on to the pieces he was learning.

'You *are* making progress, Harry.' She seemed pleased. 'Are you enjoying it? Do you get plenty of time to practise at school?'

'There's a piano in the dining hall and I'm allowed to practise on that.'

'Not when everyone's eating, I hope.'

'No. Usually in the afternoon when lessons have finished. Mr Matthews says I'm doing really well and if I want I could start to learn the organ next year. Then one day I might be good enough to play in chapel.'

'Would you like that?'

'I might be a bit nervous but I'll try.'

'Well that's the right attitude. I'm very proud of you, Harry, and so is the Colonel. I often tell him about you and Ron when I write.' Harry had never met the colonel. It was strange to have played with the old toys and dusted the study of a man you didn't know. Even stranger to be written about in letters exchanged between that man and his wife. Of course, Harry expected to meet him one day and rather looked forward to doing so. The house was full of the colonel's presence as if he was due to return at any moment. His hat and coat were hanging in the hallway, and his walking stick and umbrella were ready to be plucked from their stand as required. A tray was always laid out for him in the kitchen should he return in urgent need of refreshment. And the half-full whisky decanter in the study stood by with his nightly tipple as if he had poured his drink from it only the evening before.

'Do you miss him, Mrs Buckley?' Harry was prompted to ask.

'I do, Harry, very much indeed. It seems such a long time since I last saw him.'

'I miss Fred too,' Harry confided. 'And Father.'

Mrs Buckley squeezed Harry's hand and wiped away a fleck of dust from her eye.

The previous term, Harry had read *The Jungle Book* three times. He remembered Mr Chandler's instruction to relate the tales to Ron and so decided he had better know them particularly well. He had promised Ron that he would tell him the stories when they were back at Bottle Green and the best place to tell them was in Warren Woods, where they could pretend they were in the Indian jungle. Violet seemed reluctant to let them wander too far in the afternoons and often had things for them to do, but one very warm afternoon she said she needed to rest and they could go to the woods if they liked.

Of all the tales and all the animals, what had captured Harry's imagination more than anything was the story of the Cold Lairs, the ancient abandoned city in the depths of the jungle, where Mowgli had been imprisoned by the lawless monkeys. On the way to the woods, Harry explained to Ron who Mowgli was and why the monkeys had captured him.

'Where are we going, Harry? What are we going to do?

'We're going in search of the lost city. We'll pretend we are Baloo and Bagheera going to rescue Mowgli.'

Harry had only been to the woods when Fred or Mother had been with them and thought it would be a good idea to find the spot where the scout camp had been. He wasn't entirely sure of the way but they followed the path as best they could even though it was overgrown now, untrodden by the tramping feet of the scout patrols. At last they came to a hollow and, ignoring the fact that Kipling's fictional city was built on a hill, Harry declared they had arrived. Now that they were here, he wasn't quite sure how to continue the game. So they sat on a fallen trunk and Harry described the city to Ron, designating the trees and bushes as temples and battlements. Then he told him how the panther and the bear, assisted by Kaa the snake, had rescued Mowgli and how they had all escaped at last. Ron listened intently. But beneath the make-believe about monkeys and other animals, Harry was aware of imaginary people who had once populated this city of his invention and, though they were nothing more than shadows, he seemed to sense them living and breathing and watching the two brothers as they played.

When the boys had been home for almost a fortnight, a letter arrived from Fred saying that he was unable to get leave and what rotten luck it was when he hadn't seen his brothers for so long. Harry and Ron were bitterly disappointed. They had so looked forward to seeing Fred and have him organise games and adventures for them. It was more fun going to Warren Woods if Fred was with them. They could show him where they had carved their initials and he could add his own if he wanted to. They could tell him all about school, show him their reports, and have him listen to Harry playing the piano.

'It doesn't seem fair,' said Violet, 'but we have to learn to be patient. Poor Mrs Buckley hasn't seen her husband for a very long time indeed. The war can't go on for ever, it just can't. And as soon as it's over, Fred will be allowed home to see us. At least...' She hesitated. 'At least he is alive and that's something to be very thankful for, isn't it?'

'When will the war end, Ma?' asked Ron. 'I can't remember when there was no war. Can you, Harry?'

And Harry could, but only just.

One afternoon when the boys had already been home for a fortnight, Edith Kenton called to see Violet, who brought her out to the garden, where Harry and Ron were shelling peas on the grass. They sat down together on the garden bench, a gift from Violet to Fred when he last came home on leave. Edith had just received a letter from Robert, which she invited her friend to read. This sharing of letters from Fred and Robert had become a routine for Violet and Edith, a means for the anxious mothers to increment their scant knowledge of what their sons were doing and how they were keeping. Harry watched the two women, his mother intent on what she was reading, and Mrs Kenton intent on Violet as if her facial expressions might provide clues to Robert's well-being and even to his fate.

'Do you think he seems well?' Edith asked.

'Yes, I do,' said Violet.

'But he tells me so little, and I don't think he's received my last three letters.

'He doesn't want to worry you,'

'But it makes me worry more. Not knowing the truth is worse than anything.'

Harry considered this statement, remembering once more the gathering he had witnessed in Mrs Kenton's sitting room, an event which he had now concluded was, without doubt, Mrs Kenton's attempt to communicate with her dead son Albert, to be reassured that he was safe and well in another life. Perhaps there was more consolation to be had from her dead son, whom she could apparently contact, than from her living son, whom she could not.

'I must be going,' said Edith after a while. 'Jessie will be home.' She stood up.

'Thank you for coming,' said Violet. 'And I'm sorry again about this evening.'

'Next time,' said Edith, and squeezed her friend's hand.

That evening after tea, Harry and Ron washed the dishes and cleared the kitchen table so they could all play cards. When they were ready, Harry went out to the garden to fetch his mother. She was sitting on Fred's bench, looking down at her lap and twisting her wedding ring gently round her finger. She looked up and smiled when Harry approached.

'What were you thinking about?' Harry wanted to know.

'About the war. About Fred. About Father.'

'You said in one of your letters that Fred took you to Warren Row. That's where you and Father met, isn't it? Will you tell me what happened?'

And she told him the story of the sign at The Old House at Home.

'But the sign Father painted has gone, hasn't it?'

'That's right. There's a new one there now. But you could say that Father's sign served its purpose, couldn't you?' She laughed to herself.

'Did you want to go to Mrs Kenton's this evening? Ron and I can manage on our own.'

'It doesn't matter, Harry. Come on, let's go and see what Ron's doing.'

At last, when Harry and Ron had returned to school and the autumn term was no longer new, the war came to an end. Harvest and spud-picking had passed, and the cold weather had already set in. A week or so earlier, the boys had once more watched their effigies perish in the Guy Fawkes bonfire. Christmas was almost in sight. News that an armistice had been signed travelled quickly around the school on that Monday morning: no one knew who had broken it first, and no one cared. In class, the teachers read the newspapers to the boys and let them make flags or simply talk about this momentous event. At eleven o'clock the bell was rung and lessons were suspended. The boys flooded out of their classrooms and along to the dining hall where they were served mugs of tea with bread and jam, a treat usually reserved for Sundays. The din was silenced briefly for an announcement that there was to be a parade before lunch, and a special chapel service at six o'clock.

The boys emerged from the dining hall to find the school band had assembled outside and was playing a patriotic march. The scouts had changed into their uniforms and were formed up ready for the parade. Reverend Bell and the headmaster, Mr Oddy, appeared on their bicycles and led the band off along Top Road. The scouts followed, and then staff and boys fell in behind them, a few more teachers on bicycles following up the rear. Round the school grounds they went, with no one to watch them but the cows and horses on the farm. Everyone was taking part in the celebration, whether they truly understood its significance or not. Harry and Ron marched along together, waving their flags, and preoccupied with the thought that Fred had lived through the war and would soon be on his way home. After a complete circuit of the grounds, the parade came to a halt on the little green by the school entrance. Everyone gathered round the flag staff for the raising of the Union Jack. Then they sang *God Save the King*, and gave three cheers for the monarch and his armed forces.

The afternoon had been designated a half-holiday, which the boys spent in their houses. They were supervised by the matrons in their common rooms, some playing games, while others sat down to write letters to relatives. Harry and Ron agreed to share their letter-writing responsibilities. Harry wrote to Violet and to Mrs Buckley, while Ron wrote to Fred. 'You must be very glad it's all over,' Harry wrote to his mother, 'and that Fred has come through.'

The reflections of the chapel service that evening seemed to Harry more in keeping with his mood that day than the triumphant parade of the morning. 'Never forget what has been lost,' the Reverend Bell warned the boys, 'never forget the sacrifices made by those men dear to you and dear to our community.' Everyone sat with their heads bowed, configuring their remembrances. Harry thought how the war had diminished his life and the lives of those he knew. Even Father's decline and death he was unable to disentangle from the war and Fred's departure for the army. Mr Chandler had watched his nephew suffer and die, never again to sit with him in the worn old armchairs of his study. Mrs Buckley had forgone four happy years with the colonel Harry had never even met. Mrs Kenton, estranged from this world, lived only on the thoughts of her dear dead Albert. And poor Rudyard Kipling had not only lost his son, but had no prospect of visiting a grave at which to mourn for him. Much disaster met with, Harry concluded, and very little of triumph.

III
1945 – 1946

Early September 1945

On the deck of the troopship transporting him from India to Singapore, with the rising moon revealing the vast emptiness of the sea, Harry found himself thinking back to that final day of the previous war. How vivid that day still seemed, the earlier part of the morning marked out in minutes and seconds as teachers and pupils waited for hostilities to cease, and the later hours filled with celebration in so many forms, the elation made sweeter by thankfulness and relief. How different it had felt when, in the oppressive heat of India, Harry had heard that war with Germany was once more at an end, news which seemed less poignant, less momentous to him as an adult than it did nearly twenty-seven years earlier as a child a long way from home. No overwhelming sense of relief this time, very little beyond the lassitude he felt from his fever and from all that had preceded his departure from England. Besides, even though the tide had turned and victory was likely to follow, the fighting in Asia was not yet over and there was a lurking suspicion that the continuing struggle of the armies in India, Burma and the Far East had been forgotten by those who were celebrating victory in Europe. But now, at last, with the capitulation of the Japanese, the global war had officially ended and Harry allowed himself some time to reflect on what this meant for him. More months abroad, certainly, time to acclimatise to this new continent. Time too, perhaps, to assimilate the circumstances which had caused him to be cast adrift and, for the second time in his life, to find himself an exile.

Gazing out to sea, an involuntary image came to him of that dreadful night nearly five years before when the Germans had bombed Coventry, the brilliant but treacherous moon lighting the way to their undefended target. An unwelcome thought, not because of the human suffering, although heaven knows that was bad enough, but for other reasons that lurked uncomfortably just below the level of full consciousness. Leaving England had subdued these potent recollections, but not eliminated them, or their power to unsettle him. Harry forced his attention towards his brothers, thousands of miles away, their days just beginning. They were probably at work, or maybe having breakfast with their wives and children. He tried to work out the time difference. No, definitely at work by now. How he missed them, Ron in particular. It was nearly seven months since the formal occasion when he had last seen Fred, a little less since he had last met with Ron, just a week or so before he embarked, in fact, although what they talked about that day eluded him. He wondered how often Ron reminisced about their schooldays at Farningham. Lately, Harry had found himself returning to them often, seeking shelter there, in those early years, from the blast of more recent memories which would otherwise have unmanned him. Did Ron remember the exhilaration of the victory parade on that chilly November morning, or the simple delight of writing letters home that holiday afternoon? How shocking it would have been then to have had a revelation of the coming years, of this other long war, and of the random sequence of events that would cause Harry to be standing here now, in the moonlight, surrounded by the waters of the Indian Ocean.

A few days later, the SS Strathmore arrived in Singapore. The docks were crowded, partly with carts and oxen, but mainly with local people who had come to welcome the troops. A large Union Jack fluttered and flapped from the ship's railings, as if in coy response to the rising cheers of the crowd below. Harry stood on an upper deck with his pals, Joe and Norman, somewhat moved by the reception. For the first time, he felt that the war was truly over, and he marvelled at the fact that he was to play a small part in the restoration of order and normality to this tiny precious colony on the far side of the world. And he marvelled too at the evidence of so much humanity on the move, one contingent of troops following fast in the wake of another, each man and woman with a unique story of what they had seen and experienced, and what had brought them together in this place.

For some months now, Harry had considered Norman and Joe his firm friends. He had never possessed that ready facility for friendship that Ron had, but in these past few months, either at sea or during their posting in India, he had started to get to know and to trust them. The sharing of confidences did not come easily to Harry and even now he had held back much of his own personal war story. They knew that he had spent several years working in an aircraft factory, hating the monotony of the work and being confined indoors, away from the gardening he loved, but that his work as a volunteer for the Red Cross had eventually led him into the Medical Corps for training as an orderly. His posting abroad, Harry hoped, needed no further explanation and he was grateful for his friends' lack of curiosity, or maybe their forbearance in not asking.

It was Norman he had teamed up with first, on the long journey from Southampton to Bombay. He had noticed him once or twice in the mess, having finished his meal, tapping his fingers on the table, as Violet used to on the kitchen table at Bottle Green. Some days later, when Harry went up on deck for a cigarette, he found himself standing next to Norman, who was doing finger exercises along the railing, as if in imitation of a demented crab.

'Missing your piano by any chance?' Harry asked him.

'All the time,' said Norman, surprising Harry by pulling a photograph of it out of his top pocket. 'Here. Don't know what possessed me to abandon it like this. Do you play?'

'Yes, I do, but not especially well, I'm afraid.'

Norman, it turned out, was a professional pianist and had trained at the Royal Academy of Music. He wasn't what you would call a household name, but before the war he had counted himself lucky to be earning a decent living the way he had always hoped to. When the war had started, much of his work had dried up and, having no inclination to take up arms, he decided to join the Medical Corps.

'Funny how a war makes people hungry for music,' he said. 'I remember going to hear Myra Hess play one lunchtime at the National Gallery, after they'd removed all the works of art. Had to join a long queue and then sit on the floor. But it was worth it. More than worth it. Inspired me to put on a few concerts at our local church. Annoying really, getting called abroad like this. Had to cancel a good show. I was hoping to play the *Liebesträume*. Liszt. Do you know it?'

Harry did indeed know it. Keen to share his enthusiasm for music with Norman, he let slip that he had been learning part of it before he left England.

'Number 3, I assume,' said Norman. 'One of the most beautiful melodies I know. And one of the saddest.'

'The fingering was giving me some difficulties, though.'

'I'll tell you what we'll do, Harry. As soon as we're billeted we'll go in search of a piano and I'll give you a lesson or two.'

It was Norman who introduced Harry to Joe. Harry understood immediately why they had become friends. They shared that open, straightforward manner with people they hardly knew, although Joe's interests were somewhat different from Norman's. In civilian life, Joe was a carpenter like Ron but the similarity did not end there. He spent hours dismembering broken artefacts, anything he could get hold of, laying bare their component parts for scrutiny, repair and reassembly. Harry recalled the many and various dissections Ron had performed at Bottle Green

– watches, clocks and wireless sets on the kitchen table, a motorbike engine and a lawnmower on the grass at the back of the house. Norman had first got to know Joe when he had offered to repair his broken wristwatch. Norman introduced Joe to Harry as an heroic mender of anything broken. 'But I don't do bones, I'm afraid,' said Joe. 'We'll leave that to the experts.'

'What about hearts?' Norman quipped.

In India, the three men spent what they could of their off-duty time together. They sat in the shade and played cards or talked about gardening. Their complaints about the weakness of the tea developed into a game of stranger and stranger suggestions about its provenance. They exchanged anecdotes and information about their working lives but, apart from this, they made very few personal disclosures, and Harry preferred it that way. When he succumbed to the Indian climate and was confined to quarters with a serious fever, it was Norman and Joe who took turns to drop in and see how he was doing. The piano lessons remained a promise, but privately Harry didn't feel like playing, not just yet anyway.

And now they were in Singapore. Their unit was to be billeted near the large British government hospital where they would be working. The day after disembarking, they were ordered to report for duty, Harry and Norman in the same ward together, Joe just up the corridor. In Ward 5B Harry found two nursing sisters hard at work, preparing for the influx of prisoners of war from Changi jail. There had been plenty for the nurses to do to bring the ward up to the stringent standards required by Matron. When they had arrived the hospital was deserted. Well, not exactly deserted, but overrun by monkeys. It was hard to believe it had been as dirty and insect-infested as the nurses described, given that now it was almost gleaming. But there was still a great deal to do, cleaning out the lockers, airing the sheets and blankets, gathering together and storing the limited medical supplies that were arriving daily. In the neglected and overgrown grounds of the hospital, Harry found tropical flowers, red, pink and yellow hibiscus, which he picked and brought into the ward.

The nurses, Sister Turner and Sister Kirwin, like their counterparts in India, were members of Queen Alexandra's nursing corps and had the status of officers. They were efficient, disciplined, determined. Harry rather liked them. They were a little aloof and that was easier. He didn't mind taking orders from them or the matter-of-fact manner in which they explained the daily routines to the orderlies and showed them where everything was kept. No fuss, that was their way, and when they realised Harry's capabilities, they largely left him to his own devices.

Within a couple of days, the patients from Changi started to arrive in Ward 5B. Harry watched as the nurses led them in and helped them to bed. They were weak and emaciated, their bones painfully visible beneath their flesh. Swollen knees and ankles and the uneven patina of their skin bore further witness to their malnourishment. Several were covered in sores. What else was wrong with them was clearly evident in some cases, less easy to diagnose in others. Many were barely able to walk, and Harry was called to assist two men who needed to be carried in on stretchers. Whatever their condition, they were all young soldiers for whom fear had now subsided into relief. One of them wept openly as he stepped into the ward and saw the glorious flowers which shifted his world from grey despair to hope. Another came doddering towards his bed where Sister Kirwin stood neatly in her white uniform and starched lawn veil. He walked with a makeshift crutch, looking down as he did so. But when he reached the bed, as if alerted by the pool of brightness that seemed to spread around her, he looked up and said, 'I have come from the depths of hell and am greeted by an angel from heaven.' Then he got into bed and, as far as Harry could tell, said nothing more for many days.

The surrender of the Japanese was to be formalised with full military pomp. Admiral Mountbatten had arrived in Singapore to officiate. Harry was curious to see him. Some of the orderlies were off duty and went to watch the parade. Outside the Municipal Building, Lord Louis inspected the naval guard of honour. Harry, Joe and Norman were some distance away and it was hard to see much of what was going on but the bright ranks of naval men in their stark white uniforms were almost startling. So much whiteness amid so much devastation. Lord Louis was the most resplendent of them all in his immaculate uniform. Lord Louis Mountbatten, who was related to the King, and who had already been immortalised on screen by Noel Coward. How could Harry forget seeing the film, with Celia Johnson as the captain's wife. After the signing ceremony, which took place behind closed doors, the Japanese commanders walked down the steps, dull, subdued. It was hard to think of these humiliated men as perpetrators of the atrocities which had taken place in the last few years, atrocities which everyone seemed to know about, but no one wished to discuss.

After the march-past, there was a little time left to look round the city before they had to be back at the hospital. A short walk took them to St Andrew's Cathedral. When they stepped inside, away from the tropical heat, it was hard to believe they weren't back in England. They wandered apart, the transepts and colonnades allowing each of them some privacy in their explorations. It was surprising that the cathedral was virtually empty given the number of people out on the streets. Harry wandered over to inspect the organ console. He expected to find the cabinet locked but it had been left open. The stops, the pedals, the array of manuals seemed invitingly still. He climbed onto the bench, sliding up and down it a little to gain the right position. One switch, and a faint vibration indicated the instrument was ready. Harry thought for a moment about what he should play and chose the hymn that he had sung that first day at Farningham and which, with a satisfying sense of completion, he had played for the Duke of York at the close of his school career. *Now thank we all our God*, he played, softly at first, getting used to the registration, then louder and richer until the tune resonated through the splendour of the Victorian edifice. When he had finished, he slipped gently from the organ seat and went to meet his companions.

'We must find that piano,' said Norman. 'By Christmas at the latest.'

That evening back at their billet, Harry took out the three books he had brought with him, each carefully wrapped in brown paper for protection. He knew the books by their size and thickness. He selected *The Jungle Book*, unwrapped it, and flicked two or three times through its pages, where he had inserted various folded pieces of paper. 'Patience, Harry, you know you put it in here,' he said aloud to himself. Eventually he pulled out an old newspaper cutting and unfolded it carefully on the bed. The article was about the Annual Festival at Farningham in June 1926, Harry's last official day at school, the day when Frank Chandler had given him the Kipling. He reacquainted himself with the faded photograph that accompanied the article, holding it close for inspection.

From a slight vantage point, the camera looked down the main drive, which disappeared at the top right hand corner of the picture, round a gentle bend, towards the unseen entrance at West Hill. An important personage was arriving in a Daimler. The younger boys of the school, pristine in their uniforms, lined the route, white Eton collars delineating their ranks. They were all intent on the spectacle, except for one lad who seemed more interested in looking up at the photographer. Visitors to the school were gathered behind the rows of boys. It was high summer and the ladies protected themselves from the sun with their parasols as they watched the stately progress of the visitor's car. Two long ropes had been attached to the front bumper and the car was seemingly being pulled up the gentle incline of the drive by a group of boys from the scout troop. Were it not for the slackness of the rope, the photograph might have given the illusion that the vehicle had broken down and the scouts had come to its rescue. But the car had no need of assistance in this pageant, the boys in their practical brown uniforms being required simply to demonstrate the respect and duty they owed to the school's royal patron and all he represented. Nine scouts pulled each rope, and it would have been hard to identify most of them from this blurry image except that Harry had marked out Ron with a cross. He wondered now why he had done so when he would never fail to identify his own brother, but it struck him that the mark might be of assistance to some future generation. Seventeen years old, almost too old by this time for the scouts, Ron stood out as one of the tallest lads. He too seemed to be looking up at the photographer, pleased perhaps that the moment would be recorded for posterity.

Harry could remember where he was standing when the Duke of York's car went past. Earlier that morning he had delivered a large wheelbarrow filled with flowers to the dining hall, which Mrs Shepherd and some other helpers were waiting to decorate in honour of the Duke and other dignitaries. A few hours later he went back to see the results. The hall was rich with floral scents. He complimented Mrs Shepherd on the display. 'You grew them, Harry,' was all she said. As he walked back to Moore House, the Duke's car was coming up the drive, preceded by the two lines of scouts. Harry was on the same side as Ron, and they caught each other's eyes as Ron went past. Harry suspected his brother would rather be playing cricket on a perfect summer's day like this, but it was quite a spectacle, a sight he was unlikely to forget.

That afternoon, Harry had an unanticipated conversation with the royal visitor. There had been a special service in the chapel, at which the Duke had given the address. Harry had played the organ. He had practised for weeks and it seemed to have gone well. He liked playing for services. He liked the transition at the end of the service as the congregation gradually petered out. At the start of the voluntary, the chapel was full. By the time Harry played the final chord, he was alone. He could sense the chapel emptying as the acoustic changed. There was a relief in looking round when the music was finished to see empty pews and to be able to slip away quietly without attracting attention. So when he came out into the sunshine, he was surprised to find the Duke still there, talking to some of the other guests, Reverend Bell hovering nearby.

'Ah, the organist,' said the Duke, coming over to Harry to shake his hand. 'Splendid performance. Very well played.'

'Thank you, sir. That's very kind of you.'

'Do you practise often?'

'As often as I can, sir. I enjoy it.'

'Very good. Keep it up. Well done.'

Harry often thought about the Duke and his kind words that day. He was a handsome man, only a few years older than Fred. He had recently married the beautiful Lady Elizabeth Bowes-Lyon and Harry wondered how a man who, according to the newspapers, seemed so retiring and diffident had first approached a woman of her beauty and popularity, his royal status notwithstanding. And now, through a twist of fortune that was both unexpected and undesired, he was King. Harry tried to work out how Lord Mountbatten and the King were related but he wasn't entirely sure. Distant cousins, he thought. Joe or Norman would probably know. But he did know that the King's grandmother had laid the foundation stone for Farningham School and also founded the nursing corps to which Sister Kirwin and Sister Turner belonged, bestowing the weight of her expectations on schoolboys and nurses alike.

Unsurprisingly, such brushes with royalty did not normally play a part in Harry's life. Today's ceremony was the first such occasion he had witnessed since that Annual Festival in 1926. Back then, the Duke's visit had seemed something grand, a recognition of how he valued the school of which he was the president, an acknowledgement of all the school had done to prepare the sons of the empire for whatever lay ahead. But now it seemed more like a dress rehearsal for times like these when British men would need the custom of ritual and pomp to bring order once more to a world that had fallen apart.

The piano Norman had wished for was found only a few weeks later. Joe and some other orderlies had been sent off to a local school, currently abandoned, to see what they could salvage which might be of use to the hospital. The piano was in what presumably had been an assembly hall. It was badly out of tune but relatively undamaged. Norman got permission for a group of volunteers to retrieve it from the school and re-house it at the hospital. The music would be beneficial for the patients, he said. It would take them out of themselves, cheer them up. It took six men to manoeuvre the instrument into the back of an ambulance. They drove along the damaged roads, leaning their weight against it to prevent any knocks. At the hospital it was agreed that the piano be kept in a small lobby where it could be heard from several of the wards, or wheeled into a different area if needed. Harry, Joe and Norman made it their project. Joe meticulously cleaned the mechanism to unstick some of the keys. He repaired the music rest and oiled the pedals to stop them squeaking. Norman tuned the piano as best he could using makeshift tools, a spanner borrowed from the army mechanics as his tuning key and swabs from the operating theatre for the mutes. It wasn't perfect, but it was playable. Harry polished the wood and brass, and gave the piano an appearance that would be acceptable to Matron, who watched disapprovingly as the piano returned to active service.

Liebestraum would have to wait a little longer, Harry realised with some relief, but the piano was nevertheless a wonderful addition to their lives. Matron had not wanted it at first. 'This is a hospital, not a concert hall,' she had been heard to remark to the Brigadier. 'We have no time to be tripping over musical instruments lying around in the corridor.' In the end, she softened. On Sunday mornings Harry was permitted to play hymns for the patients and, once a week, Norman was allowed to give an hour's recital. Matron had forbidden any interim practice on the grounds of disturbance to the sick, but Norman played as if their return to health depended on it, while the orderlies and the nurses listened in private admiration as they went about their work. And for that brief hour, Harry noticed, the faint tincture of horror which permeated Ward 5B was somehow, mysteriously, sweetened.

Sister Kirwin later told Harry and Norman more about the state of the hospital when the nurses arrived, not long after the Japanese surrender. Everything that could be of any use to the Japanese had been taken away. There were no beds, no bed linen or blankets, no instruments, nothing useful at all. The x-ray machines were broken and beyond repair. It was largely thanks to Matron's determination and, apparently, the help and intervention of Lady Mountbatten, that the hospital had become functional again so quickly. The sisters had worked round the clock to get everything ready for their patients.

'One of the most satisfying things I've ever done,' said Sister Kirwin, 'getting this place back in order. You need to have seen the chaos to believe it.'

'It must have been exhausting,' said Norman. 'You nurses are superhuman.'

'You'd have done the same, I'm sure.'

Far worse than the efforts needed on the ward, she said, was going to Changi to help assess the medical needs of the liberated soldiers before moving them to the hospital. Hundreds of men were in need of long-term care. Some had been fortunate, if that was the word, in being admitted to an overcrowded prison hospital while other sick men were left to languish in their cells. She found it hard to believe how many had survived for so long on little more than rice and tea, eked out with whatever fruits or vegetables they managed to procure. Those most in need of nourishment were the first to be denied it, the Japanese refusing to provide rice for men too sick to work, men who now, like babies, needed to be slowly weaned back onto solid food.

In the tiny cells, where four had occupied the space originally intended for one, she had started to understand the mental state of the men they were caring for. Here were the trappings of a collective determination to survive – makeshift beds knocked together from old wooden crates, threadbare sacks filled with grass for pillows, and lamps made from tins of diesel and pieces of string. Brutal, stark accommodation, privacy out of the question, bad enough for one or two nights, unthinkable for months on end. On a noticeboard in a corridor, she happened to add, someone had pinned a typed copy of 'If', and Harry wondered what Kipling would make of his poem hanging there to urge those exhausted men, tired from waiting, to find the will to hold on. Nurses, too, had been imprisoned in the jail and many of them were recuperating at Raffles Hotel. If she knew any of them, Sister Kirwin didn't mention it.

She and some other nurses had also been taken to see the cemetery, where, in the early days of the occupation, the British prisoners had been told to clear an area of jungle so they could bury their dead. 'That was the worst place of all,' she told Harry and Norman. 'They'd tried to make it look like a country churchyard back home, with the mounds properly turfed over and with crosses, and you went through an archway with a gate, and it seemed quite peaceful. But then I thought of how many had died so unnecessarily. If only they'd had better medical care or simply better food and conditions, something could have been done...' She tailed off, and turned away from them.

'Please don't talk about it if it upsets you,' said Harry, and gave her his handkerchief. She nodded and blew her nose.

'Thank you,' she said. 'Better get back to work.'

That evening, Harry was reminded of something else Sister Kirwin had mentioned, something one of the patients had told her, how deeply despondent the men in Changi became when months would pass without letters arriving from home. Only occasionally were they allowed to write the briefest of cards themselves and for all they knew these were tossed into a sack and forgotten. Harry realised he hadn't written a single letter since his arrival in Singapore, and, although he had no particular reason now to worry about Ron or Fred, it suddenly occurred to him how much they might be worrying about him. So he wrote Ron a long letter, interspersing his account of Singapore with wry observations about Matron and the food and the monkeys. 'I'm in good health and good spirits,' he told his brother, which was closer to the truth than it had been for many months, but only in part. It was true he was feeling much better now he had acclimatised to the heat and got over the stomach upsets which had left him so enervated. And now

130

he had settled into a routine at the hospital and seen the initial signs of recovery in some of the patients, he felt a stronger sense of purpose than he had for some time. But for all this, he could not shake off the discomfiting awareness that the natural promptings of his heart reached out to nothing but an empty space.

Ron's letter concluded, Harry wrote a similar but distilled letter to Fred, the same events but without the additional remarks that only his younger brother would fully appreciate. When he had finished, he found he was now very much in the mood for writing, so he began a third letter, this time to Frank Chandler who, unbelievably after so many years, was still working, as far as Harry knew, as a teacher at Farningham. He might have retired by now had the war not given him an opportunity to stay on in a place he clearly loved, undertaking the work he still relished. He and Harry had been regular correspondents since Harry had left school, by which time Harry felt his teacher had become his friend. He had been back to Kent on a handful of occasions to visit Frank, the last time being nearly a year before the declaration of war against Germany. He deeply regretted not having seen him for so very long, almost seven years. Frank was still living in the same house at the edge of the school grounds, his study now virtually overrun by books, and the two armchairs, like a pair of old companions, were faded and threadbare, even more of a contrast to the spare chair Frank brought in for additional guests.

'I expect this letter will take some time to reach you,' Harry wrote, 'but I know you'll be keen to hear about my work here, as well as my posting in India.' Harry had long ago stopped feeling like a schoolboy working at his composition whenever he wrote to Frank, although it would never have surprised him to have his letter returned with corrections, but he always considered how to assemble his news. So he began by recounting what had happened since his arrival in Singapore, trying to anticipate what would interest Frank about the colony and holding back what he knew would be of far more interest to him, the time he had spent in India. He described the hospital, how efficiently it had been put back into operation, and told him about some of the patients he was caring for, including Ralph, who had remained virtually silent since he was admitted to Harry's ward. He told Frank about the day of the surrender ceremony when he had caught a distant glimpse of Lord Mountbatten. He described St Andrew's Cathedral and how he had been unable to resist playing the organ. 'It felt like being back in England, but not quite like playing in school chapel,' he wrote. And naturally he mentioned 'If', still, he assumed, adorning the wall of that now deserted prison.

Only then did he turn his attention to India. 'You'll be pleased to learn that I have *The Jungle Book* with me and read it once more while I was in the land of Kipling's birth.' He paused, uncomfortable with this formal tone, and put down his pen. It weighed on his mind, the knowledge that Frank, who frequently proclaimed his preference for home, had always nursed a desire to visit India, a pilgrim paying homage to his favourite writer. Having been directed to India for a very different purpose, Harry nevertheless felt as if he were there on a vicarious mission, in which he had failed. What would be best? To compose an invented tale of India, one that would go some way to satisfying his friend's unfulfilled ambition, or to tell the plain truth? And what was the truth exactly, now he looked back on that time? For one thing, Harry had hardly been well enough to absorb many of his Indian experiences. The ants and the mosquitoes, the stomach upsets, the itchy rash of prickly heat, these all beset him within days of his arrival. Later, convincing himself there was nothing seriously wrong, and equally concerned not to make a fuss, he worked on in the grip of fever long after he should have taken to his bed. After that, it took him several weeks to recuperate and by the time he was feeling more like his old self, his 'English self', as he called it, the war was over and his unit had been reassigned to Singapore.

Was India as he imagined? There was no simple answer to that question. In many ways it was just as he anticipated. The heat, the disease, the traces of the war. And so much of what he saw seemed unremarkably familiar. The ordinary people he encountered, the dhobis and the char wallahs and the postmen, well, they were just going about their daily business. And of course there was no getting away from the fact of the British Raj. The shops attested to it with their signs in English, and then the railway stations, the racetrack at Poona, where he had made a brief visit, so many places were just like England – if it wasn't for the extreme brown dryness and the heat. It was the first time Harry had set foot on foreign soil, and it didn't seem entirely foreign, this distant jewel of the British Empire.

What was it then which left Harry with that constant sense of dislocation? How much could he really attribute to the unfamiliar animals – the monkeys, snakes and tree rats – and the exotic fruits and vegetables he saw on the market stalls? The temples and shrines with their different intricacies, beautiful in their own distinctive way, were they capable of causing him to feel so strangely separated from everything he took to be normal? No, he was unsettled, disorientated before he had even arrived. The deep yearning which India almost promised to satisfy was, he realised now, only to be stilled by something India could not provide. He was doubly displaced, his restlessness compounded by a tantalising sense of an effective but elusive cure. How could he explain all this in a letter?

As for Kipling and his stories, they might just as well have been written and played out on the moon. Harry had wandered around Bombay trying to picture Frank's idol, as a small boy and as a young man, exploring its streets, its people, its way of life, absorbing images that would generate ideas for years to come. In every Indian child's face, he looked in vain for the face of Mowgli, who stubbornly evaded incarnation. Naively, he had half expected to turn a corner one day and find an almost hidden path that would lead him out of the city, away from its everyday traffic, and, after many hours' walking, deliver him to the Cold Lairs, that lost city, where the tumbledown battlements and half-open gates hanging on rusted hinges still whispered of its former inhabitants. But he realised now he was no nearer to Kipling's fictional world than when he had first read of it as a schoolboy in Kent or when he had conjured it up in his own words for Ron that summer in Warren Woods.

In the end, his letter-writing mood evaporated and he curtailed his letter to Frank. There was far too much to tell him about India than he could put in a letter, he said, and he promised that he would try to visit when he was back in England, presumably some time the following year. Already that visit seemed an inviting prospect, sitting by the fire, drinking tea or beer, whiling away a long afternoon as they gradually unravelled their news for each other. By then, Frank would almost certainly have retired, and perhaps have a new perspective on his long years of service at the school. By then, Harry would know how to tell the story of those difficult months in a manner which would not disappoint his attentive listener.

The debt which Harry felt he owed to Frank had accumulated steadily during his school years, starting that first spring when the teacher had introduced him to Kipling's famous poem. On that last day when Harry had met the future king, Frank had invited him out to the local hostelry, an outing which seemed designed to put their friendship on a new footing by taking place away from the confines of the school grounds. The Annual Festival had kept them both busy throughout the morning and the afternoon, but now the excitement and the heat had subsided into the calm quiet of a warm summer's evening. They met at the school gates and strolled down into the village, evaluating the day's various events. Once settled in the bar with their pints, Harry told Frank his plans for the future. He was to return to Bottle Green where he had been offered a post as junior gardener on a private estate.

'Well, I think we can say you've turned out alright then.'

'Not bad. I've learnt a bit about gardening anyway.'

'Perhaps you could give me some advice about my roses before you go. They're in a bad way.'

'I'm only a junior gardener remember. Don't expect me to have all the answers yet.'

'No. The pressure to have the answer is the teacher's unhappy lot.'

After a couple more pints, Frank suggested they make their way back up the hill. He invited Harry to his house. He had something he wanted to give him.

They were silent as they walked up West Hill. The time of day and the descending sun seemed to demand it. They entered the school gates and passed the chapel where someone was practising the organ.

'I'll miss that,' said Harry. 'I'll miss playing the organ for services.'

Frank didn't respond immediately. Then he said, 'I've never forgotten a question you once asked me when you were still quite new, one afternoon when you helped me tidy the chapel. Do you remember? You asked me if the dead could communicate with the living. I avoided replying. But I feel I owe you some kind of response now, before you leave us.'

Harry did remember, all too clearly. He waited for Frank to continue.

'The truth is, I didn't know what to say. I've never known precisely what to believe or how to explain it. So it was impossible to give you a satisfactory answer.'

'Which you felt obliged to do as my teacher.'

'Yes, but that obligation no longer exists.'

'So what do you think?'

'I believe the dead watch over us, stay with us in some way, as if they perceive our need for them. I don't know if they can truly communicate with us. But I do believe we can sense their presence. Sometimes... Sometimes I feel my nephew is with me. In my study. When I'm sitting reading, I sometimes look up and it's as if he is sitting in the other chair, watching me. As if I can almost see him, more than simply with my mind's eye.' They walked a few more yards. 'But that's all. It's not an answer, Harry. It's just telling you what I feel. Nothing more than a hunch, really.'

'Thank you,' said Harry.

The gift which Frank had given Harry that evening took him by surprise, that blue leather volume of *The Jungle Book* which his teacher had lent him so many years before. He remembered taking it back to Moore House with Ron and the empty feeling it gave him when he opened the cover to see that the flyleaf was blank. But now the book had an inscription: 'To Harry, leaving school. May the earth be yours. With best wishes from Frank Chandler. June 1926.'

Harry remembered walking back from Frank's house that evening carrying his gift. He walked to the school gates, breathed in the night air and what little he could still see of the view across the fields and down to the village. The chapel was silent now. The door was locked, or he might have been tempted to enter and play the organ himself one last time. How strange to be thinking of this here in Singapore, so many years later. How vivid that last day at school seemed this evening, as if he could slip out of his billet and, in the near distance, discern the outline of the silent chapel rather than the faint glow of the lamps in the hospital.

He sealed and addressed his letter to Frank and thought of him receiving it one chilly morning in the very near future, putting it down on his armchair unopened, saving it until the evening when he would enjoy Harry's news sitting by the fire after supper, a glass of beer on the table beside him. Harry often imagined Frank sitting there, night after night, the company of his books supplemented perhaps by the presence of his much-loved nephew. And maybe sometimes others came too, boys he had taught, even lent books to, who had gone away to war and never returned. Boys who, like Harry, owed Frank a pupil's debt of gratitude. How many had he taught over the years, and how many lost in that first war, now possibly superseded by a new generation of unspeaking visitors to that worn-out armchair?

And what about the recuperating patients of Ward 5B, lying there trying to sleep in the virtual darkness, with only the faint glow of the night nurse's hurricane lamp reassuring them that help was at hand? Did they feel the presence of their lost comrades? Silent Ralph, who, according to Nurse Kirwin, had helped to prepare the graves and bury the dead of Changi, and Taffy with his terrible burns - who came to comfort them and sit by their bedsides in the lonely hours of the night?

Harry thought of Kipling, creator of so many magical tales and characters, powerless to conjure again the son for whom he grieved so bitterly. As for himself, he could hardly bear to admit his own longing, his need for a lost presence to return and connect him once more with the life he had left behind. During the day, his work at the hospital brought some purpose to his waking hours and restored his sense of self by degrees. But as night and the hours of sleep approached, he felt once again diminished, more acutely aware of the loss he had suffered than when he awoke in the morning with duties to perform. Lying bereft in his bed, sleep eluding him, he tried not to feel anger towards the God who seemed, inexplicably and without warning, to have withdrawn his countless gifts to Harry.

Within a few weeks, things were running as smoothly as could be expected at the hospital. The patients of Ward 5B slowly began to recover their bodily strength, although it was hard to judge to what extent, if any, the deprivations and horrors of the jail had receded from their memories. Somehow, they seemed a little less bowed, less tense, but there are some experiences, Harry reflected, from which you never fully recover. The conditions and injuries of the patients were various. Two of the boys (and they were really boys still) had no specific injuries but were suffering from exhaustion and serious malnutrition. Most of the others had been wounded before being captured and had received only makeshift treatment during their imprisonment, prolonging their recovery by many months. They were all thin, fragile, walking uncertainly. But by November, they were all well enough to take a stroll in the hospital grounds or to sit outside in the sunshine. Harry came out with his camera. The lads who were strolling around came over to where the others were sitting in deckchairs and lined up behind them for a photograph. Taffy, his face still wrapped in bandages, insisted on standing in the middle. Harry had not seen his facial injuries, having never been present when the nurses changed the dressing. Sporting this curious mask, holes cut for eyes, nose and mouth, and his hair flopping rakishly over the top of the bandages, Taffy seemed full of confidence, laughing and joking with his fellow patients as they posed for Harry's pictures. It was sobering to wonder whether he would present such a brave face to the world once there was no longer a need for the dressing.

Harry enjoyed his work on the ward and in the hospital. Much of it was fairly mundane, looking after the supplies, keeping the areas clean and tidy, serving meals to the patients, and helping them to get in and out of bed. Mostly he dealt with the living. The men in his ward were likely to recover and be repatriated, and for this he was grateful. His conversations with the patients were brief and intermittent, a few words exchanged while serving a mug of tea perhaps, but gradually he got to know a little more about each of them, almost always about their families back home, almost never about their experiences in South East Asia. Harry appointed himself the provider of flowers to the ward. Every few days he would fill the makeshift vases with fresh flowers, at first from the overgrown hospital grounds, but later from the village near his billet where the local children got to know him and sometimes assisted him with his flower gathering, helping him to select the most colourful and eyecatching orchids. And every Sunday morning he played hymns on the old piano, many of his own choosing, and some as requests which he had collected from his and other wards.

The nurses were formidable. It was impossible not to admire them. They worked long hours without complaining. Many of them had returned to Singapore after the years of occupation, having been among the luckier ones who had escaped relatively unscathed from the terrors of the Japanese invasion, although nurses like Sister Kirwin and Sister Turner were on their first posting there. It was extraordinary to watch the transformation in the patients when the nurses were near them, hovering like angels as they administered their tender mercies and brightening the ward with an almost unearthly light. Many of the sisters were barely older than the patients themselves, but their care had a maternal air, Harry noticed. They spoke to the recuperating soldiers with an authority lent to them if not by their age, then by their relatively privileged social backgrounds. With the orderlies they might have maintained a similar stance, but as the weeks went on Harry found them increasingly friendly, approachable. When everything was in order and Matron was known to be elsewhere, they would often take their cups of tea outside, and sit and talk with Harry, Norman and the others about how their patients were doing, or exchange tiny rags of news and gossip about hospital life.

Christmas approached. Norman and Harry came up with the idea of a small concert for the patients. They went to see Matron, feeling not unlike supplicant schoolboys.

'Yes, why not?' was Matron's response, 'but I'd better clear it with the Brigadier.' As the weeks had gone by, and clear signs of the patients' regeneration had seemingly rewarded her efforts, she too had relaxed, settled into her role. There was no doubting her authority so she had little need to assert it. They were, after all, working together for the common good. The plan was to hold the concert in the ward. The piano would be wheeled in and patients from nearby wards would be invited to attend. The concert would be in two parts, popular favourites followed by a selection of Christmas music. Norman made some posters advertising vacancies for performers, whom he would audition. This was how they discovered that Sister Kirwin, Beatrice as she now insisted they call her, was something of a singer. She admitted to having taken lessons while she was at school, and to having won a prize in a local competition. Harry was appointed her accompanist, a role he felt somewhat diffident about.

The first challenge they faced was deciding what she should sing. 'It'll have to be something I know well,' Harry said. 'We've no music.' He ran through his repertoire. She looked doubtful.

'I don't suppose you can play *Love's Old Sweet Song*, can you?' she said. 'It was one of my mother's favourites so I know all the words.'

'I can indeed,' said Harry. He wondered whether to go on. 'It was one of my mother's favourites too. I think she learnt it from her mother.' But he stopped there.

'Well, that's our decision made, then,' said Beatrice.

The next challenge was where to rehearse. The performers didn't want the patients to have heard the whole programme before the big event, nor did they want them to hear the inevitable mistakes they would make while practising. So they waited for the warm afternoons when

143

most of the patients were outside, taking a stroll or sitting in the sunshine. Norman had put together a small choir of privates from the medical corps and was coaching them in the secrecy of their billet.

Harry and Beatrice managed to have three impromptu rehearsals for their turn. Beatrice had written out the words of the song, just to be sure, and they spent the first half an hour getting the tune and tempo right. It was ragged, but promising, Beatrice said. By the third rehearsal, it was sounding far more coordinated, almost professional. They ran through it one final time.

When they had finished, Beatrice said, 'How long ago did your mother die?' She had this curious gift of sounding matter-of-fact but looking sympathetic. 'If you don't mind me asking.'

'A few years ago now. The war proved too much for her, I think.'

'Mine died when I was away at school. We knew she was ill but my father didn't expect her to go so quickly or he would have called me home. I hated not being able to say goodbye. Still, one has to get on with it, that's what I was always taught.'

Harry was glad at this point to see some of the patients coming back into the ward needing his attention. He had an uncomfortable feeling that he should tell Beatrice more about Violet's death and what had happened subsequently. Her brusqueness almost seemed to demand it. But for now, he much preferred to keep it to himself.

The concert was to take place on Christmas Eve. A few days beforehand, the orderlies decided to decorate the ward. With considerable tenacity, the patients had made yards and yards of festive paper chains from old newspapers. Taffy had taken charge of this project, seeming to enjoy giving orders to his companions about the dimensions of the links, and exercising a rigorous level of quality control over them. Even Jim, whose right arm was still in a sling, was expected to help by handing out the cut strips ready for sticking.

The only patient who took no part in the paper chain cooperative was Ralph. Ralph, who had shuffled in that first day, seen the angelic vision of Nurse Kirwin, and retreated into a silent world of his own. He would come and sit outside with the others, he would seem to make a slight response to their jokes and light-hearted insults, but he remained apart from the group, choosing to be with them, but not of them. Now he sat in the corner of the ward at a table used by the nurses for writing their nightly reports, and spread out before him some items he had somehow acquired from around the hospital: a broken piece of broom handle, some other odd-shaped blocks of wood, some scraps of white linen, and a Swiss army knife. For three days, he sat at the table, slowly carving and assembling the wood. When his carpentry was done, he turned tailor, cutting and sewing the white rags slowly, meticulously, his hands trembling slightly as he did so. He sat with his back to the ward. If he sensed someone coming towards him, he covered his work with his arms or with a sheet of newspaper. Finally, late one afternoon, when the paper chains had been hung and the window sills festooned with greenery, he turned from his work and caught Harry's eye as if summoning him. Harry put down the tray he was carrying and went over. On the table, the newspaper covered whatever it was Ralph had been making. Shakily, Ralph lifted the sheet as gently as if drawing back a silk bedspread to reveal the doll he had fashioned, all dressed in white, linen strips swathing her head like a curious cross between a halo and a veil. With both hands, he lifted the doll gently, lovingly, and, resting it on his open palms, handed his creation to Harry.

In the opposite corner of the ward, a crowd were gathered round a makeshift Christmas tree which Joe had cut from the hospital grounds and brought into the ward as the centrepiece for the concert. The patients were passing the nurses pieces of gauze and nuts and fruit to decorate it. The Brigadier had phoned the recently resurrected local newspaper and asked them to send a reporter, who had made some notes about the forthcoming concert and was now photographing patients and staff as they adorned the tree. When Joe saw Harry walking towards them with Ralph's doll, he went and fetched the stepladder and some tape, took the doll reverently from Harry, and tied it to the top of the tree, a guardian angel of the ward, watching over sick and healthy alike. From the table, Ralph looked on, his hands no longer trembling.

*

Patients started to gather early for the concert on Christmas Eve. Some sat on the beds, and extra chairs were brought in to fill all available spaces. Norman was the first on, playing a jazz medley as a lively start to the proceedings. Other medical staff followed, performing music of the previous decade, Irving Berlin, the Gershwins, Cole Porter. 'What a swell party this is,' crooned two of the doctors, 'a swell-e-gant, e-le-gant par-ty *this is*.' Harry listened anxiously, wondering if he had made a poor choice. So much of the inter-war music seemed to have passed him by. The soldiers were too young to know his piece. They preferred tunes that were lively, modern. He glanced at Beatrice, waiting in the wings, and grimaced. She smiled back as though nothing was wrong. Why hadn't their song been programmed first rather than as the last item before the interval? When their turn came, as it quickly did, they were given a round of applause as they took their places. Harry cleared his throat and, before sitting down at the piano, he turned to the audience. 'Ladies and gentlemen,' he said, 'something a little different. A trip down memory lane. We hope you enjoy it.' After only a few bars, it became apparent the audience were indeed enjoying it, swaying gently to the lilt of the music, and accompanying the final chorus in a quiet, almost imperceptible hum. They forgot the swell party and were carried softly along by the sweet song of love. Nurse Kirwin's voice had them spellbound, and Harry played the best he could remember. After the hectic jazz, after the busy song and dance hits of more recent years, he found himself, in this strangely

147

incongruous setting, transported back for a few brief moments to the calm shade of an English garden one happy summer long ago when he was still a child.

In a flash, the song was finished and the audience burst into applause. Harry stood up and stepped forward next to Beatrice to take a bow. As he did so, she reached out and took his hand, squeezing it lightly before letting go. If he had looked to his side, he would have seen her turned towards him and smiling, but he was too busy taking in the looks of the patients, Taffy grinning behind his bandages, Ralph smiling as if he were at the gates of heaven, all of them gazing at the wondrous angel who stood beside him.

When the concert had finished after a rousing rendition of *The Twelve Days of Christmas* and the patients had all been returned to their wards, Harry went outside for a cigarette. Beatrice was out there with some of the other nurses. She came over to him. 'We should have done an encore, you know.'

'One song was quite enough for my nerves. And my piano-playing.'

'Thank you for accompanying me. I enjoyed it.'

'Glad to be of assistance. I enjoyed it too.'

The next morning, when he had five minutes to himself, Harry's thoughts drifted back yet again to his years at Farningham School. That first Christmas, when he had been briefly overwhelmed with homesickness, but had somehow managed to put on a brave face and, as it happened, have quite a good time. Now he was so much further away from home, so much more had happened, but the homesickness didn't come. If he was honest, he was glad to be here in the hospital rather than in England. Even Christmas with Ron and his family would have been difficult for him, and all in all it was easier not to have to make excuses. Not that Ron would have made an issue out of it, but he would have insisted Harry join them anyway. And if Ron hadn't succeeded, then Ivy certainly would have done. No, it was better to be here where duty and routine would map out his day for him and the unfamiliarity of the setting would help him forget about the Christmas he might have had.

A few days into the new year, Harry, Norman and Joe found themselves off-duty together and decided to walk to the cathedral, now a favourite destination, and then down to the sea. It was hot and sticky but good to be away from routine tasks for an hour or two. Norman had found something he wanted to show the others. Halfway down St Andrew's Road he had discovered a tiny secluded graveyard where a broken ring of kranji trees shaded several rows of neat white crosses, shoulder to shoulder like a guard of honour. Norman had made some inquiries. 'Soldiers and natives killed by the Japanese when Singapore fell. A naval officer discovered the graves with nothing more than wooden pegs to mark them, so he got permission to tidy the place up a bit.' They went in. The crosses stood out ultra-white in the darkened green shadows. Norman and Joe sat down under one of the trees while Harry wandered along the rows, looking at the names of the fallen, Chinese, Indian, Australian and British. *Edwards*, he read, *Bignold, Spencer, Newton, Holloway...* Holloway. He had almost forgotten. Standing there in the Singapore heat, he was suddenly reminded of the young soldier he had met that afternoon in Mrs Shepherd's parlour. Lieutenant Holloway, who had asked him how he was settling in and who had known about Kipling's son. But that first memory was inextricably connected to another afternoon in late November, only two weeks after the armistice, when he arrived back at Moore House to find Mrs Shepherd sitting at her table weeping.

When he asked if there was anything he could do, she simply pushed two letters across the table towards him, and gestured with a nod of her head that he should read them. The shorter one was from Holloway's commanding officer, writing to Mrs Shepherd to tell her of the circumstances of the soldier's death and to proclaim what a brave young man he had shown himself to be. The other letter had been found among Holloway's belongings ready to be posted. 'I wish to thank you from the bottom of my heart,' Holloway had written, 'for all your care of us boys at Farningham. You brought us up to be strong and self-reliant. You shared our troubles and our joys. You have been like a mother to me, and thanks to you I have somehow found the strength to get through this dreadful war. I pray it cannot go on for much longer and as soon as I return to England I shall hurry to Farningham to see you again...' Mrs Shepherd continued to weep as Harry read. Her grief reminded him of his mother's desolation when she was widowed. He went into the kitchen and put some water on to boil. He spooned tea into the teapot, and placed a cup and saucer and a jug of milk on a tray. Then he went back to the parlour and put his arm around Mrs Shepherd's shoulders for a few moments before slipping out quietly and closing the door.

Holloway had died on the last morning of the war, between the signing of the armistice and the 11 o'clock ceasefire. As the boys of Farningham rejoiced at the conclusion of the war and the end to the loss of life, he was just hours beyond their earthly celebrations. Looking down at the grave of this unknown namesake, Harry's heart rose in fresh and abundant grief for the young soldier he had hoped to meet again, and whose death first struck him with a child's incipient awareness of wasted life. I have already lived twice as long as he did, thought Harry.

March 1946

Early in the new year, Sister Turner became engaged to one of the army doctors. It was a whirlwind romance. They had met, apparently, at a Twelfth Night party in the officers' mess and now they were to be married just as soon as they could both be granted leave. Sister Kirwin was delighted for her friend and glad of a little diversion, and the orderlies sometimes caught her humming a wedding march when Sister Turner walked past. The patients soon got to know about the forthcoming wedding and Taffy, bold behind his mask of bandages, asked Sister Kirwin when they could expect to hear of her engagement, drawing attention to his own availability should she be interested. She smiled sweetly and told him to tidy his locker.

Harry wondered how many of the nurses would go home from the war with husbands or fiancés. Outwardly, they were so professional and matter-of-fact but perhaps in private they considered their war service as a better opportunity to find a suitable marriage partner than they would have back in England. After all, so many young men would not be going home, and he remembered the gradual depletion in the male population of Bottle Green as the previous war had progressed. Poor Jessie Kenton, she had not married, as far as he knew. On the basis of simple statistics, it seemed as if the nurses in Singapore had an almost limitless choice but of course that was very far from the truth. For one thing, a relationship between a nursing sister and anyone other than a commissioned officer was openly frowned upon. For another, many of the officers were already married with families or had girlfriends waiting hopefully for their return. By the time you whittled it down, only a tiny proportion of the many men the nurses encountered could be viewed as potential and suitable husbands.

It was a random and chancy business, Harry knew that, meeting the right one. He remembered the story of how his parents met. It had occurred to him many times that if Violet had not had the courage to go out into the yard and speak to George when she did, the moment would have passed and she might never have seen him again. What would have happened to them then? In what different directions would their lives have taken them? Oddly, he couldn't remember how Ron had met Ivy. Or perhaps he had never said. One day Harry and Violet were unaware of her existence, and then suddenly she was part of the family, her introduction to the Elston household a domestic episode Harry was unlikely to forget.

Ron had announced one morning at breakfast that he would like to bring a young lady home to meet Violet. It was 1936, a momentous year. Rudyard Kipling and King George had both died in January. By the time Christmas came, the new king had abdicated and his brother, the shy and charming duke who had congratulated Harry on his organ playing, had ascended to the throne. Ron must have met Ivy during the summer months and it was early September when he brought her over to meet Violet. The arrangement was that Ivy should come for afternoon tea. Violet had gone out earlier in the day to visit Mrs Buckley, now elderly and not in the best of health. When Violet reached Linden Hill, she had found Mrs Buckley very poorly indeed and unable to get out of bed. By the time she had fetched the doctor, made her friend comfortable and instructed the maid, it was already late afternoon. So when Ron arrived with Ivy, only Harry was at home. Harry liked her immediately. She was friendly, straightforward, nicely but not ostentatiously dressed. She told Harry how pleased she was to meet him and asked him to show her the garden, having heard a great deal about his gardening skills from Ron, who had definitely not inherited green fingers. It was late summer and the garden was abundant with flowers and vegetables. Harry led her down the path, pointing out what he was growing, what had done well, what had let him down. At the bottom of the garden, the elder tree was in full flower. Fred's bench, its wood turned pale and flaky now, offered an inviting seat in its shade.

'What a lovely spot. Do you come and sit here often?'

'Sometimes. It's mother's place really, said Ron. 'We leave her in peace, don't we, Harry? She likes sitting here when she's missing Father or just feeling worn out.'

Ivy admired the elder tree, saying how it reminded her of the house where she grew up.

'Well, while we're waiting for Mother, perhaps you'd like to try my elderberry wine,' said Harry. 'What do you think, Ron?'

'Sounds like a good idea to me. Shall I go and fetch it?'

'No, you sit here with Ivy. I'll go.'

A few minutes later, Harry was back with their refreshments. The tray had been covered with a white lace napkin. There were three glasses and a full bottle of wine.

'I ought to warn you it's quite strong,' said Harry, pouring moderate amounts. He passed Ivy and Ron their drinks and sat down on the grass. It was a perfect afternoon, the sky cloudless, the air sweet with the scents of the garden and the occasional flurry of birdsong from the bushes and from the fields beyond.

Ivy talked about her brothers, where they lived and what they did for a living. She came from a large family. Some years before, her youngest brother, Maurice, had died of septicemia. He was only sixteen. He'd gone swimming in the canal and cut his leg. She still missed him a great deal. He'd been such fun to be with, always planning some scheme or other. Harry noticed her empty glass. 'What did you think of the wine, Ivy?'

'It was delicious, very refreshing. And not *very* alcoholic, was it?' Harry and Ron exchanged a look.

'Would you like some more?'

'Well, just half a glass maybe.'

They chatted on, Harry pouring more wine whenever their glasses were almost empty. After a while, Harry and

Ron seemed to be doing most of the talking. Ivy had become very quiet.

'Are you alright, Ivy?' said Ron. 'Would you like to go indoors?'

'I would like to go indoors, yes, I would. I think I should.' She stood up, swaying just enough to indicate how the wine had taken its effect. Ron took her by the arm and led her back up the garden path towards the house. She walked tentatively, like a young child. She tripped on the back doorstep but recovered herself. Ron and Harry took her into the sitting room where she slumped down on the sofa.

'I'll fetch you a glass of water,' said Ron. But when he came back, Ivy was asleep, one leg stretched out in front of her, her shoe kicked off, the other leg tucked awkwardly beneath her, shoe still on.

'Probably best to leave her to sleep, Ron,' said Harry, and they went into the kitchen, where they had barely sat down before they heard Violet opening the front door.

Harry was having a smoke in the hospital grounds and reliving that scene when he was interrupted by Beatrice Kirwin.

'Sorry to spoil your daydreams,' she said, 'but some of the patients are ready to go now.' Another contingent of soldiers was being taken to the port to embark on the hospital ship that would take them home, including two of the patients on Harry's ward. Beatrice and two of the orderlies were to accompany them. For the next few hours, Harry was completely occupied with this task. He helped the men, still weak, but so much stronger than when they first came to the hospital, to climb into the ambulance, although they were capable now of managing by themselves. He loaded their few belongings. There was only room for the driver and two others in the front, so Harry volunteered to sit in the back with the patients.

'It must be good to be going home at last,' Harry said to them. They looked back at him blankly. 'I suppose so,' was the only answer that one of them gave and he realised then the inappropriateness of his remark. He had learnt enough in the last few months to understand why his passengers looked so unmoved by the prospect of their journey. They had been away so long, known and experienced unspeakable times in Changi prison. England and home must have seemed not only remote, but no longer imaginable. Loved ones might, intentionally or imperceptibly, have allowed the ties which bound them to the absent to loosen. For these long-suffering men, the certainty and safety of their hospital ward was the reality they lived by now, not a life distanced by time as well as miles, spoiled by the expectation that they would not find it as they remembered. He sympathised. He had no immediate wish to return home either, although he supposed this would be inevitable in a few more months. Harry too had come to find the hospital the reason for his existence, his work providing a routine he could depend on, that would get him safely to the end of each day. But, unlike the men in the ambulance, he knew for certain that when he returned he would find everything exactly as he had left it.

After the soldiers had been delivered to the hospital ship, a protracted and complicated process given the number of troops, trucks and ambulances on the dock, they were ready to return to the hospital. The other orderly said he would walk, as he was off-duty now and felt like stretching his legs, so Harry travelled in the front of the ambulance with Beatrice. She was very subdued. Harry sensed what she was feeling about saying farewell to the patients she had nursed for the last few months. Her anxiety about them didn't stop there, at the dock. But she would probably never know what happened to them in those post-war years, and whether their lives returned to something which could pass for normality. After a few minutes, she asked the driver if he could do a detour to Thomson Road camp so she could briefly say hello to a friend who was nursing some civilians there.

'Do you mind?' she asked Harry. 'I won't be long.'

'Be my guest,' said Harry.

When they arrived at the camp, Beatrice got out and went to find her chum. The driver said he would wait in the ambulance. Harry decided to look round. The area near where they had parked was full of Indian women and children. It was curious, being so used to the male population of the hospital, to hear the higher pitch of their voices, and to observe the way they socialised, so different from the camaraderie of the men. Beatrice was over at the other side of the compound. She'd found her friend and they were deep in conversation, probably about Sister Turner's wedding. At a low table under some awning sat a group of children, bowls of fish and rice in front of them. Harry watched these young experts with chopsticks, something he had yet to master. He went over and crouched down at the end of their little table, admiring them as they scooped up every last grain.

'Was that good? It certainly looked it.' He nodded encouragingly at one of the little girls. After a moment or two of uncertainty, she replied with a ricey grin, and showed him her empty bowl. It was the simplest of responses. Not quite knowing what to do next, Harry waved goodbye to the little diners and went back to the ambulance where the driver was taking a nap. Beatrice returned a few minutes later and they set off. She was in a brighter mood now.

'Sorry to keep you waiting. We were discussing the outrageous cost of lipstick.' Harry noticed the driver smiling to himself. He thought how disappointed Ralph would be to think of his heavenly angel concerning herself with such earthly matters.

'I saw you with the children. Aren't they adorable?' she said.

'It must be very different for your friend, working in a camp like that.'

'Yes, in some ways. But we're all aiming for the same outcome, as Matron constantly reminds us. It must be nice to work with children, though. I'd like that.'

Harry thought about the children he had seen in the streets on the day they arrived in Singapore. They were waving at the open trucks of soldiers as they drove past, but they looked tired, neglected, bewildered. The smiles on the faces of those children at the camp, no longer hungry or afraid, were heartening.

'I really miss my niece and nephew in England. They're both at school now. I can't wait to see them again. I'm worried I won't recognise them or that they won't remember me. I miss my sister too, but I miss the children the most. What do you miss about England, Harry?

'I miss my garden,' said Harry, thinking of the garden in Bottle Green that he had nurtured for so many years. When he left school, he had returned home to take up his job at Hall Place. Fred had married and moved away many years before and Ron was still at school, so for two years it was just Harry and Violet. Then when Ron got his first job as a carpenter, he moved back too. Violet was glad to have them both there, although now of course their roles were very different. It was just like old times, she joked, looking up at the two boys who had grown into men. Violet complained she was getting too old to work. She still helped at Mrs Buckley's but now the Colonel had retired they had a new housekeeper and Violet was 'let off' as Mrs Buckley termed it. Harry had taken charge of the back garden almost immediately, and Violet was glad to be free of the responsibility. That first autumn Harry had dug out more beds and planted a host of vegetables and flowers. The following year he made an archway and trained rambling roses to grow over it. They moved Fred's bench down to the bottom of the garden beside the elder tree. Then he turned his attention to the front garden, training more roses up the side of the door and over the porch. He planted hollyhocks and delphiniums and anything that would grow sufficiently tall to give the cottage an air of privacy and seclusion.

He was happy in his work and happy at home with Violet. On Sundays he went to church, and in the week he would sometimes go for a drink with one of his workmates, or later with Ron. Vaguely, he hoped a time would come when his life would change and he would have a wife and a family too, but for now he was content enough with the way things were. Besides, what would Violet do without her sons to keep an eye on her? One summer he bought a stone birdbath and placed it where Violet could watch the birds from the kitchen window. There was an inscription around the edge of the bath. 'One is nearer God's heart in a garden than anywhere else on earth,' it read and Harry felt this to be the truth.

It was still a pleasure to think about the garden at Bottle Green at that time, to imagine it at its best as it was that summer when Ron brought Ivy home to meet his family. But that was almost ten years ago and it was hard to avoid asking the unpalatable question of who was tending it now? Harry could never have left it were it not for the events which had made it impossible for him to stay. Giving up his precious garden was a small price to pay in order to escape the constant awareness of all that had changed, the shrivelled roses waiting for Violet to dead-head them, the empty bench waiting to creak with laughter from Ron and Ivy, the open fields beyond the garden which had absorbed so much childhood shouting and whooping, and now lacked even the wisps of smoke from Harry and Ron's cigarettes. And here, where Harry had indeed felt close to the heart of God, Harry's own heart had risen at the approaching tread of the most loved one of all. Surely better to have exiled himself entirely than to listen in vain to hear those gentle footsteps once more.

Back in the ward, Harry got on with his duties. Now two more lads had gone it was starting to feel empty. The time was coming when all the patients would be repatriated and Harry would be free to go home. He went over to talk to Ralph, sitting by his bed reading the newspaper. The angel he had made for the Christmas tree had been handed back to him on Twelfth Night and he had it tied to his bedstead to watch over him as he slept. How he had changed since Christmas. Still thin, but no longer malnourished, he barely shuffled at all now when he walked. His skin was less yellow, less drawn, and he appeared younger too, although he would never look as young as his twenty-four years. If you looked closely into his eyes, there was still a distant haunted expression, but his trembling had ceased and he could look back at you face to face. From silence, he had progressed to a willingness for short conversations. He even smiled as Harry approached.

'Is there anything you need, Ralph?'

'No thank you. How did it go today?'

'Very busy down at the port but they're aboard now. Usual stifling quarters below decks but I'm sure they'll be fine. Won't be long now before we're seeing you on board.' After his experience of the afternoon, it occurred to Harry that this might not be a welcome reminder.

'My mother will be pleased to have me home. But I'll miss everyone here. What will I do without you and Sister Kirwin?'

'Take your angel home to remind you of her.'

'Oh, I won't forget her. You're the one who needs an angel to accompany you.' And he looked at Harry, holding his gaze, and in that moment Harry realised that Ralph, always so silent, was the most observant, that it was Ralph who had detected Harry's residual grief, the grief of a man who had walked side by side with his heart's companion but was forced now, with faltering steps, to journey alone.

Some months later, when summer had arrived
wholeheartedly in England, Harry found himself walking
up the path to Ron and Ivy's front door, his jacket over his
arm. A child watched him from the window, half-hidden by
the curtain, but she disappeared before he had put down his
suitcase and lifted the knocker. Ivy opened the door, and
the little girl stood close behind her.

'You're back. You made it.' Ivy pulled him into the
house and gave him a hug. 'How lovely to see you, Harry.
Come in. Let me help you with your case. Go and sit down
and I'll make you a cup of tea. How was your journey?
You must be exhausted.'

Harry was tired, and he submitted to Ivy's fussing over
him. Three days had elapsed since he had arrived in
Liverpool, where he had been demobbed. It was a relief to
get to Hedingham. A relief, but also strangely bewildering
for his long posting abroad to finally end here, in Ron and
Ivy's hallway. He followed the little girl into the sitting
room and gave himself up to one of the armchairs. His feet
ached and he was glad to sit down. Ivy brought tea and
cakes and sandwiches and told him to tuck in. But it was
hot and he had no appetite. He drank his tea while Ivy
talked and sampled her own baking. Her daughter stood
resting one elbow on her mother's knee, coyly assessing

this newcomer to her life, ignoring encouragements to go over to him and say hello.

'Goodness, is that the time,' said Ivy, jumping up as the clock struck five. 'I must get dinner on. Ron'll be home soon, Harry, and I'm sure he'll want to take you for a pint. What do you say?' Then she showed him up to his room and left him alone for a while to unpack his things. This was not the room he had stayed in last time, but a smaller one at the back of the house, from which he could just see the keep of the Norman castle standing proud above the trees, a flag flying from one of the two turrets which had withstood the ravages of wars long, long ago. In one corner, there was a pile of boxes which Harry recognised as the ones he had packed a few weeks before leaving Bottle Green and which contained his papers, some photographs and pictures, and his sheet music. He opened the wardrobe and found some of his clothes already hanging there. Ivy must have done that for him. From his suitcase he added the rest of his clothes. He took out the precious books which had been his travelling companions - his Bible, *The Jungle Book*, and the *Treasury* of poems which had belonged to Violet - and put them in their accustomed place on the bedside table. Travelling light has its benefits, he thought, when his unpacking was finished after ten minutes. He stood for a few minutes more looking out of the window towards the castle, and then he went downstairs to his sister-in-law and niece.

Ivy flatly refused to let Harry help her with the meal, and insisted he sit and read the newspaper until Ron came home, which he did some minutes later. Harry was so relieved to see his brother, he felt like weeping when Ron shook his hand.

'Let me just get changed,' said Ron, 'and we'll nip down to The Bell for half an hour. I expect you could do with some beer.'

Harry didn't mention the pints he had shared in Liverpool with Joe and Norman. That was different, a token of being back on land, a receipt for having exchanged the humid climate of the Far East for the comfortable warmth of England in July. It was good to sit and drink and talk with Joe and Norman at the end of their long voyage, confident that he would see these friends again in the near future, but from the moment their ship had left Singapore, Harry had looked forward to this moment of companionship with his brother, when, for the first time in well over a year, he would feel the tightening of a thread that attached his heart painlessly to the past.

The next day was another working day and Ron had left before Harry was up.

'What would you like to do, Harry?' said Ivy, when he had finished his breakfast. 'Make yourself at home. I've got some errands to do but here's a key. You can come and go as you please.'

'I think I'll take a walk,' said Harry, glad of the prospect of some time by himself.

'To the castle?'

'Yes, I think so. I'd like to see it again.'

It was some years since Harry had last visited the half-ruined castle which he could see from his bedroom window, a very happy day, he recalled, gazing out that morning before coming downstairs. And beyond the castle, hidden from view, was the parish church. He might go in and see if he could play the organ for a while.

The castle keep, a model of solidity and yet elegant, dignified, had always struck him as a remarkable building, but today its setting was what appealed to him, with the trees and the nearby lake, a composition which seemed so unmistakably English, a picture postcard view which, ironically, now confirmed his homecoming. The keep was reached by an old bridge across a moat which had long dried up and was instead lined with soft, verdant growth. Halfway across the bridge, he stopped to smoke a cigarette. How peaceful the world seemed today, almost unnaturally so, the wisps of his cigarette smoke the only discernible movement against the stillness of his view. Then he leaned his arms on the parapet, and gazed into the green gulley, as if into water. He thought of the hours he had spent on his return voyage, leaning on the ship's railings and staring down at the surface of the sea, trying, but failing, to decide what he would do when he reached England.

He thought of that last day in Singapore, markedly flat after the excitement of his arrival. When the time came, he had few farewells to say. Most of the patients he knew had already embarked for home. Joe and Norman were coming with him on the same troop ship. Sister Turner had left shortly after her marriage, moving with her husband to a posting back in England. Beatrice Kirwin had left in May, planning to return to civilian nursing, glad to be free of the heat and the mosquitoes, she said. He remembered her insistence when she left that Harry give her his address. He explained that he would be lodging with his brother and sister-in-law in Essex, and he didn't know how long for.

'I can write to you there. And if you've already moved away, presumably someone will forward my letter to you? I'd like to keep in touch. You know, shared experiences and all that.'

Harry wasn't sure if he wanted to keep in touch with Beatrice. He was mildly surprised that she wanted to write to him. He didn't feel he knew her particularly well. Perhaps it was their performance at the Christmas show which had clinched the matter. Still, it would be rude not to give her an address. He helped her with the rest of her luggage. One of the army trucks was taking her down to the port. Matron was there to shake hands with Beatrice and commend her for her sterling effort.

'Goodbye, Matron. I've learnt a lot here. Thank you.' She turned to Harry. For a moment she hesitated as if she might kiss him goodbye but instead she offered her hand. 'Goodbye, Harry. I will write. See you in England perhaps.' Then she got quickly into the truck and was gone. Turning to go back into the ward, Harry noticed Matron had been watching them.

'Not long before you'll be following her, is it, Private?'

'I don't think so, Matron. Just a few more weeks.'

Well, enough goodbyes. Time to get back to work.' And off she went.

A squawking crow launching itself from the top of the keep made Harry look up, as if in answer to someone calling him. He walked to the other side of the bridge. He would see if the castle was open. A wide and surprisingly shallow flight of stone steps on the side of the keep led up to the solid archway which was its only entrance. Harry tried the wooden door, which rattled, but was locked. A pity. He would have liked to stand in the airy space of that vast banqueting hall, and, painful though it might be, to imagine he was there once more with Ella, who had enjoyed the castle so much. But the memory brought him no pain, embracing him instead like a puff of the warm breeze, soothing, comforting. The mood of those many months abroad, when involuntary thoughts of her troubled him with a deep sense of her absence, was suddenly reversed and she returned to him as before, fully, if differently present.

It was approaching noon, and the sun was high in the sky. Harry went in search of some shade, taking her presence with him, down to the lake where they had walked hand in hand to the bench which provided a cool resting place by the water, but where the castle could still be seen beyond the lake, between the crowns of the trees. Only then, sitting in the shadows, looking out across the water, did Harry realise that the anguish which had travelled with him had evaporated and he was at peace, and ready to make some decisions.

*

In the pub on that first evening of Harry's return, Ron had diplomatically refrained from asking about his plans for the future. He sensed that this would be pointless anyway. Harry would tell him of his intentions, if he had any. So he simply told Harry he was welcome to stay as long as he wanted in Hedingham, that he and Ivy were both glad to have him there, and he was sure little Mary would be too, just as soon as she overcame her characteristic shyness. It was true that Harry had not yet made up his mind where to go or what to do. The recent weeks at sea had given him plenty of time to contemplate these questions, but he had been unable to see the way forward any more than he could envisage at that stage how it would feel to be back in England. All he knew was that he was determined to work as a gardener. Nothing else would suit him so well. But where to live? That was something he had been unable to decide.

'I think I've had enough of bandages,' he told Ron. 'I need to get my spade out and do some digging.' That was all he had said by way of a hint about the future. Meanwhile, he had found the gardening tools in Ron's shed and been tidying in their garden. Ivy was very grateful.

'I don't seem to have time for the garden these days,' she said, tousling her daughter's hair.

Ron's diplomacy about Harry's future extended to the recent past too. Understanding Harry's natural reserve, it wouldn't have surprised him to discover that Harry had

170

told no one about his terrible loss until the very end of his posting abroad. It was about two weeks into the journey home, after a communal singsong on board, that Harry finally told Norman what he had previously been disinclined to tell anyone. They were sitting out on deck, smoking. It was unbearably hot down below and they were reluctant to turn in for the night.

'Fifteen more days and I shall be reunited with my piano,' said Norman. 'What bliss. But I shall always think fondly of that old joanna we had in the hospital. What about you, Harry, will you be reunited with your piano and finally master the *Liebestraum*?'

'Well, it's in storage at the moment, so I may have to wait a while.'

'In storage? How come?'

'I vacated my house just before I came out to the Far East. Most of my stuff's in storage. The smaller, more valuable things are at my brother's. I'll have to find somewhere new to live.'

'Why did you give up your old place? Sounds like you've made a lot of bother for yourself.'

'I could have stayed there. Maybe I should have done. But something happened. I was married, you see. My wife died. That's why I volunteered for the posting, to get away.'

'I'm so sorry, old chap. I had no idea.'

It's okay. I wanted to keep it to myself. It doesn't matter so much now.'

'Well I hope we can stay in touch when we get home.'

171

'I'd like that.'

'Thanks for telling me, Harry. You didn't have to.'

'I'm glad I did,' said Harry.

Over the next two or three weeks, Harry went back to the castle and the lake many times. Mostly, Ivy let him go alone, sensing that he was strengthened by the solitude, but sometimes, when Ron was at work, she and Mary went with him. Walking between her mother and her uncle, Mary gradually became used to this new grown-up who was living in her house, and one day she took his hand and led him down to the side of the lake to help her feed the ducks. One particularly warm Sunday they all had a picnic at the edge of the grassy moat. Ron and Ivy sat on the blanket, smoking and drinking lemonade, while Mary insisted again and again that Harry stand at the bottom of the dip to catch her as she ran headlong down the slope, where he would pick her up and swing her round, her legs flopping out like a propeller. And as Harry became more and more part of his brother's family, so he became increasingly certain that very soon it would be time to leave them, to go back to Bottle Green, where he and Ella had been so happy.

He mentioned this plan to Ron a few days later, when they were having another quiet pint at The Bell.

'It's up to you, of course,' said Ron, 'but don't you think you'd be better somewhere new? And if you could find a job near here, we'd still be able to see plenty of you.

172

Mary would like that. And if you need anything... you know.'

'I'll chew it over a bit longer,' said Harry, not wishing to appear ungrateful, 'but I don't think I'll change my mind, not now.'

Privately, Harry had already decided. Things would be fine. Not perfect, but he would manage. Life would be calm. No more calamities. He set about making enquiries for somewhere to live. The cottage had been let and it was almost impossible that the tenants would be vacating it in the near future. He would look for somewhere nearby, maybe in Knowl Hill. It would probably be better to start again in a new house, not in that old home that held so many memories. Then there was the question of finding a job. Hall Place had been handed back to its owner, he had heard, and maybe there would still be work for him there. He knew what Ron and Ivy would think about this, but he felt drawn to the place where he had first met Ella and to which, so it now seemed, she was urging him to return. He no longer had any wish to avoid it.

While all this was going on in Harry's mind, a letter arrived from Beatrice. Ivy had been the first to get to the post and she teased Harry gently about the identity of the sender. The handwriting looked like a woman's. The postmark was London.

'Who's it from, Harry? Someone you met abroad?'

'Yes, I think it's from one of the nurses on my ward. She insisted I gave her an address. I hope you don't mind.'

'Not at all. Invite her to visit if you want to.'

Harry was embarrassed by the length of the letter. It must have taken Beatrice some time to write and he supposed he would have to reply somehow. But it was interesting to read what she had been up to.

'Dear Harry (no more Private Elston now Matron's not around!)

I hope this finds you well. I don't know when you're returning to England but I imagine it must be sometime soon if you are not back already. It's good to be home although I do miss everyone at B.G.H. I have been so busy, catching up with my sister and taking her children on the outings they are constantly demanding. But we've been having a top time and it's wonderful to be free of the mosquitoes and the rice!!

I got home at the end of May, so I was able to take part in the victory parade. Did you read about it? We were drilled for days on how to march properly. They seem to think women don't know how to walk in step. It was quite a day we had, waiting for what seemed like hours ready for the off. Such a long parade, and we were quite near the back, led in by the Home Guard Band, which was very jolly. It was such a shame it was raining but there were thousands and thousands of people on the streets waving and cheering. There were flags *everywhere*. Eventually we got to the saluting base and I caught a glimpse of Churchill in his top hat. The princesses were there with the King and Queen. Didn't you say the King used to be the president of your school? He's very handsome. On and on we marched. My feet were killing me and we were all soaking. But it was grand to take part. I wouldn't have missed it for anything.'

Her letter went on in this vein, and as he read it Harry started to reassemble this lively popular young woman in his mind. He'd forgotten how much the patients liked her, how they brightened up when she came into the ward. Beatrice explained that since she had been demobbed she had been living with her sister in Battersea, but she had a new job to go to shortly, in a civilian hospital in Redhill. 'I think I'm looking forward to it,' she wrote, 'but it will never be as much fun as Singapore. Still, at least I won't be bored and, to be honest, I am getting a bit bored here with nothing much to do apart from spend time with the children and write long letters to the Singapore crowd. Of course, I would have written anyway, not just because I'm at a loose end...'

Ivy was itching to read Harry's letter, or at least find out more about its author. Ron kept his thoughts to himself.

'You can read it, Ivy, I don't mind,' Harry told her. 'It's just news about what she's been doing since she left Singapore. I expect I'll get letters from the others sooner or later.' He was hoping to hear from Norman in particular.

That evening, Harry resolved to tell Ron and Ivy his decision. It was after dinner. His little niece had finally agreed to go to bed, leaving the radio to entertain the adults instead. Ivy was darning socks and Ron was doing the crossword. While he listened to the music on the Home Service, Harry was thinking he ought to reply to Beatrice's letter but he wasn't sure what to say or how to say it. He got up and fetched some writing paper, and got as far as writing 'Dear Beatrice', but that was all. Instead, he doodled on the pad as he hummed to the music in the background, nothing remarkable, all pleasant enough, as he thought vaguely about how to begin his letter. But then a song he knew only too well brought his pen to a standstill. Even Ron looked up from his puzzle and saw his brother smile to himself, put the writing materials down, lean back in his chair and close his eyes as the sweetest song of all carried him back, not to his childhood or to that evening of the Christmas concert in Singapore when he had accompanied Beatrice, but to those latter years with Ella, who awaited him in the dim shadows.

'I've made up my mind,' he announced before he went to bed. 'I'm going back. I'm going to look for a job near Bottle Green.'

'I understand,' said Ron.

'You're welcome to stay here until you sort something out,' said Ivy.

'I don't want to impose. You've been so kind already,'

'It's no imposition. Stay as long as you like.'

Some weeks later, Ron and Ivy helped Harry move into his new house, a cottage in the next village from Bottle Green.

'It's just like your old house,' said Ivy, when she saw it.

'That's why I like it,' said Harry.

They unpacked the belongings he had brought with him and in the afternoon a van arrived bringing the items he had placed in storage. Ron helped him manoeuvre the furniture into position. He and Ivy had to get back that evening – their neighbour was looking after Mary – but they were reluctant to leave Harry.

'Are you sure you'll be alright, Harry?' Ivy was clearly anxious. So gregarious herself, she found it hard to understand why Harry wanted to isolate himself in this way.

'Don't forget, let us know if there's anything you need,' said Ron as he shook Harry's hand.

Harry was sorry to see them go but glad to have the place to himself. He sat down in an armchair and looked around him. Yes, this would do. He could be content with his lot here. He thought back over the last year. He had been half way round the world, seen places and people he had never dreamed of seeing, but he had no wish to travel again, or turn away from the life that defined him, which had been reclaimed and found ready for him to inhabit once more.

The next day, he rose early, made tea, and took it outside to the overgrown garden. There was nowhere to sit, so he wandered along what he could find of the path, considering where he could clear a patch of lawn for the birdbath. How he had missed mornings like this in Singapore, surveying his tiny estate, making plans for what he would do with the garden. This one had been sadly neglected. He felt as if he had come to its rescue, just in time. He would soon have it under control again, and flourishing. He inspected it closely to see what was growing. Rambling roses, white, almost pink, had taken possession of the hedge. The sight of them filled him with a comforting sense of familiarity. Later that morning, he picked a bunch, wrapped them in newspaper, and set off for the church at Bottle Green. Ron had given him an old bicycle but it was only a mile or so and he decided to walk, it would give him time to compose himself. And so, almost thirty years since he had stood by his father's grave before going away to school, he came to be standing in another corner of the same graveyard, whispering softly that he was home, and home for good, as he laid the roses on the newest of the graves of his loved ones.

When Ron and Ivy visited Harry a few weeks later, they found him comfortably installed, as though he had lived in this new house for many years. If Ron was disconcerted by its similarity and proximity to the cottage of their childhood and youth, as well as by the many reminders of that earlier time, he didn't let on.

'Make yourselves at home,' Harry told them, and they settled down on the tiny sofa in the sitting room while Harry was making tea in the kitchen. The room faced west, just like its counterpart at Bottle Green, and the afternoon sun was already seeping indoors. With its dark green furnishings, the room was vaguely reminiscent of a clearing in the woods or the shade of a spreading tree in the corner of a garden. All the furniture was familiar to Ron, the sofa, the two armchairs, and the piano which Mrs Buckley had given Violet not long after Father died.

For the first week or two after moving in, Harry had done very little in the way of unpacking, as if allowing himself time to get used to the house before entrusting it with his more personal belongings. Besides, he had been preoccupied with his return to Hall Place, and found himself unexpectedly tired at the end of each working day. But in the week preceding Ron and Ivy's visit, one by one he unpacked the boxes he had brought from Hedingham, lifting everything out carefully, as if in a ritual, reacquainting himself with the possessions which connected him to the time before he went away. Finding places for these items, he granted them permission to release their sentimental hold over him once more.

In one corner of the sitting room was the oak cabinet which George had made nearly half a century before as a wedding gift for Violet and above it hung his portrait, as if enabling him to keep watch over his handiwork. Harry had filled the cabinet with his sheet music and his small collection of books. He had two framed photographs which were particularly precious to him. The first was the studio photograph of Violet and Fred with George's portrait on the wall between them, taken the year after the boys went away to school. Harry had put it on top of the cabinet, aware that it was rather strange to have the image of his father in the photograph echoed in the portrait which hung behind it, but liking the effect nevertheless. The other photograph was of himself and Ella, the one which Ron had taken that summer in the garden at Bottle Green. This had been placed on the piano.

Mrs Buckley, having outlived the colonel by several years, had died about the time of Hitler's annexation of Austria, as far as Harry could remember. The Buckleys had no children, so Linden Hill had passed to a distant cousin of the colonel's. Mrs Buckley had left most of her money and personal possessions to her younger sister in Norfolk, but she had bequeathed Violet a small annuity and the pair of ruby lustres which Violet had always longingly admired. Mrs Buckley had joked to Violet that, having dusted them so lovingly for so many years, she was already their custodian. These glass ornaments were also displayed on George's cabinet, either side of the family photograph. They reminded Harry of Violet and of Mrs Buckley, but most of all of that day at Linden Hill when he had first dared to try the piano.

'The lustres look lovely, Harry,' said Ivy, as he came in with the tea tray.

'Don't they? I washed them very carefully. Mother would have been so upset if I'd broken anything.'

'That's just the right place. The afternoon sun really sets them off.'

'Yes, I think she'd approve, don't you, Ron?'

Harry enjoyed having Ron and Ivy to stay. He showed them round the garden and explained what he intended to do with it. The birdbath was still stored in the shed, but Fred's bench was already positioned beside a hawthorn tree. Ivy sat down ceremoniously.

'No elder trees in this garden, then, Harry?' She chuckled to herself. 'Do you remember that afternoon Ron brought me home to meet your mother?'

'He's not liable to forget, is he?' said Ron. 'Poor Harry. She didn't speak to you for a week at least.'

'It wasn't even Harry's fault. It was my fault for drinking too much.'

'No, it was my fault for offering it to you. Well, that was Mother's view. Anyway, talking of drink, what can I get you?'

181

'I'll have another cup of tea, please, Harry,' said Ivy and he laughed.

Harry was glad that Ron and Ivy had seen for themselves how settled he already was. He didn't want Ron to worry about him. There was no need to, not now. The house suited his needs and his job back at Hall Place was going well. He had a new routine, and that was enough to stave off any unnerving sense of vulnerability, should it come, which he doubted. Every afternoon, as he cycled back from Hall Place to the quiet seclusion of Knowl Hill, he planned how to spend his evening. His possessions were all unpacked but the photographs from India and Singapore were still waiting to be mounted in the album he had bought for this purpose. 'That's your entertainment for tonight, Harry,' he said to himself as he turned the corner into his lane the day after Ron and Ivy's visit.

After supper, he went upstairs and fetched his photographs and the unused album from the spare room. Back in the kitchen, he poured himself some beer, and spread his archive out on the table. It was strange, he'd hardly thought about his months abroad since his move here. He hadn't even felt any particular inclination to talk about them to Ron and Ivy, or to anyone else for that matter. No, they had served their purpose, but now he was back on familiar ground, at home, and he saw the future years stretching out before him, years of uninterrupted peace, when he believed he would feel something at least of the contentment he had known before.

Harry was not a diary keeper, but while he was in the medical corps he had kept a small notebook in which he jotted down brief comments as reminders about places, people, activities. He had also recorded dates to help him organise his pictures, such as the surrender ceremony when he had glimpsed Lord Mountbatten from afar and even the day on which he first photographed some of the patients in the hospital grounds. Using his notebook, he began putting the pictures in order. First, India. Street scenes mainly. Exotic fruits, mangoes, jackfruit and durian, on a market stall. A snake charmer, his cobra emerging threateningly from its basket. Almost nothing of the temples and shrines which he had been patently unable to connect with Kipling's fictional world. Then, many photographs of Singapore, some of which he had taken himself, some he had bought before leaving. There were several snaps of 'the hospital crew', as he had come to think of them. The boys, with Taffy's bandaged face very bright in the tiny photos. Joe, Norman and some of the other orderlies. And the photograph which Joe had taken of Harry and Norman with two of the patients, and Sisters Turner and Kirwin completing the ensemble. When the pictures were in order he put them into groups according to what would fit on each page of his album. He cursed his clumsiness as he tried to handle the tiny metal corners he was using to secure them.

This operation finally finished, Harry poured himself another glass of beer and set about labelling the photographs, again with the help of his notebook. It was a tedious process, in all honesty, but the album would be better for containing this information. The picture with the nurses was one of the larger snaps and took up almost a whole page of the collection, but it was an unwelcome reminder to Harry that he had still not replied to Beatrice Kirwin's letter. There she stood, Ralph's angel, her hand resting on the shoulder of one of the patients. Harry inscribed below the photograph rather formally:

47 B.G.H. S'PORE

WARD 5B   NOV. 1945

SISTER TURNER   SISTER KIRWIN

TWO PATIENTS

Pte ELSTON   Pte FULLER

Well, he would write to Beatrice the following evening, after he had written to Norman and Joe. He wanted to invite them down to see the house.

When all the photographs had been mounted and labelled, there were still some blank pages in the album where Harry stuck the news clipping about Christmas in the hospital and some Japanese banknotes from the time of the occupation which he had kept for their historical interest. He had picture postcards of the ships in which he had sailed to and from South-East Asia, and he pasted these at either end of the album, adding the dates of embarkation and arrival. Under his breath, he made some mental calculations. 'Over a year and a half now,' he said quietly. His task completed, he took the finished product into the sitting room and settled into his armchair. He browsed through his collection, pleased with his effort, and looked forward to showing the album to his army chums.

The following evening, as he had determined, Harry wrote his letters to Joe and Norman. They were both living in London, where Norman was once again making public appearances and Joe was busy at his carpentry. The letters were simple and short. 'Come and visit while it's still mild enough to sit in the garden,' he put. There was no point in writing several pages when he would almost certainly see them in a few weeks' time. Replying to Beatrice was less straightforward. He couldn't remember where he'd put her letter, which would have her address. He rifled through the kitchen drawer where he kept items that needed attending to. If it wasn't there, he had no idea where it was. Lost in the move, more than likely. Well, he didn't suppose she would be that bothered if he failed to reply, although he didn't want her to think him rude. She was bound to have plenty of other Singapore correspondents. So he settled down instead to read the newspaper and half an hour later remembered he had tucked her letter for safekeeping inside *The Jungle Book*. And having found it there, he felt obligated to write a reply at long last.

He began with an apology, how he had put the letter in a safe place and then forgotten where that place was, joking that he must be getting old. He would have written sooner but he had been in the throes of moving and settling into his new home and returning to his former place of employment. He hoped she was well and enjoying her duties at the hospital. He too was well and hoping to see

185

Norman (whom she would remember) and Joe (whom she might not) within the month. And he signed off with best wishes and considered his obligation fulfilled. By the time he had finished the letters it was almost dark outside but still warm. Harry put on his jacket, lit a cigarette and went out to sit on the garden bench. He surveyed his twilight plot, marvelling at the many plants which had emerged since he had cleared the weeds and trimmed back the overgrown bushes. In time, it could be just like the garden at Bottle Green. He simply had to be patient, he reminded himself, as the soft yellow glow of evening primrose faded into the shadows and the tolling of the church bell drifted across the fields from Bottle Green, telling him it was nine o'clock.

Harry often recalled Norman's comment about being reunited with his piano. Now he was back in England and settled in his own place, he too felt the joy of being able to play again, but for him it was a private, contemplative act. Thanks to Mrs Buckley's sound judgement and relative wealth, Harry's piano was a good investment and had aged well. Within a week of Harry moving in, the tuner had paid a visit and taken a great deal of trouble to get the poor instrument, rather out of sorts after its months in storage, fully back in tune. Harry could barely wait for him to finish his work and leave. As soon as the tuner had gone, he replaced the photograph on top of the piano, and sat down to try it out. After all this time, he couldn't decide what to play. He let his fingers wander gently up and down

186

the keys. They felt stiff. It was a long time since he had played more than simple songs or hymn tunes. A long time indeed since he had been practising the *Liebestraum*. Well, he would give it a go and see how he got on. If Norman was coming down in a few weeks, he wanted to impress him. But more than that, he wanted to play for the smiling woman in the photograph, something to evoke that faint awareness of her presence, and as he moved into the first rising cadence, he sensed over his shoulder that she had come into the room and taken her place by the fireside.

After that evening, Harry spent many hours at his piano, applying himself to the pieces he had had to abandon when he left England. Gradually his renditions became more assured, more technically accomplished, and he found himself able to express through the music sentiments he would have been unable to put into words. Sometimes, though, he noticed a degree of reluctance in his fingers and particularly his thumbs, a slight stiffness that would delay a note by the mere fraction of a second, the same sensation he sometimes noticed while weeding and digging, when he would lose his grip on a fork or trowel. He attributed this stiffness to the wind being in the wrong direction and determined not to pay too much attention to it.

Despite this minor difficulty, Norman was impressed with Harry's playing. He had told Joe what Harry had confided in him on the voyage from Singapore. They saw and registered the photograph on the piano but neither of them mentioned it to Harry himself, who seemed happy enough, as far as they could tell. It was good to meet up again, the three of them. They talked about the hospital, and wondered what had happened to the piano there. They strolled around the garden, and admired Harry's work in progress. He suggested they went for a drink and, since they all had bicycles, they found themselves twenty minutes later in The Old House at Home, where Harry related the story of how his parents had met.

'I think mine met in the village shop,' Norman said. 'They were both buying boiled sweets. Not terribly romantic. What about yours, Joe?'

'No idea, I'm afraid,' said Joe. 'By the way, I wonder how Sister Turner's getting on, whether married life agrees with her.'

It turned out that Norman had also, but more recently, received a letter from Beatrice Kirwin. Sister Turner, now Mrs Gardiner, was apparently very well and living in Basingstoke.

'She asked after you, Harry. She said she'd written and you hadn't replied.'

'I have now. It just took a while, with the move and everything.'

'Jolly good. She seemed quite keen to hear from you. Why don't you go and visit her? I'm sure she'd like to see you.'

'I expect she's got more interesting things to do in her spare time,' said Harry.

'Maybe, but you should go anyway,' said Norman. 'Another pint, anyone?'

A few beers later, it was almost time for the train. Joe and Norman said their goodbyes to Harry outside the pub and set off for the station. Cycling slowly home, Harry chewed over the day's events. It had been gratifying to know how much Joe and Norman had liked the house. The piano playing had gone well, and Norman had been very enthusiastic about it. And they'd clearly both enjoyed looking at the album and reminiscing about what they'd been through together, laughing about Harry's encounter with a wayward monkey, and the day Matron tore Norman off a strip over something so trivial they couldn't even remember what it was. Funny how those times seemed to have been much more enjoyable when recollected in the comfort of an English pub with the friends they had been shared with. All in all, a very pleasant day. Norman's suggestion that Harry should pay a visit to Beatrice Kirwin he had already forgotten.

It was dark, and the house seemed a little empty when Harry got back, but he made some tea and sat in the kitchen listening to the wireless. The photograph album was still on the table and Harry browsed idly through it, almost for the last time. The experiences seemed so remote already. If he hadn't seen Norman and Joe with his own eyes less than an hour or two ago, he might be inclined to believe he had imagined the whole episode. He felt noticeably matter-of-fact about his period abroad. He had had a useful job to do, he had got on with it, and for the most part it had kept him occupied. But he knew he had been unresponsive to all the situation had offered. He had watched the nurses, some

189

years younger than himself, caught up in the intensity of their experience, both in their work and their play. Their consciousness of the unfolding drama of war heightened their responses to whatever they were doing. For Harry, the drama of his life was over, done with. No, he would look back on the months in Asia with affection, with appreciation of the rigorous routine which had helped him through, but in the end his memories would be consigned to the unopened pages of his photograph album.

One Saturday in November, Harry decided to resume his attendance at the church in Bottle Green. This had always been his vague intention, but until now he had felt little real inclination to step inside the weathered stone building which had been part of his life for so long. Besides, he had preferred to spend his weekends clearing and preparing the garden. Today, suddenly, there was a chill in the air and the ground was growing colder and harder. He wouldn't work in the garden tomorrow. He'd attend the service in the morning and spend the afternoon reading the paper or playing the piano. It wasn't a long walk to the church, hardly further than from the old house, but the next morning he left especially early, carrying a small wreath he had made of holly, ivy and mistletoe gathered from the garden and the lane.

He had come to the graveyard many times since his return, nearly always in the early evening when the long shadows marked out the resting places of the sleepers and a tiny stone angel near the gate seemed to be taking up her watch for the night. He liked it best at this time, the noise of the day having retreated from the road, and stillness having settled like a mist among the elms and yew trees. Rarely did he see other visitors then and he could remain undisturbed by Ella's grave, absorbed in solitary contemplation. Often, Harry stayed for an hour or more, smoking a cigarette or two and sometimes, somehow, reaching out to his wife, not always in words, not always in silence. Ella had been buried on the other side of the graveyard from George and Violet, and Harry was glad of that, grateful for a kind of privacy. He still tended his parents' graves, made sure they looked neat and cared for, but he seldom lingered there now. They would understand why not. To Ella, on every visit, he took flowers or some other greenery to adorn her resting place, determined it would never be left bare or forgotten.

This Sunday morning, there was a winter dew on the ground and a sprinkling of autumn leaves had settled on the grave. As he was brushing them aside, he became aware of another presence standing over him. Startled, he looked up to see a woman he faintly recognised, older than himself, and sadder too, he thought, although the quality of her sadness was distinct from his own.

'Harry?' the woman said. 'It's Jessie. Jessie Kenton. We haven't seen each other in such a long time. I saw someone at the gate and I thought it was you. I heard you'd come back to the area. I'm sorry about...' she glanced down at the grave, '...what happened.'

Harry stood up and smiled. 'Jessie, how are you? I didn't expect to see you here. I thought you'd moved away.'

'I had. It's a long story. Are you going to church? Shall we go together?'

It was reassuring to walk into church with Jessie. They sat in the Kentons' usual place. The church seemed emptier than it used to be and there was a new vicar, but the distinctive sound of the organ and the comfortingly familiar rituals were enough for Harry to feel glad he had come back, like putting on a worn, but perfectly fitting overcoat. The present organist wasn't up to scratch, though. Maybe he should offer to play sometimes. He'd think about it.

After the service, Jessie had to rush off. 'But mother would love to see you. Why don't you come to tea this afternoon?'

Harry walked home, thinking about what Jessie had told him before the service had started. It was a long time since Harry had spoken to her. He had barely seen her during the war years, when she had been away, doing some kind of voluntary work, although he couldn't recall ever knowing what her exact role had been. But now she had come home again, and was planning to stay. Her recently widowed mother, just turned seventy, needed to be looked after. She had never truly recovered from the shock of Albert's death, thirty years ago now. Jessie wanted to make sure she was well cared for. Jessie herself had aged, thought Harry. She looked so like her mother now, it confused the passage of time. And he realised the cause of his hesitation in the graveyard when, for a moment, he wondered if it was Edith standing before him.

At home, Harry considered whether he should take some kind of birthday gift when he went to tea. It was too late in the year for flowers from the garden. There was

193

nothing suitable in the house. 'You'll have to do, Harry,' he said. He made himself a simple lunch and played the piano for a while before it was time to go. His hands were still occasionally stiff, he noticed, but the weather was definitely turning colder. Probably best to cycle over to the Kentons. It would be dark by the time he came home.

This was the first time he had gone over to Bottle Green since his return. Until now, the church had been his boundary. He wasn't sure how he would feel passing the old house - there was no other route to the Kentons - and being unable to go inside. He had met the new occupants briefly but could think of no valid reason for knocking on their door in the hope of being invited in. Well, it was probably better that way, he thought, as he cycled past, trying to keep his attention on the road ahead.

Jessie welcomed Harry warmly when he arrived and led him into the sitting room where Edith sat in an armchair, a blanket over her legs. The immediate impression was of a woman who was losing her battle against the attrition of time and loss. She reached out her hand to him. 'Harry, how kind of you to cycle all this way. You look perished. Come and sit here by the fire. How are you?'

Edith and Jessie wanted to hear all about Harry's time in the medical corps. He should have brought his photograph album. They wanted to know about Ron and Fred and their families, and about Harry's new home and job. He answered their questions and they listened intently as they all sat by the fire drinking tea. When at last there was a pause, Harry said to Edith, 'I was so sorry to hear about Mr Kenton. I didn't know until Jessie told me this morning.'

'Thank you. It was difficult. We'd been married a very long time. But nothing could ever be as bad as that other time. Losing a child, there's nothing as terrible as that.' Harry didn't know what to say. 'But we have found some comfort, some solace over the years, haven't we, Jessie, thanks to Mrs Leath.'

Harry looked at them blankly.

After a short silence, Edith went on. 'She was such a help to Violet too, you know, Harry, after your father died.'

'Perhaps we should explain who she is, Mother? Harry, you're looking rather puzzled.'

'Did Violet never speak of her, Harry, never mention Mrs Leath?'

'No, she didn't. I'm certain she didn't.'

'Then you must meet her for yourself.' Edith smoothed her blanket more tightly over her lap. 'Then you'll understand. Come over again next Saturday afternoon. Can you do that?'

Cycling home, Harry wondered why on earth he had failed to ask Edith more about this Mrs Leath he had never heard of. Why had Violet never mentioned her? Or maybe he'd forgotten. That was possible. Yes, he must have forgotten. After father died, she seemed to have so many women friends in the village. She must have been one of those. Nevertheless, the niggling question of Mrs Leath's identity returned to him on and off the whole of the next day as he worked in the park at Hall Place. Apart from this, it was a peaceful day. The sun shone and they had a wonderful bonfire of dead leaves, from which Harry drew long inhalations of their sweet melancholy smoke and almost started to look forward to his first winter in the new house.

When he returned home that evening, there was another letter from Beatrice Kirwin. He knew this from the handwriting. He was reluctant to open it, beset once more by the vague but unwelcome anxieties which her previous letter had triggered. He put it on the kitchen table, deciding he would open it after he had eaten. It was cold outside and he was hungry. He switched on the wireless and listened to some music while he cooked his meal. He liked this stage of the day, work over, and some hot food to look forward to. He had even come to enjoy cooking it, although he had to admit to some memorable disasters in the last few weeks, potatoes boiled to burning, and a stew seasoned with so much salt it was inedible. But he was learning and, on balance, didn't think he was doing too badly.

The contents of Beatrice's letter were much as before. News of her sister and her sister's children, and a tremendous amount about the hospital where she was now working and having a wonderful time but still missing all her friends from the Singapore days. 'It was so kind of you to write when you were obviously still busy getting settled into your new home. How nice that Norman came to visit you. You were both so kind to me when we were in Singapore. I shall never forget that day when I was telling you about Changi and you gave me your handkerchief.

Nothing as bad as that in deepest darkest Surrey, thank goodness.' As before, the letter went on for several pages of her large enthusiastic handwriting. Finally, she wrote: 'Now you must be wondering how I knew about Norman's visit. Well, he wrote and told me what a very fine day you all had and how much he liked your home. But he's a bit worried you don't have enough fun and thinks a trip to London would do you good so I have a suggestion.' The proposal was that Beatrice and Harry should attend one of Norman's concerts in London. Beatrice made it sound quite settled, not really a suggestion at all. Harry supposed he must accept but he was unsure, hesitant. He had the vague feeling that Beatrice and Norman had cooked this up together. Well, he would think about it.

Harry spent the next week thinking about it. It nagged at him while he was at work, nagged in a different way from the mystery of Mrs Leath. Something about the proposed arrangements made him uneasy and he couldn't put his finger on it. He was very keen to go to Norman's concert but he detected an element of pity in Norman's attempt to 'get Harry out more'. He didn't want pity. That was why he so rarely told anyone anything about his catastrophic loss, let alone the full story. A sudden thought occurred to him that Norman might have told Beatrice what little he knew. The 'suggestion' for the outing definitely had something of the air of a conspiracy about it. Or maybe Harry was imagining it. 'Get a grip, Harry,' he told himself and carried on with his ground clearing. Despite his misgivings, he finally decided it would be rude not to accept the invitation. He wanted to hear Norman play, especially the Elgar, and an evening spent with Beatrice wouldn't be so bad. In fact, it would be rather pleasant, if he could just get over the feeling they had set him up. Maybe they were right. Maybe he did need cheering up, although, all things considered, he thought he was doing alright. Well, Beatrice's cheerful demeanour and Norman's music would doubtless do the trick. By the end of the week he had written his acceptance and posted it.

When Harry looked out of the window on Saturday morning, there was a thick frost on the ground. This time last year he had been sweltering in the heat of Singapore, accustomed by then to the flies and mosquitoes. Presented with these bare branches and drifts of fallen leaves, silvered by the frost, it was hard to imagine. His album was still on the kitchen table and he turned to the photographs he had taken last November. There were the pictures he had taken of 'the boys' and the team of Ward 5B. There was a picture of himself with Joe and Norman, the three of them barefoot in some jungle clearing, sitting astride a tree trunk which had been strategically placed across a stream. They looked like they were having fun. He must have enjoyed himself sometimes, Norman and Joe had reminded him of this, but in all honesty he could remember feeling little more than that predominant sense of damage, of having survived, but only just. His chums and colleagues had been good to him. He must make an effort when he went to London.

Feeling clear-headed, he set off in good time for the Kentons, deciding to walk, despite the cold. He had put on a jacket and tie, uncertain of what would be appropriate, but better to be on the safe side. He decided he might as well take the photograph album. He wrapped it in brown paper and put it in a small shopping bag that had belonged to Violet, along with a torch which he was bound to need later on. In half an hour, he reached the church but, unusually, felt no compulsion to go into the graveyard. In another twenty minutes or so, he was outside the old house. He was glad he had decided to walk as it gave him the opportunity to slow his pace and see if he could look inside. But there was nothing to give him an indication of the life which was being lived within its walls or the people who were living it. This did not bother him unduly, not today. His mind was on seeing Jessie and her mother. As for Mrs Leath, that feeling of conspiracy was creeping up on him again, but this time he was unconcerned. He carried on down the lane absorbing the thin wintry sounds of nature as though they were the richest gifts in the world. As he came within sight of the second bend in the lane, he knew exactly how much further there was to go, and quickened his pace.

When Harry knocked on the Kentons' door, Jessie welcomed him as before and led him into the sitting room. Mrs Leath had not yet arrived. Edith was there, not sitting by the fire, despite the cold, but at the dining table, which had been moved into the centre of the room. Here she sat upright, poised, as if in readiness for something imminent, important.

'Come in, Harry, How are you? We're just waiting for Mrs Leath to arrive.'

There was a faint glow in the room from the weak afternoon sun but Harry noticed the curtains had been partially drawn, making the room darker than it had been on his previous visit. Edith invited him to sit beside her and she asked him how his week had gone. They talked for a while about nothing in particular and then Mrs Leath arrived. Harry hadn't heard her knock. The sitting room door was pushed open and in she came, a woman about Edith Kenton's age, perhaps a little older, but more assured, much less desolate.

'You must be Harry,' she said. 'Good. How are you, Edith?' She sat down on the other side of Edith and took her hand. Jessie came in with the tea and sat between Harry and Mrs Leath.

'I knew your mother, Harry, said Mrs Leath. 'Did she ever mention me?'

'I don't think she did,' said Harry, 'not as far as I remember. But I may have forgotten.'

'I met her first in 1916. And she never mentioned our meetings?' Harry really couldn't understand how he had never known about her. But then he had been away at school for many of those years. Now he came to think about it, Violet did visit Edith a great deal and Mrs Leath could have been present on any number of those occasions. Mrs Leath turned to Edith. 'Shall we begin?'

Harry wished someone would explain to him what was going on. He looked at Jessie hopefully, but she simply smiled and looked down at the table. In a few moments more, when Mrs Leath had placed her hands on the table and looked upwards as if at a fixed point above Harry's head before half closing her eyes, a childhood memory came flooding back and the precise purpose of her visit began to dawn on him. Jessie and her mother sat very quiet, very still. Moments passed, moments that seemed long and full of expectation. When Mrs Leath spoke again, it was not to Edith or Jessie, as might have been supposed, but to Harry, comforting words that he would remember for the rest of his life.

Like an exhausted traveller who has reached his destination but cannot empty his mind of reflections on his journey, Harry found it almost impossible to sleep that night. His own exploration had started that dark night of the Great War when Ron was ill and he had been sent to fetch mother from Mrs Kenton's house, and now, many years later, had finished in the place where it began. At last, he was certain of the answer to the question he had posed Frank Chandler in the school chapel when he was still a child, and which Frank had half answered for him the day he left school. Now he felt he could give Frank his own answer, complete and unhesitating. In the early hours, he finally fell into a deep sleep filled with dreams of happy times, and he awoke feeling fully refreshed, and utterly certain of Ella's presence with him.

Over the coming weeks, this enhanced sense of Ella's presence did not weaken or fade. As the days grew shorter and Harry was forced indoors, he looked forward more and more to the solitary hours when he would play the piano or read the paper with the quiet contentment of those former days when he knew she was moving about in another room of the house. He saw Jessie at church and usually sat with her and always talked to her, but she never alluded to what had taken place other than to mention that Mrs Leath would be visiting again before Christmas and he would be welcome to come for tea. Having accepted her invitation at once, he found himself calculating how many days would pass before he would once more be seated at the Kentons' dining table. He had almost forgotten about Norman's recital until a Christmas card arrived very early from Beatrice telling him where to meet in London. 'I'll expect you at 4 o'clock,' she wrote, 'and we can have a cup of tea before the concert begins.' It was all arranged and Harry supposed he had better go along with her plans. It was probably too late to make alternative arrangements and, being so settled now and calm, he felt a greater readiness to accommodate her customary ebullience. In fact, he found he was looking forward to seeing her, and to having her company at the concert.

Harry arrived early at the tea shop Beatrice had designated. He had some faint notion that she had detected his previous reluctance to write or to meet and now he wanted to compensate for being stinting with his friendship. He was at the location with fifteen minutes to spare but Beatrice was already there. He saw her from across the road. She was sitting at a table by the window and looking down, as if at a book or magazine. It was getting dark, but her figure was illuminated by the lamp post immediately outside the window, and her crown of fair hair shone under the light's gentle gleam. An earlier snowfall had left its soft surface like muslin on the pavement and windowsill.

A bell tinkled as Harry opened the door of the tearoom. Beatrice looked up and smiled when she saw him.

'Gosh, you look exceptionally well,' she said as they shook hands.

'And so do you,' said Harry. 'The Surrey air must agree with you.'

The waitress brought tea and plates of sandwiches and cakes. Beatrice stirred the tea vigorously and poured out dark brown liquid.

'I like my tea strong these days,' she said. 'A reaction to that awful weak stuff we had to drink in Singapore, I imagine.'

And inevitably, they fell to talking about those Singapore days, as Beatrice liked to call them.

'Strange, isn't it,' she said, 'to think about what we were doing this time last year? You know, preparing for the

203

concert and decorating the ward for Christmas? Have you been doing much playing, Harry?'

Harry told her a little about some new pieces he had been practising.

'What are you doing for Christmas?' she wanted to know. Beatrice was going to her sister's. She was on duty at the hospital on Christmas Day, 'just my luck', but she would be there for Boxing Day and the family had decided to celebrate Christmas then in her honour. She had been buying books for her niece and nephew and took out *Lollipop Wood* and *Our Friends Next Door* to show Harry. 'Oh, and this,' she said, reaching into her bag and pulling out a copy of *The Jungle Book*, much to Harry's delight.

'You're smiling?' said Beatrice.

'It's an old friend,' said Harry. He told her how he had first encountered the stories at school and, almost expansively, about Frank Chandler's enthusiasm for Kipling and why Harry had taken his copy with him when he was posted abroad.

'Well, I hope Billy enjoys it. If he does, I'll buy him *The Second Jungle Book* for his birthday.' Now Harry was not so much delighted as surprised. Reluctant to appear ignorant, he changed the subject. He had no idea there was a second collection. How on earth had he missed that? True, He was not a great frequenter of bookshops, but he was almost appalled by his ignorance. 'Pay more attention, Harry,' he told himself.

The venue for Norman's concert was a short walk from the tea room. It was snowing again when they set off, and they walked briskly through the busy streets, past the glamorous stores of New Bond Street and Oxford Street where shoppers were in search of Christmas gifts. The concert hall was somewhat smaller than Harry had expected, but grand nevertheless. They took their seats in the third row back from the small stage which was set up with chairs and music stands for Norman's quintet. Harry had never seen such a beautiful piano, a Bechstein, in first class condition by the look of it and polished to perfection. How wonderful it would be to play such an instrument.

'Are your fingers itching?' said Beatrice, as if reading his thoughts.

'I couldn't do it justice,' said Harry.

The lights dimmed. The members of the audience had a final fidget and cleared their throats. Accompanied by much applause, the players came on, bowed, and took their seats. When the hall was silent and still, they took up their playing positions, froze momentarily like elegant statues, and then, with an almost indiscernible nod from the first violinist, they began their performance. Harry was instantly transported, enthralled by the skill of the players as they wove the melodies - some calming, some energising - of Brahms, Webern and Elgar, passing the threads as it were from one to the other with the most finely judged intuition. It was remarkable. And to hear Norman playing on a decent piano at last was a joy. What a contrast to the old instrument they had found in the Singapore school and their makeshift music-making in the hospital. But of course then they had been thankful for small mercies, and moved by the power of music to help heal the sick men in their care.

When the concert was over, they went to the stage door to meet Norman. They were effusive in their praise of Norman's playing and he graciously accepted their compliments. There was just time for a quick drink before Harry and Beatrice had to go for their trains.

'What did you think of the Webern, Harry?' Norman asked.

'A bit newfangled for me, I think. But I enjoyed it. I feel on safer ground with Elgar though.'

'I know what you mean. Well, you must both come and hear the group again. If you'd like to.'

'That would be lovely,' said Beatrice eagerly. 'Wouldn't it, Harry?'

Norman looked from Beatrice to Harry and back to Beatrice.

'When an angel beckons, how can he refuse?' said Norman. Beatrice blushed and looked at her watch. 'I must go,' she said. 'I'll miss my train.'

Slightly flustered, Beatrice said her goodbyes and was gone, admitting a sprinkling of snowflakes into the pub as she hurriedly closed the door behind her. They rested briefly on the wooden floor before melting.

'You know she's sweet on you, don't you?' Norman said to Harry as they stared at the starry trail to the door which she had left in her wake.

'I beg your pardon?'

'Come on, Harry, you must have noticed. Ever since that concert last Christmas.'

'You must be mistaken. I haven't done anything to encourage her,' said Harry.

'It doesn't work like that,' said Norman.

Time was getting on, and Harry was glad he had the excuse of making his train.

'Good to see you, Harry. Happy Christmas. And think about what I told you,' said Norman, as he shook Harry's hand outside the pub.

Harry didn't think about Norman's disclosure until he had reached Paddington and was sitting waiting for the train to depart. He trusted Norman's judgement, and on reflection he was possibly correct in his assessment of Beatrice's emotions. For the second time that day, he was struck by his own inexcusable ignorance. But that was all. It troubled him to think a sweet and popular young woman like Beatrice should experience any disappointment in her life, but even if Norman was right, and he had to admit this was a possibility, he had no intentions towards her. How could he?

Christmas approached, and Harry prepared to spend his few days off with Ron and Ivy, after which he was also hoping to pay a visit to Frank Chandler in Kent. There was little to do at Hall Place that week so he spent some time choosing and buying their Christmas gifts. He pushed his conversation with Norman to the back of his mind. There was nothing he could do, no action he would take. He wished Norman had said nothing, but he supposed the revelation was unpremeditated, an involuntary response to Beatrice's hasty departure. A few days before Christmas, he returned home from work one evening laden with parcels, presents for Ron and Ivy and their daughter, and also for Frank, Edith Kenton, and Jessie. He was expected at the Kentons' one last time before Christmas, and he wondered whether he should have bought something for Mrs Leath. But what could he possibly give her which was not inappropriate to the nature of the extraordinary gift she was able to bestow on him? How could he match that? He unpacked his purchases and set them out on the kitchen table. At the bottom of his shopping bag was one final item, which he had found, much to his delight, in the bookshop and had purchased instantly. A blue leather volume, secondhand, a little dusty, but in very good condition. He gently blew away the dust, cleared a space on the table, and set the volume down squarely in front of him. He turned to the title page and saw, with some satisfaction, the name of *The Second Jungle Book* and beneath it the name of the author. He took his fountain pen and in the space below he wrote: 'H G Elston: to himself. Christmas 1946.'

'Happy Christmas, Harry,' he said aloud, when he had completed his inscription.

Christmas at Ron's had become a less worrying prospect to Harry. If the happy circumstances of his brother's family life made him envious, he was strengthened by the knowledge that his own life had taken on a beneficial, if unexpected dimension since the time when he had been staying with them several months previously. Then, many aspects of his life had been unresolved which he now felt had been settled. He was settled. He had no plans to do anything which would precipitate a significant change to his life and he liked it that way.

Ivy was her usual hospitable self, producing wonderfully tasty meals and pressing Harry to generous helpings of seconds. He was waiting for her to mention Beatrice again, but this time she was more circumspect.

'Have you heard from any of your Singapore colleagues lately, Harry?' she said to him on Christmas Eve as she was spooning jam roly poly into his bowl.

Harry was relieved that she had not focussed her attention on Beatrice, despite her previous interest in that first letter.

'Do you remember me mentioning Norman, the pianist? I saw him only a couple of weeks ago. I went to one of his concerts in London.'

'That must have been nice. Did you go alone?'

Harry wondered how much to say. 'No, one of our other chums came along too, and we all went for a drink afterwards.'

'Bit of a reunion then? That must have been fun.'

'It was a very pleasant evening. I wish I could play the piano as well as Norman.'

'I bet he's not as good as you at gardening, though,' said Ron.

Christmas Day came and went without any shifts or dips in Harry's mood. The emotional exposure of spending Christmas in England with Ron's lot was a risk worth taking. Truth to tell, he thoroughly enjoyed himself. He felt relaxed, at peace, not alone. On Boxing Day, Ivy sent him and Ron out for a drink together while she cooked the dinner. As they walked to the pub, Harry wondered whether he should tell Ron about Mrs Leath. After all, Ron knew the Kentons as well as Harry did, and he was bound to remember that dreadful day when Edith turned up at their house, grief at the death of her son having turned her into a woman they barely recognised as they looked on bewildered. But trying to explain the difference Mrs Leath had made to his outlook, well, he wasn't sure he would find the words which would convince Ron that his older brother hadn't become just the slightest bit cranky. So he told Ron about Edith Kenton, and how Jessie was looking after her now, about his regular visits to tea at their house and how he usually saw Jessie at church, but of Mrs Leath he made no mention. Nor did he mention Beatrice Kirwin, although he found himself thinking about her fairly frequently over Christmas, not so much on account of Beatrice herself but because of the letter he had received from her just before he came away and which was lying, abandoned and unopened, on the kitchen table.

Harry didn't know it at the time, but his trip to Kent to visit Frank Chandler was the last he would make for many years. It was about 4 o'clock and almost dark when he stepped off the train at Farningham Station. The tiny platform at West Hill which used to save the schoolboys a long walk with heavy suitcases had been closed some years before, and it took Harry nearly thirty minutes to walk down into the village, along by the great arches of the viaduct, crossing the river as he went, and up the hill to the school entrance. Frank had arranged for Harry to stay at the Old Boys' Lodge and once he had deposited his holdall and overcoat, he set off through the school grounds to Frank's cottage, carrying only the Christmas gifts he had brought for him. The lights in Moore House made Harry think fondly of Mrs Shepherd and all the kindness she had shown him when he was a young lad. She had died many years ago now and on one of his visits shortly after her death he had taken flowers to her grave in the village churchyard and been heartened to see that others had been there before him.

Frank welcomed Harry warmly and ushered him into the cottage. The hallway was dim and it wasn't until they were inside Frank's study that Harry saw how gaunt his former teacher had become. For a moment he was reminded of the Changi prisoners he had nursed in Singapore. Frank had aged far more than the eight years or so which had elapsed since they last met. When Frank went out to the kitchen to put the kettle on, Harry noticed how he shuffled, pulling his faded old cardigan around him for warmth. The study was more densely populated than ever with Frank's books, and the dust on the shelves and any available surfaces, where it was lit up by the table lamps, reminded Harry of a soft layering of snow on hard ground.

Frank brought in tea, and later beer, bread and cheese, and they sat talking by the fire for several hours. When the fire burned low, it was Harry who got up to fetch the coal scuttle and rake the embers. Frank had retired the previous summer. The relief of VE Day was, for him, not just the relief of another long war finally coming to an end, but also the pretext he needed to relinquish his teaching post. He had loved his work, but in the last year or so it had started to become too much of a burden.

'Just didn't seem to have the energy for it anymore,' he told Harry. 'But I did my bit for the war effort. Now I can settle down and really do some reading.'

Harry returned home from Kent with a strong sense that he would not see Frank Chandler again. Even though Harry was staying the night, Frank had excused himself from meeting the next morning. Harry had an early train to catch and just as he was leaving, a boy came knocking on his door with a parcel, a rectangular object wrapped in brown paper, larger, thinner and heavier than a book. Harry had no time to open the package so he gently placed it in his holdall, padded it with his pullover, and set off for the station. The train, fortunately, wasn't crowded, and rather than risk the luggage rack, Harry sat with his holdall next to him all the way to London. On the tube train he sat with it on his lap, and on the last stage of his journey, when the train was much busier, he held it to him as if the parcel had become more precious as the journey progressed and took him further and further away from his old friend.

The house was cold when he arrived back. He pulled the curtains, lit the fire in the sitting room and then the kitchen range, and made some tea before opening his parcel. By now, he was certain he knew what it was, but he would savour opening it nevertheless. He took his penknife and cut the string, then folded back the layers of brown paper reverently. The picture frame was face down and Frank had tucked a letter under the wire. Harry placed this to one side, wiped his hands on his trousers, and then carefully turned over the frame feeling no surprise to discover he had been right about the gift. He knew just the place for it and he would hang it there tomorrow morning. Frank's letter was short and to the point. 'This is for you, Harry. This is your poem, and has been since I first read it to you in 1918, I think it was, never mind all the others who have heard it and treasured its message. Of all the pupils I have taught, I have always associated it with you. I'm sure there will be a place for it on the wall of your new home. With all best wishes, Frank.'

'God bless you, Frank,' said Harry, before he blew his nose and took off his glasses to wipe his eyes. Then he took his poem into the sitting room and propped it up on one of the fireside armchairs. Back in the kitchen, he scrunched up the brown paper, took that into the sitting room too and threw it into the grate. His sadness made him careless of what he was doing and he failed to notice that Beatrice's letter had been scrunched up together with the paper and consigned to the flames. The next he was to hear of her would be several months later when Norman told him that she was engaged to marry a doctor she had met at Redhill Hospital.

Harry was not expected back at work until early January. The days following his trip to Farningham he spent quietly indoors, sometimes reading, sometimes listening to the wireless or playing the piano. On New Year's Eve, he finally memorised the *Liebestraum* note-perfect. He wished Norman could have been there to hear his performance, but it was only a faint wish, since all that truly mattered was to have the awareness of another audience, someone who would know what it meant to Harry to have mastered the difficult music and absorbed it into himself, *their* music, *their* memory. After he had played, he closed the piano lid and remained with his hands resting there for some moments, filled with a sense of satisfaction and completeness. Then he fetched himself a drink and sat dozing by the fire as the last few hours of the year moved steadily on. At last, over seven years after it had begun, he felt the war and all its attendant tribulations were over and peace had been restored somewhere deep inside him.

IV
1939 – 1944

September 1939

On the Sunday morning when Neville Chamberlain
announced to the nation that Britain was once again at war
with Germany, Harry had gone to church as usual. It was a
glorious late summer's day. He had got up as soon as it was
light and made tea for himself and Violet. They took it out
to the garden and sat together on Fred's bench. Preoccupied
with thoughts of what might transpire that morning, neither
of them had very much to say. Instead, they drank their tea
and stared at the abundance of vegetables, ready for
harvesting, ready for a crisis.

'Are you going to church, Harry?' Violet looked at him
anxiously.

'I think so. I'd like to. Are you going to come?'

'Not today. I'll stay here and listen to the wireless for
the announcement.'

'Do you mind being left alone?'

'No, I don't. I think it would be better.'

This was Violet's way of saying she feared the worst,
that 11 o'clock would come without any response to
Britain's ultimatum, and the whole country would find
itself reeling from the shock of peering at last into the
abyss. Violet felt she had no resources for surviving
another war. The deprivations it would bring meant nothing
to her, nor would any prospect of personal danger to

217

herself, but the possibility of harm to those she loved, or of endless weeks and months of separation and waiting for news, that was almost unbearable. And who knew how long it might go on? A few months of conflict could somehow, perhaps, be tolerated. But last time the promised months had turned horrifically into years and, when the armistice finally came, her nerves were almost shattered. If the news was bad today, if she was to discover that the safety of her little world in Bottle Green was irreversibly compromised, then she wanted to hear it alone.

For some years now, Harry had shared the role of church organist with the long-serving incumbent who was now getting too old and frail to perform his duties every week. Mr Leonard was reluctant to give up entirely – 'Playing in church keeps me going,' he had told Harry – but happy to let his deputy take over at least twice a month. This particular Sunday, he had insisted he would play. The difficult times in which they were living demanded it. If war were to be declared, it was his duty to play for the congregation as they moved forward into the darkness. Harry had conceded that it was probably the older man's prerogative to pick and choose his weeks, so he took his place with the rest of the congregation. Seated at the back of the church, it was easier to look around without catching the eyes of fellow worshippers. The church didn't seem any fuller or emptier than usual, but several familiar faces were missing and several unfamiliar ones had taken their place.

The service progressed as normal, its opening penitential tone seeming somewhat at odds with the mood of righteous indignation which so many villagers had recently expressed towards the aggressor. But, as always, there was something comforting about the familiar liturgy. Its cadences had been known to Harry before the outbreak of the previous conflict and, he had no doubt, would comfort and calm him through any war which might now come, and even, beyond that, to the end of his days. After the confession, the absolution, the psalms and the Bible readings, the hymn was announced. 'We will sing hymn number four hundred and fifty,' said the vicar. 'O God, our help in ages past, Our hope for years to come.' As he spoke, he was looking not at his flock, but beyond them to the west door where a woman had slipped into the church and was now waiting there, only a few feet from Harry. It was the vicar's housekeeper. She looked serious, impatient, as if waiting to convey a message. When the organist began to play, the vicar moved from his position by the lectern and, trying not to attract attention by retreating along the south wall rather than coming down the nave, walked briskly to the back of the church to join her. When the hymn finished, he was still absent from his place. The congregation remained standing, silent, facing towards the altar. After a few more moments, the vicar's step was heard returning to the chancel, this time moving heavily up the nave and up the tiny flight of steps into the pulpit. He motioned for the congregation to sit before he cleared his throat and told them of the Prime Minister's announcement.

After the service, Harry was anxious to get back to Violet. He slipped out of the church without speaking to any of his acquaintances, omitted to pay his usual visit to his father's grave and set off home half walking and half running. As he cleared the bend, he could see his mother standing in the lane, looking out for him. But she didn't wait as he approached. Instead, she turned without acknowledging him and stepped back into the front garden. When he reached the cottage she had disappeared indoors and he found her sitting at the kitchen table.

'Have you heard the news?' she asked him.

'Yes. Are you alright, Mother?' She didn't look at all alright. Her mouth was pinched and her greying hair was dishevelled, making her look older as if from neglect. Harry put the kettle on.

'What will happen to us, Harry? I can't go through it all again.' He knew what she meant.

'Let's not dwell on it today. Come on, the garden's looking lovely. Let's not waste the sunshine.' He gently took her arm and, shaken though she was, she complied by getting up from the table and letting him lead her outside. After an hour or so, she rallied and became almost talkative, but she carefully avoided the subject that Harry knew was weighing most heavily on her heart.

That evening, a vague sense of misery descended on Harry. All day he had tried to stay cheerful for his mother's sake, but at sunset his mood lapsed from determined cheerfulness to uncharacteristic gloom. He played the piano for a while, rather listlessly, while Violet sat with her untouched sewing on her lap, staring at the window.

'I suppose we must think about the blackout,' she said, when the room was almost in darkness and Harry could barely see even the white keys of the piano.

'Yes, we must. We'll do something about it tomorrow,' said Harry.

It was almost impossible to sleep that night even though the morning's news had now left Harry with a sense of intense weariness. There was a great deal to consider. Most pressing was the question of whether he or Ron or Fred would be called up. The scramble to prepare for war had exposed the shortfall in the British forces and conscription was bound to come. It was simply a question of when, and who, and how many. Fred had been demobbed not long after the end of the previous war and had worked for many years now as an electrical engineer. He was a likely conscript, perhaps, although his age might have been against him – or in his favour, depending how you looked at it. But Harry and Ron might expect to receive their papers, if not at once, then perhaps within the year. It was not impossible that all three brothers could find themselves serving in the forces if the war was a prolonged one. No wonder Violet had been so upset, so fearful. And in the event of Harry being called up, being sent away, who would look after Violet? He supposed if she had to manage on her own, she could, but he had noticed in her over the last year or so those first traces of the fragility of age which he knew would take hold and accelerate if she was left alone without his support.

Which brought Harry to another concern, the far more private and nebulous question of his own future, a concern which he had never mentioned to Violet, and certainly wouldn't now when even the suggestion that he might turn his domestic attentions elsewhere would seem like a betrayal. Ever since he had returned from school to Bottle Green, he had hoped that one day he would meet a woman he would like enough to marry. In the first years of work, when his attention was largely given to the gardens and grounds of Hall Place, he had been willing enough to believe that this would happen sooner or later. At first, the cycle of the seasons, watched so carefully as part of his working life, barely alarmed him at all on his own behalf. But then they started to acquire the nature of a reminder that time was passing and, as he watched his mother starting to grow old, he feared for himself that he too would grow old and find himself alone, unmarried, and disappointed. This feeling deepened not long after Ron met Ivy. Despite Ivy's inebriated introduction to Violet, her future mother-in-law had liked her enormously and encouraged Ron to pop the question, which he had every intention of doing in any case. Their wedding had followed less than a year later, at which point Harry could not help but tell himself it was his turn next, especially since Ron had rather impertinently jumped the queue. Fred had been married for many years, had two sons already, but his marriage had made less impact on Harry having taken place while his much younger brothers were still at school. Harry had never compared himself to Fred in the way he compared himself to Ron. But someone had to look after Violet, and that was possibly that. Besides, the war changed one's priorities, and maybe he had no business worrying about personal aspirations when the bombardment could begin at any moment.

The following morning the keen concerns of Harry's largely sleepless night had lost their edge but had settled instead like a headache which dulled and inhibited his thoughts. When he left for work, Violet was already up, sitting reading the newspaper, her posture suggesting she did so almost against her will.

'Don't worry, Mother,' Harry said as he left, knowing the remark was pointless. 'What will you do today?'

'Make jam, I suppose,' Violet said. 'Make jam and listen to the wireless.'

Despite Violet's fears, she would have to admit that for the first few weeks after that dreadful Sunday, it was hard to believe the nation was at war. She and Harry went about their everyday lives as usual. The subject of conversations with their neighbours had shifted, but almost imperceptibly, the focus now being not when war would happen but when the might of the enemy would first become evident. At Hall Place, where Harry was now the senior gardener, the younger employees came and went as normal. One or two of them talked about joining up, but patently failed to do so. Their employer asked Harry to see that some additional provision be made for growing fruit and vegetables, and Harry designated an unused area of the walled garden for this purpose. In the evening, Harry would still sometimes go for a pint after work, often to The Old House at Home where his parents had met. Business there seemed to be thriving. Maybe talking about the war made people especially thirsty, or simply gave them an excuse for drinking. The only concession to the possibility of a German attack was the nightly ritual of blacking out the windows before lights could be lit indoors, something which was a major headache for the owner of Hall Place, but which Harry and Violet could achieve together in less than ten minutes. It was a shame, though, Violet said, to have to shut out the last of the evening light so soon.

On Sunday mornings, the customary patterns of churchgoing underwent some small modifications. The vicar adjusted the content of his sermons to include some guidance to his flock on their moral position with regard to the enemy. Prayers were included to petition for the deliverance of the nation and its monarch, and the vicar, who had always had intercessionary tendencies, introduced an additional prayer to St George, presumably to be on the safe side. He selected hymns which would either stir up national feeling or, through their invocation of various saints and martyrs, keep his parishioners' minds on the advantages of the next world. Mr Leonard told Harry that he had decided to play for all the services for the foreseeable future, especially since it was only a matter of time before Harry would be called up. Mr Leonard, on the other hand, was ready to engage with Hitler from his organ console.

The first significant change in the village came in the form of the influx of evacuees from London. One afternoon, a WVS member knocked on Violet's door and asked her if she would be willing to take in a child, or even two siblings. Violet was doubtful. She would have to ask her son. They discussed it when he came home from work that evening.

'We must try to help,' said Violet, 'and we do have a spare room. We could maybe take one child.'

'Won't it be a lot of work for you?' said Harry. 'Would you be able to cope during the day?'

'Well, there would be school, so it wouldn't be all day. Then you can help me in the evenings. Anyway, I think I'd like to have a child here. It'll remind me of when you and Ron were small. And I did miss out somewhat when you went away to Farningham.'

'But with all due respect, Mother, you were a little younger then.'

Eventually, they agreed they could take one child if necessary, boy or girl, they had no preference. Although Harry had been concerned to spare Violet the additional work and anxiety that a lodger might cause her, he was touched to think she would like to compensate herself for the lost years with her own children. For himself, Harry found the prospect of a young charge rather appealing. It would be pleasant to have a taste of fatherhood. The possibility of acquiring a liking for something he might never again experience he pushed to the back of his mind.

In the end, the number of children who arrived in Bottle Green was considerably fewer than expected and Harry and Violet's spare room was not required. The dozen or so children who did come were much in evidence around the village. The Kentons took in two brothers, Victor and Sidney, very distressed at leaving their mother in Clapham. They were nice boys, Edith told Violet, but they were constantly arguing with each other. Their brotherly banter was wearing her out. Harry offered to take them for a walk. Seeing how miserable they looked, he began by telling them how he and his younger brother Ron had been sent away from home during the previous war when they were barely older than Victor and Sidney, and it was a relief to see the evacuees smile when he said it had turned out alright. In fact, he and Ron had had rather a good time. Harry introduced the boys to his favourite spots in the area, showed them how to select the best conkers for tournaments and advised them on the range of sweets for sale in the village shop. One afternoon, he gave them a guided tour of Warren Woods, the scene of his own childhood games and explorations. He told them about the scouts who used to populate the trees on fine spring or summer evenings. When he discovered the boys didn't know the first thing about orienteering, he dug out Fred's old compass and showed them how to use it to find their way out of the woods, spinning them round with their eyes closed and letting them work out the direction home. He

226

told them how his older brother Fred had signed up for the army, leaving him and Ron to visit the woods on their own, and how, that first summer holiday back from Farningham, Harry had made up stories for Ron based on the characters of *The Jungle Book*, when they would imagine themselves coming to rescue Mowgli from the monkeys in the Cold Lairs.

When Edith came to tea with Violet, she usually brought Victor and Sidney with her. So that the women could talk undisturbed, Harry took the boys into the garden and started teaching them the names of the trees and flowers. On the occasional evenings when Violet went to visit Edith, and Mr Kenton took himself off to the pub, Victor and Sidney were sent up the lane to the Elstons' cottage and Harry entertained them with card games or let them play with the wooden toys that George had made so many years before. He found the box of lead soldiers that Mrs Buckley had given him and Ron that Christmas, and let Sidney and Victor play with them, marvelling at the years that had passed since he and Ron had done the same, although he was sure they hadn't argued as much as the evacuees seemed to. One evening when they were very restless, he read them a tale from *The Jungle Book*. They curled up together on the sofa, Sidney with his thumb in his mouth, and listened wide-eyed, only interrupting when they had questions about the story. The next time they saw Harry, they pestered him for another one, and before long they were making up their own stories of Mowgli's adventures in Warren Woods which they related to Harry with muddled enthusiasm.

Edith was extremely grateful. 'I can't thank you enough, Harry. You've really helped them to settle in. I was so worried.' Despite this, Edith, he noticed, looked as if she was enjoying the experience of having the evacuees rather more than some of the other villagers who had been complaining apparently about bedwetting and other forms of bad behaviour. But in a month or so, the children had calmed down and been absorbed into village life. When the harvest festival came round, they were all brought to church carrying their harvest offerings, pumpkins and swedes, apples and potatoes, as if they had always been a part of the gentle rhythms of this community, so far mercifully unscathed by the process of war.

Information about conscription was not long in coming. All men between the ages of eighteen and forty-one, other than those in reserved occupations, could be called upon, unmarried men first. Those under twenty-three were required to register for availability at once; older men would have to register in due course. Violet by now had had time to become accustomed to the possibility of all three of her sons being called up. Fred had turned forty just a few months earlier. Surely he could not be required now. In Violet's mind, his experiences at the Somme exonerated him from further service but, more superstitiously than that, she feared his luck might have already run out.

'You used to say he knew how to take care of himself,' Harry reminded her.

'Yes, but it was easier to say than to believe.'

A letter arrived from Ron. Violet breathed a sigh of relief when she read it. He was in a reserved occupation, as it turned out. Rippers, the expanding and successful woodworks where Ron was now employed as a foreman, had been commissioned in the production of Mosquito bombers. He had plenty of work to keep him occupied, and he had signed up as a special constable, which entailed doing the rounds at night on his bicycle. Harry was rather amused at the thought.

'I hope he doesn't crash,' he said, wondering how Ron would find his way in the blackout.

A few days later, Fred also wrote to say he was unlikely to be called up, thanks to his work at the electricity company. He had been busy constructing an Anderson shelter in his Croydon garden, deeper than the recommended minimum. The deeper, the better, he explained. That was something he had learnt in the trenches of the Somme. He was rather pleased with the finished result, which he had fitted with a ventilation shaft and electric light.

Violet's relief at the news from Ron and Fred, at least as far as conscription was concerned, sharpened her fears about Harry. Gardening was hardly an essential wartime occupation, even if he had been directed to increase food production on the estate. And he was single. Nor was she so old and frail that he might get let off on compassionate grounds. Harry himself was philosophical.

'Don't worry, Mother,' he found himself saying yet again. 'It might not happen. And anyway, who knows, I might find myself a wife.'

'What was it like, those first few weeks of the last war?' Harry asked Violet in the opening days of this new conflict.

'Unreal, in many ways. I suppose it was only when Fred enlisted, you know, that I first felt the shock of it.'

'All that football. Do you remember?'

'Yes, well, and football at the root of the problems, that's what I think. Having to get used to Fred being away, that was difficult. And then Albert died. I'll never forget that day. Poor, poor Edith. Then your father... And you and Ron going away to school... I wondered sometimes where it was all going to end.' She stopped, and looked out of the window, but Harry could tell she was still running through those unforgotten events in her mind. She said so little normally about the past. This short speech was almost remarkable in its length.

'I wonder when we'll hear from Frank,' Harry said, trying to draw her back to the present.

'Mm, yes, I wonder when,' she mumbled, still gazing towards the garden.

Now the war had started, Harry was especially glad that he had taken his mother to visit his old school and to meet Frank Chandler, a trip which seemed as if it would be almost impossible now. Harry himself had been back on a number of occasions since leaving school, normally in the summer for Old Boys' Day. Violet had always expressed a desire to go but somehow over a decade had slipped by with her wish unfulfilled. Then one dull October evening in 1938, well over a year after Ron and Ivy's wedding, Harry said, 'Let's go to Farningham. I want to show you around, and you must meet Frank at last.'

A few days earlier, the newspaper had been full of the Prime Minister's visit to Munich to negotiate with Adolf Hitler, or at least to buy Britain time to prepare for war. From that point onwards, despite the signed promise of a halt to aggression, war was in the air, there was no denying it. The nation was bracing itself for the inevitable conflict to begin, or so it seemed to Harry from the demeanour of the people around him and the snatches of conversation he overheard at work or in the pub. If he didn't take Violet on the long talked about visit now, it might never take place at all. Harry wrote to Frank Chandler and it was agreed that they would be there for the first weekend in November. Harry could stay at the Old Boys' Lodge, and one of the school cooks said she could let Violet have her guest room for the night.

They arrived at Farningham that Saturday just in time for the Guy Fawkes parade and bonfire. Frank had invited them to come for tea first at his house. When Harry introduced his mother to Frank, it struck him for the first time that they were a very similar age. He wondered it had never occurred to him before. But when he was a child, he had always seen his mother as younger than her years, as the beautiful young woman he imagined her to have been when she first met George. Frank Chandler's age, when he first knew him as a teacher, was indeterminate, his authority over the boys adding to rather than reducing his years. And they had aged in different ways. Frank had become slightly stooped, shabbier, as dusty as the piles of books in his study, whereas Violet still had the bearing of a younger woman, even if her greying hair betrayed her actual years. In both their faces, however, Harry could trace the irreversible lines of bereavement and grief.

It was a memorable weekend. Frank and Violet got on even better than Harry could have hoped. His mother was invited to sit in Frank's companion armchair while Harry took the additional seat. They talked and talked, almost oblivious to Harry, who sat listening to them with amusement as they picked over the highs and lows of Harry and Ron's school careers like an old married couple. It was almost dark when they had finished tea, and they went outside to watch the boys display their effigies, marching with them down to Big Field, where the bonfire was ready to be lit. Harry stood with his mother and former teacher, enjoying the spectacle as if he were a boy again, while thinking how quickly and seamlessly the last twelve years had passed. The following morning, they attended chapel, and Harry pointed out to Violet the exact spot where his brief conversation with the King had taken place. After the service, he introduced her to Reverend Bell, who, like Frank Chandler, had served so many years at the school that he had become as sturdy and solid a part of it as the buildings themselves.

'Thank you so much for all you did for the boys,' said Violet. 'I always hoped I'd get the opportunity to thank you in person.'

Then Harry walked with Violet around the school grounds. He showed her Moore House, although he hesitated to call, having never met the new matron. 'Go on,' said Violet, and when Harry explained who he was, they were welcomed in and given a brief guided tour. Violet stood in silence, nodding to herself as she took in the domestic scenes of this other home where her boys had grown up in her absence, as if something had finally been satisfied inside her. Harry was overwhelmed with reminders of those years, pointing out to his mother many things which related to Ron, but saying very little about his own memories. Upstairs, the room where he had first slept had been redecorated and rearranged but Harry saw none of these changes, standing close to the spot where he had sat and copied out his favourite poem, the vision of his younger self oblivious to the man who peered over his shoulder. The new matron was clearly busy, so they politely refused her offer of something to drink and left after hardly more than fifteen minutes. Harry took Violet to the school house, where she stood on tiptoe to look into the empty classrooms, next to the dining hall, the smells exactly the same he told her, and then down to the tiny farm, passing the workshops where Ron had learnt his trade of carpentry and joinery. Violet was delighted by everything she saw, the places she had only read about in their letters, or imagined in the descriptions they had given her when they came home for the summer vacation.

'It's hardly changed,' Harry remarked as they wandered around. But there was one tell-tale sign that peace for their time was likely to be very short-lived and that the school was as vulnerable to attack as any other location. Between the boarding houses, in the plots where Harry had learnt how to plant and nurture flowers and vegetables, and in the lawns where he had swept up the leaves for Mrs Shepherd every autumn of his school life, deep trenches were being prepared to shelter the boys in the event of an onslaught from the air. As it was Sunday, digging had been suspended, but the pits were already long and deep, their sides reinforced with wood and concrete. Large mounds of chalky earth had accumulated next to the trenches, making them appear more like enormous graves awaiting a burial party. A shovel and spade lay criss-crossed on the ground, ready for the resumption of labour the following morning.

Ever since Frank Chandler had met Harry's mother, he had addressed his regular letters to them both. It was the November after the outbreak when they received the first of his occasional reports about the war's effects on the little community on the hill. This year there had been no bonfire for Guy Fawkes because of the blackout. Instead, the effigies had been displayed in the dining hall and a prize given as usual for the best one, which bore a remarkable resemblance to the German Führer. Slowly, the school's ranks were depleting, as the senior boys started to enlist.

Mr Reynolds, the mathematics teacher, was running special classes in trigonometry to help those who wanted to apply for the Air Force. Every morning before school, the teachers read the daily newspapers so that lessons could begin with a briefing on the progress of the war, of the battles won and lost. The boys followed the news eagerly, as they would an adventure story. Much had been made of the sinking of the Royal Oak at Scapa Flow, not least because it had given them their youngest ever pupil, little Jimmy Parker, barely two years old, probably too young to remember the father who had gone down with his ship in the icy Scottish waters. 'But school carries on,' wrote Frank, 'and the food is probably no worse than usual, so the boys have little to complain about.'

That first winter of the war was a bitterly cold one and Harry became very worried about Violet. She took to going to bed exceptionally early, claiming she could no longer stand the blackout.

'But it's always been dark, even with the curtains open,' said Harry.

'You can't see the moon and stars,' she said. 'I used to like to sit here and watch the moon, and it's too cold to go outside.' The only evenings when she would venture out were the occasional visits down the lane to Edith's house. She insisted on going, even when the lane was covered in ice or snow, and was anxious about arriving at Edith's by the predetermined time. Harry offered to accompany her, which she allowed only because he was coming to collect the evacuees, and when he walked back with them a couple of hours later, she was usually glad of his arm to help her home. Despite her increasing physical frailty that winter, she always seemed energised, animated when she returned from Edith's, an improvement which Harry attributed to the strength of the women's friendship.

The possibility of Harry being called up remained with them, but it was rarely discussed, although Harry could see how it weighed upon his mother, her constant tenseness a sign that she was waiting for the worst. Christmas brought little respite from the lurking anxiety of conscription. The farmer at Wonnacotts had promised Edith a chicken and she invited Harry and Violet to join them for Christmas lunch. The boys would like it too, she said. Christmas Eve was a dismal affair. The day had been foggy and grey. There was to be no midnight mass, no light shining in the darkness, and Harry and Violet sat at home together as they did most other evenings that winter. Violet had knitted scarves and socks for the boys and Mr Kenton, and had made a colourful rag rug for Edith, all of which she wrapped in brown paper while Harry played carols on the piano. Despite the frost outside, Violet was miserable about not attending church. The next morning, she cheered up a little when she heard the bells ringing. She and Harry visited George's grave before the service, taking a Christmas wreath they had made.

'I don't expect you're sorry to be missing all this,' Violet said somewhat bitterly as she placed it down.

Christmas lunch was a muted affair but the adults did their best to entertain the boys. Edith poured glasses of sherry for Harry and Violet and they toasted their absent loved ones. Edith had very much hoped that her daughter Jessie would be home for Christmas, but she had been sent away on a detachment. Like Ron and Fred, Robert had decided it was inadvisable to travel and was staying at home with his family. Harry was particularly sorry not to have seen Ron. Last Christmas they had all had such fun together. Still, he enjoyed playing games with the boys, and promised them that as soon as the snow came again he would help them build a snowman.

With January came the first ration books, but by this time Violet had lost interest in eating and hardly cared about the shortages. As long as her son was with her, she would gladly forgo any number of meals. Eventually, the letter they had been expecting was delivered, the contents of which would make very little difference to Violet's life but cause a great deal of change in Harry's. He was directed to work at an aircraft factory near Reading, where they were expanding their production of training aircraft for the RAF. It could have been much worse, Harry told Violet. At least she would still have him at home. It took a while for the contents of the letter to sink in. He was rather bemused when he thought of himself and Ron as tiny cogs in the vast machinery of wartime aviation. Neither of them had ever been particularly interested in flying. Harry had always felt he wouldn't mind a sea voyage, but taking to the air had never had much appeal. Still, there it was, and he must get on with it, although he would miss his work at Hall Place. There were rumours it would be turned into a convalescent home. But first the gardens were to be sacrificed in the interests of national security. Supporting the forces was an obligation, a duty: he could hardly complain about the deep sadness within him that the roses and other flowers he had nurtured so tenderly would bloom unseen, if they survived at all, under what must be an inevitable invasion of weeds.

If forced to be honest, Harry would have admitted he disliked every moment of his work at the aircraft factory. Simply having to spend his day inside was bad enough. When he had been employed at Hall Place he never looked at his watch. The rising or setting sun told him all he needed to know about the transit of the day and he never felt any impatience for his tasks to come to an end. In the factory, every hour seemed to drag and within minutes of starting work he longed for it to be over. He hated the noise and smells of machinery, so much worse he supposed when one had been accustomed to the sounds and scents of nature. When the day was dragging more than usual, he would recite Kipling's 'If' in his head in an effort to manufacture the steadfastness he sadly lacked. When he came home in the evening, he said little to his mother about his day and instead went to sit by himself in the garden.

His only consolation was that he had not been sent for military training. His unskilled work at the factory was a long way down the chain of production which ultimately resulted in the possibility of inflicting harm on the enemy. Even this sometimes felt a little close for comfort. Harry would not go so far as to call himself a conscientious objector - defending the nation was, after all, a necessity – but he knew he lacked the mettle of his brother Fred, who would have killed a man at short range if he had had to. Did this make Harry unmanly? Were those who protested on moral grounds cowardly, or principled enough to brave the derision of others who were prepared to fight? He couldn't decide, but he knew he was glad he could support the war effort on the home front and hoped that this would be duty enough.

By the summer of 1940, the war began to proclaim its presence in Harry and Violet's lives. The church bells were silenced, only to be rung in the event of an invasion. The skies of southern England were infested with fighter aircraft, although Harry knew this more from Frank Chandler's letters than from the occasional evidence of his own eyes. 'The boys are obsessed with aircraft identification,' wrote Frank. 'A Hurricane has come down in Forty Acre Field and there is a black market in souvenirs.' Ron's next letter described a brief encounter with the enemy himself. One night after doing his round as a special constable, he had been at the police station writing up his report when a German pilot shuffled in looking disorientated and bewildered, and gave himself up. They had all felt rather sorry for the young man, and Ron poured him a drink from his hip flask. 'I had no idea what he said to me, but he sounded very grateful.'

'I'm sure he *was* grateful, and not just for the whisky,' said Violet.

*

As Harry had anticipated, Hall Place was given over to the army as a convalescent home and began receiving wounded soldiers who had been rescued from Dunkirk. Work on the gardens he had so lovingly tended came to a halt. Harry's predecessor as the senior gardener was brought out of retirement to help increase food production. Harry had always got on well with William Allington. The older man had been Harry's mentor when he first went to work at Hall Place. He encouraged Harry's talent and passed on to him the lifetime's wisdom he had gleaned there. From William, Harry learned so much more about planting, understanding when was the best time to plant and the best time to prune, which soil was preferable, in sunlight or shade, which plants made good bedfellows and which would cause him horticultural headaches. William lived in the gardener's cottage tucked away behind the big house. When the time came for him to retire, his philanthropic employer hadn't had the heart to evict him after so many years of faithful service and offered to let him see out his days there if he wished to, an offer which was gratefully accepted.

Harry took to cycling over after his daytime shifts at the factory to see what was going on, a pleasure he allowed himself every two or three weeks. The sense of delight he felt when he turned off the main road onto the long tree-lined drive that led up to the grand eighteenth century house never failed him. Always, he had this sense of entering a secluded world. It had never felt like going to

241

work at all. His former employer had moved into the attic servants' rooms of Hall Place leaving the Red Cross to have the run of the rest of the house, but it was William that Harry went to visit. The old gardener was always pleased to see Harry and offer him a beer. One evening, Harry arrived to find that William was out. He decided instead to wander round the grounds. On the east side of the house was a large formal garden where steps led down from the terrace onto a lawn. Tables had been set out on the grass and here sat some of the patients, the Dunkirk evacuees, playing cards or reading. Others were walking tentatively, supported by nurses, up and down the terrace. It was warm, even within the shade of the lime trees, from where Harry thought he could watch inconspicuously. The peaceful scene before him almost belied the terrible siege which had taken place only weeks before on the French beaches. So far Bottle Green had been spared any enemy attack, but even here was evidence of the displacement of humanity imposed by war. Soldiers from who knows where sent out to France and now brought back to this unknown corner of England to recover from their experience. Young women packing their suitcases and leaving their comfortable homes to come and look after them. And then there were the children, wrenched from their parents, loaded onto trains and deposited as strangers in the countryside. Throughout the land, all over the continent, humanity on the move. He was glad for the privilege of being able to remain at home.

Suddenly, Harry had a sense of someone else's presence and he turned to see one of the nurses standing beside him.

'Oh, I didn't mean to startle you,' she said. 'I was just getting some fresh air. It's been a long day.' Harry noticed how the leaves of the lime trees formed a perfect backdrop to her dark hair and smiling face. 'You look lost. Are you looking for someone?'

'No, I'm not lost,' said Harry. 'I used to work here, as a gardener. I came to see William Allington but he seems to be out so I thought I'd have a stroll round my old patch.'

'William's inside, I think, playing darts with some of the patients. Why don't you come in?'

'I'd like to,' said Harry, 'if you're sure it's no bother.'

'No bother at all,' said the nurse.

They set off across the lawn and she continued to talk, gently, thoughtfully. 'It must have been a wonderful place to work, before the war. I love it here. It's so peaceful. I often sneak out and wander round the grounds. I must have admired your efforts a hundred times. The patients are happy here too. Heaven knows they deserve some peace and quiet after what they've been through.'

'That makes me feel so much better,' said Harry. 'I can't tell you how much I miss working here.'

When they reached the terrace, which they seemed to very quickly, the nurse stopped by the French windows to let Harry go first.

'Your friend's in there,' she said. 'Do go in. I'm afraid I've got to run off and do some errands upstairs.' She paused and turned towards him. 'I'm Ella,' she added, offering her hand.

'Harry. Harry Elston. Pleased to meet you.' And he clasped her hand warmly in both of his before reluctantly letting her go.

The next time Harry saw Ella was equally unexpected. It was Sunday, and news was coming through on the wireless of the wave of attacks by the Luftwaffe, lasting through the night, on the London docks and the East End. Violet sat at the kitchen table listening, pulling her handkerchief tight between her hands. Harry could tell what was uppermost on her mind.

'Don't worry about Fred,' he said. 'Croydon's a long way from the East End.' She looked up at him, doubtful, anxious. 'Do you want to come to church?' he asked, suspecting he already knew her answer. Since the start of the war, Violet's attendance had become spasmodic, part of her increasing reluctance to leave the house. She shook her head. 'I'll see you later then,' said Harry, sorry to have to go alone.

On what seemed now like a pretext of visiting William Allington, Harry had returned to Hall Place on several occasions since his first meeting with Ella, hoping each time that he would catch a glimpse of the nurse and maybe even speak to her, but so far he had been disappointed. He avoided rainy days, and days when it had been raining, calculating that there would be no activity outside. More than once, even though it had been warm enough to throw open the French windows, the terrace and lawn had been

245

empty. William was always glad of Harry's visits and the opportunity to tell him what had been happening on the estate. The gardens were being neglected, there was nothing he could do about it. Still, at least the house was being put to good use, and the owner was doing his bit for the war effort by giving it over to the Red Cross. In response to Harry's questions, William said he knew very little about the nursing staff or the running of the hospital, even though he sometimes went into the makeshift wards or the recreation room to keep the patients company. Together, he and Harry walked round the grounds and tried to be philosophical about the flowerbeds, which now looked as if they were being encroached upon by a stealthy miniature jungle of creeping ivy and luxuriant weeds. In the kitchen garden it was a different picture. Before the younger gardeners had been called up, they had made sure that every spare inch had been cultivated, with the result that it was now abundant with neat drills of vegetables, which William was doing his best to look after.

'The boss has told them over at the house they can have it all for the patients, but he told me to help myself to whatever I need,' he had said, pulling up a couple of leeks and some carrots and handing them to Harry, who felt it would be impolite to remind him that he had his own supply at home.

Harry always enjoyed visiting William, but recently he had come away feeling deflated, not so much at the deterioration of the grounds he had worked so hard to maintain, but at his failure to encounter once again the dark-haired woman he had so enjoyed talking to. He still remembered clearly their brief conversation as she walked beside him towards the house.

'Did you work here a long time?' she had asked. 'You must have been sorry to leave.'

'Yes, over thirteen years,' said Harry. 'But the aircraft industry needs my unskilled labour more, unfortunately.'

'That's hard, though. At least I'm doing what I've always done, and enjoying it. Working here seems so worthwhile.'

Harry had surmised from this that she must have been working in a civilian hospital prior to the outbreak of war, and found himself eager to know more about her and, unusually for him, keen to tell her more about himself. In those few brief preliminary exchanges, Harry had developed an immediate liking for the nurse. Her manner was friendly, gentle. He felt an instant twinge of envy towards her patients. And there was a certain quality about her, a steadiness, which he envied too. 'If you can dream – and not make dreams your master' were the words of Kipling that came to mind.

That Sunday morning, Harry went to visit his father's grave before church. Like the gardens at Hall Place, the graveyard was also getting overgrown, he noticed, as he picked his way over to the far corner, oblivious to the young woman standing watching him as he went. Harry no longer talked aloud to his father as he had as a child when relating his simple narrative of school life and village life. Instead, he had developed a silent form of dialogue in which he tried to articulate George's disapproving views on national and international politics. As he tidied the grave and the area around it, he considered what George's response would be to this latest turn of events in the war, and how he would deal with Violet's anxiety about Fred. Probably, in his matter of fact way, he would put his arm round his wife's shoulders and tell her plainly that if Fred could get through the Somme, he could certainly get through this.

A different quality of light settled on the grave, making Harry aware that someone was standing over him, and he looked up to see a woman's figure, lit from behind by the morning sun which shone in his eyes and prevented him at first from seeing her face. He shaded his eyes with his hand and saw to his surprise that it was Ella, dressed not in her nurse's uniform but in a smart green coat which blended with the surrounding foliage.

'Harry, isn't it?' she said. 'I'm sorry if I've disturbed you yet again. You didn't see me when you came in and I didn't like to call out, not here.'

'Ella. No, you haven't disturbed me at all. What a pleasant surprise.'

'I'm staying with some relatives nearby. They invited me for the weekend and I thought I'd go to church but I was much too early and...'

'This is my father's grave,' said Harry, helping her out. 'I usually come here on Sunday mornings.' He glanced down. 'It's as if he expects me.'

'I understand.' She looked closely at the headstone. 'Did he fight in the last war?'

'No,' said Harry. 'My oldest brother did. And survived. He lives near London now. My mother's very worried about him and his family being bombed.' He looked at his watch. 'It's almost time for the service? Shall we go in together?'

'Yes, I'd like that. I don't know anyone in this village apart from my aunt and uncle and they're not really church goers.'

The church was crowded that morning, probably the result of what had happened the night before. Edith was there with her evacuees, who gave little waves to Harry when they spotted him, before giving each other the gentlest of surreptitious thumps. Harry saw them whispering to Edith and he wondered if they were asking about the strange lady who had come into church with him. He liked having Ella sitting by his side as they waited for the service to begin. The vicar came in unsmiling, pensive. He had clearly heard the news, and the prayers that morning alluded to the plight of those who had suffered in the bombardment. Since the war had started, the hymns had been judiciously chosen, but this morning it was hard to determine whether 'Christ whose glory fills the skies' was a regrettable oversight or a clear message that the people of Britain would not be intimidated by the enemy. As they stood to sing, Harry turned and grimaced at Ella, who shrugged and smiled knowingly. But they sang with gusto and for Harry at least it was a song of thanksgiving, despite its unfortunate irony.

It was due to Ella that Harry, a few weeks later, joined the Red Cross. After church that day, anticipating that her answer would be yes, he had gathered the courage to invite her out to tea the following Saturday. The intervening week at the factory seemed more protracted than ever, but the tedium was relieved by the prospect of something very pleasant to look forward to when it finally ended. That afternoon, they exchanged brief stories of their lives so far. Harry told Ella about his childhood, and how he and Ron had been sent away to school after their father's death. Feeling in retrospect that the decade or more which had passed since he left Farningham had been relatively uneventful and therefore of little interest, he talked mainly about his schooldays, detailing the annual activities which marked out their year, the potato harvest, the Guy Fawkes parade, Christmas dinner and the annual festival. He told her about Mrs Shepherd, who had been like a mother to him and Ron, and particularly about Frank Chandler.

'He sounds delightful,' she said. 'I wish I could meet him.'

'I hope you will one day,' Harry found himself replying.

Ella was not a local girl. She had been born and brought up in Coventry, where her father was a factory manager. The family were comfortably off and there was no need for her to work, but the thought of staying at home had no appeal for her and she had begged her parents to let her train as a nurse at the local hospital. Long before the war had started, she had volunteered for the Red Cross, anticipating that when war came, as they all felt sure it would, she could do something specific for her country. Secretly, she had hoped it would provide an opportunity to get away from home and her loving, but overprotective parents. When nurses were needed for the new convalescent homes, she had only managed to persuade her parents that she would be perfectly safe in Berkshire because her aunt lived so nearby.

Harry, who knew many of the folk who lived in Bottle Green at least by name, was surprised not to know Ella's aunt and uncle, even though she had said their house was on the edge of the village, almost in neighbouring Knowl Hill.

'They like to keep themselves to themselves, I suppose,' said Ella, 'and they haven't lived down here that long. My aunt met her husband during the last war. He inherited the house from his much older cousin, an army colonel, who died childless. His widow lived there for many years on her own and then when she died, it came to my uncle. He let it out until he retired and then they decided to go and live in it. I think they're a little embarrassed at the size of the house. It's much too big for them really. Maybe they won't stay there. Why are you smiling?'

Ella was delighted when she discovered that Harry not only knew Linden Hill but had a lifelong connection with the place. She insisted he tell her all he could about the Buckleys. There was a great deal to say about Mrs Buckley, but he had hardly known the colonel, even though he was still alive when Harry left school and returned to Bottle Green. He rarely left his study, keeping the door firmly and forbiddingly closed. In winter, only a faint ribbon of light could be seen along the bottom of the door and Harry often wondered what shadowy memories he kept in there for company.

'When did you last visit the house?' Ella wanted to know.

'Oh, some years ago now. My mother helped look after Mrs Buckley until she died. I used to go and help the gardener sometimes. Or when she was well enough, Mrs Buckley used to come and sit downstairs and listen to me play the piano. It was thanks to her that I learned to play in the first place. She paid for my lessons when I was a child. Mother could never have afforded them.'

'Do you still play? I don't suppose you have much spare time.'

'When I can. It helps to keep me sane after the monotony of the factory. I used to play the organ in church sometimes but Mr Leonard has commandeered it again for the duration of the war, I think.'

'I'd like to hear you play.'

'You must come home and meet mother and then you can.' Ella looked pleased at the suggestion.

Later, the conversation turned again to Ella's work for the Red Cross. 'We're all volunteers,' she said, 'and that makes it much nicer in a way. I've met so many interesting people, and I love nursing. I don't think I've ever been this happy really.' She made it sound so appealing.

'Where do I sign up?' said Harry, half joking, half serious.

'Would you like to? Would you really like to?'

As Harry expected, Edith Kenton had told Violet about the young woman she had seen with Harry in church. The information unsettled her, bringing once more to the forefront of her mind her perpetual worry, nurtured for several years now, that Harry would meet someone he wanted to marry and she would be left entirely on her own. Now that the war had come, the thought of being alone was increasingly alarming to her. Every time she heard on the wireless or read in the papers about the almost daily air attacks which were systematically destroying London and so many other towns and cities, and thought about the dreadful shocks being endured by those citizens, it was as if the bombs had fallen in the gardens or lanes of Bottle Green and shaken her to the core of her own being.

When Harry told Violet about Ella, he tried not to alarm her. 'Don't worry, Mother, I'm not going to desert you, whatever happens. I'll invite her over and you two can get to know each other. You'll like her, I know you will.'

'No elderberry wine this time, Harry,' said Violet.

The farmer at Wonnacotts had promised Victor and Sidney that, when he had a spare moment, they could have a ride around the farm on his carthorse. They were beside themselves with excitement. They pestered and pestered him until at last, even though he was busy with the harvest, he agreed they could come on Saturday afternoon. They asked Harry if he would come with them, and Harry asked Ella if she would like to come too. When the four of them arrived at the farmhouse, the small team from the Land Army had already finished work on the cornfield and had moved on to the vegetables. The farmer was in the yard, where the patient old horse stood ready in its harness. Victor and Sidney were sent into the shed to get buckets to load onto the cart. When they were all ready to walk out to the field, the farmer beckoned to the boys.

'On you get, lads,' he said. Harry helped them mount the animal with a leg-up. Victor said he should be allowed to sit in front as he was the eldest. Sidney's face fell.

'If you sit behind, you can see over Sidney's head, and then you'll both be happy,' said Harry.

The little party set off, the farmer leading the carthorse with the boys on its back. Harry and Ella walked beside them, enjoying their laughter as they jogged up and down and tried not to fall off. When they reached the field where the girls from the Land Army were working, the farmer told the boys to jump off and help with the buckets. With a certain amount of heaving and grunting, they loaded the full ones onto the cart and replaced them with the empty ones they had brought. Then the land girls showed them how to pick the sprouts, and they each filled a bucket of their own, competing to see who could fill his bucket first. 'Steady does it,' said the farmer. Harry and Ella stood watching them, smoking cigarettes.

'They seem like nice kids,' said Ella.

'They are. You must get to know them better,' said Harry.

When all the buckets were full and ready to be transported back to the storehouse, the boys were allowed to get back on their mount. Passing him the rein, the boys asked if Harry could lead the horse this time, and Ella went round to the other side so that the animal was between them. Off they went, a little rustic procession, the land girls following the cart with their hoes resting jauntily on their shoulders. Too tired to talk, the farmer walked a few paces behind. Exhilarated by their position and the happiness of the occasion, Sidney and Victor took out their handkerchiefs and waved them against the afternoon sky.

Violet liked Ella very much and was pleased for Harry, whatever implications this situation might have for her. She could tell he was serious about Ella but determined not to ask him about his intentions. The two of them arrived from the farm and Harry excused himself briefly so he could wash and get changed. He wanted an excuse to leave Ella alone with his mother. Violet had been keen to hear about Linden Hill and she told Ella how they had come to own Mrs Buckley's piano. She wanted to know what the house was like now, and what plans Ella's aunt and uncle had for it.

'They're still settling in at the moment,' she told Violet. 'But I think they like it. Perhaps you'd like to come over one day. I'm sure they wouldn't mind. They hardly know anyone round here.'

'I'd like that very much,' said Violet. 'And I hope you'll come here as often as you can. You'd be very welcome.'

Frank Chandler's next letter was his most unsettling yet, and for the first time Harry started to worry seriously about his friend's safety. Running for cover had become a regular part of the school curriculum. 'A very effective way to keep the boys fit' was how Frank put it. The wailing of the air raid sirens would be accompanied by the teachers blowing whistles as a signal to the boys to take cover in the shelters. At the sound of the whistles, the boys would come running at top speed from all over the school grounds, those who had been out on Big Field arriving several minutes later than the rest, red-faced and breathless from their sprint, the silvery flashes of German war planes proving a better accelerant than any threats from the sports master. The army had positioned ack-ack guns in the area, and their stuttering fire was an additional soundtrack to the sprint for the safety of the trenches.

A few weeks earlier, the school had taken a hit. The carpentry workshop where Ron had learnt his trade, as well as the farm building nearby, had been partially damaged, and three classrooms in the schoolhouse were reduced to rubble. If the bomb had not fallen on a Sunday, many could have died. The boys became animated discussing the reasons why their school had been a target. Some believed that the school campus had been mistaken for an army barracks while others favoured the view that the German pilots had been aiming for the viaduct as a way of breaking communication links. A less conspiratorial interpretation was that the German bomber, bothered by the pursuit of an RAF Hurricane, had been panicked into dropping its incendiaries prematurely.

Harry tried to imagine what it was like for those young boys and how he himself would have coped. Were they thrilled to find themselves in the middle of this real-life adventure, the sort of thing they had only read about in comics? Or were they secretly, or even openly afraid as they dashed through the fields to safety when they heard the whistles blow? He thought of his own puny efforts in the cross-country runs and wondered if he could have run for cover in time, or would he have been like the few stray boys Frank had mentioned whose legs gave out and who threw themselves instead headlong into the furrows between the rows of potatoes hoping that the foliage would prove sufficient camouflage?

In November, on the night of the full moon, the Germans launched a devastating air attack on Coventry. Harry knew nothing about it until he arrived for work the following morning and found his fellow workers talking of little else. Within an hour of the raid beginning, the city had been set alight by incendiaries, followed by hours of bombing, designed presumably to destroy the factories so crucial to the war effort. Thousands were homeless, and the cathedral was reduced to a stone shell. Harry listened to the news numb with horror. Many workers, white-faced, were asking if their own factory would be the next target but all Harry could think about was whether Ella had heard the news and whether her parents or sister would be among the numerous civilian casualties. All day he fretted, fearing the worst. As soon as his shift was over, he was out of the building, impatient to make his way directly to Hall Place. When he arrived, he found Ella in tears. She had been listening to the home service. She had tried to get news of her family but their telephone was dead, as was their neighbours'. Normally so composed, she sat in the corner of the nurses' room sobbing uncontrollably. Harry bent down to put his arm round her, and at that moment he decided he would one day ask this woman to marry him. He led her out to the terrace for some fresh air. It was another clear night, and the moon was bright. Ella looked up.

'It was the moonlight that led the bombers to their targets. I used to think the moon was beautiful but now I shall always think of it as treacherous.'

'It's still beautiful,' said Harry.

She sobbed a little longer, then, when she had taken a deep breath and blown her nose, she said she had better get on with her work. She smiled at Harry. 'I'm glad you're here,' she said.

It was Sunday before news finally came through at Hall Place that Ella's parents and sister were safe. They had spent the night of the attack shivering in a field on the edge of the city and in the morning they had walked to a village a few miles away where some old friends were kindly putting them up. They would be staying there for the time being. Half the houses in their street had been bombed, they said. Theirs was still standing, but without gas and water it would be foolish to return.

'Thank God,' said Ella as she put the telephone down and reached for Harry's hand. 'That's the best news I've ever had. But those other poor people... Our neighbours...' She shook her head sadly and went back to the ward.

The photographs of Coventry which appeared in the newspapers were shocking, although they had shown the piles of street rubble which characterised the aftermath of bombing raids many times already. But there was an appalling newness about the pictures of the bombed medieval cathedral, its outer walls still partly intact and counterpointing the mounds of rubble with the delicate stone tracery of the windows. The pinnacles which had survived the blast pointed accusingly upwards. Within the walls, the debris had been partly cleared to create an uneven nave, where visitors could still pick their way, stumbling, towards what was left of the altar.

'I wonder if they'll ever rebuild it,' said Ella as they stared at the photograph. 'It's part of my childhood, going there at Christmas and other times. I can remember my first visit. I was out shopping with my mother. I must have been very young. It started to rain and we had no umbrellas so she said "Come on, let's go in here" and we took shelter in the cathedral.'

'What was it like?'

'To a child? It was wonderful. It seemed so vast to me then. We walked around looking at the statues and the stained glass. I couldn't believe a roof could be so high.

When the rain stopped, I didn't want to go outside but Mother promised we could come back another day, whether it was raining or not. After that, I made her go in every time we went shopping or happened to be walking past.'

'I wish I'd seen it,' said Harry. 'But it's better that those bombs fell on the cathedral rather than destroying even more homes, and killing even more people.'

'That's what I think too,' she said.

1941

Violet had certainly had enough of the war. Her nerves were shattered. The blitz that had struck at the heart of London and Coventry and so many other towns and cities might have come nowhere near her own home, nowhere nearer than Slough, as it happened, but the months of worrying about Fred and the grandchildren and the fear of an unknown future had reduced Violet's nerves to a wreckage.

'I'm in ruins,' she told Harry, 'like that picture you showed me in the paper of Coventry Cathedral. Inside, I'm all rubble. And the tea is so weak these days. How are we meant to withstand it all on weak tea?' She complained about Churchill and what she called his hollow nonsense. 'Unconquerable spirit indeed. Why doesn't he just come out with it and say we've all had enough? I don't care if Hitler is listening. Does he really think we aren't all sick to death of it?' Harry listened and said nothing as he watched her put away her mending and ease herself out of her armchair. She had become so thin lately, so weak. Not helped by food rationing, she had lost interest in eating, serving herself smaller and smaller portions as the days went by, and often giving up on the meal when it was only half eaten.

The one thing Violet had not done was cancel her evening visits to Edith, which Harry interpreted as a positive sign, despite her grumblings. 'If I don't go,' she would say as the designated date approached, 'the boys will be disappointed. They so look forward to their evenings here with you.'

'The boys can come anyway. You don't have to go out.'

'If I don't go, Edith will be miserable. She relies on me to go and see her.' Harry was not entirely convinced about this, thinking Edith might rather enjoy a few peaceful hours of her own company, but Violet was adamant. What was more, this was the only time she seemed to take any trouble with her appearance these days. Even on her occasional visits to church, she looked as if she had rushed out before she had finished getting ready. But for her evenings with Edith, she always made sure her hair had been washed and she had a clean blouse to wear. She would stand in front of the mirror in the hall, pinning on the delicate pearl brooch which George had given her one Christmas when Harry and Ron were still very small. When she fumbled with the clasp, she would ask Harry to help her. Kissing her goodbye, he caught faint whispers of perfume, her eau de cologne mingling with whatever it was she had put on her hair. He would stand at the front door to wave and as she walked down the path he noticed how her step was more like that of a young woman going to meet her date, as was the smile she gave Harry when she turned to wave back before disappearing without hesitation into the gathering darkness of the lane.

*

While Violet moaned and fretted about the war, Harry had never been happier. He saw Ella whenever their shifts would allow. Sometimes, his few spare hours given over to the Red Cross would take him to Hall Place, and then they would find themselves working together, Ella tending to the patients and Harry doing whatever other jobs he could to assist the nursing staff. He had started first aid training, and he recalled the rudimentary lessons of Fred's scouting days, something he had enjoyed then because he looked up to his older brother and was glad of his attention. But now, partly to his surprise, he found he had an aptitude for the course, although Ella joked that he was being too modest and that a man who was good at tending flora was bound to be good at caring for people. She had a point. The pleasure Harry always gained from nurturing a sapling into a mature and healthy plant now mutated into the satisfaction of helping with the care of the convalescent soldiers.

In their time off together, the two of them would go for a walk or sometimes out to tea or for a drink. Harry was reluctant to leave Violet on her own too much, so often he and Ella would spend their time at Bottle Green, reading the papers or working in the garden. Violet never touched the piano these days but Harry liked to play the piano for the two women, who took it in turns to make requests. He liked the way his mother and Ella got on together and Ella's willingness to accommodate Violet's needs. Every day, he considered how fortunate he had been to meet her and his determination that she would always be by his side strengthened accordingly.

Sometimes, they talked about the bombing of Coventry, Ella often wanting to rehearse the unspeakable shock of hearing the news, followed by those terrible protracted days of anxiety, then at last the relief of knowing her family were safe. 'I don't know how I would have got through that time without you, Harry,' she told him. She was thoughtful for a few moments. 'It's extraordinary, though, isn't it, how resilient people can be? You'd imagine no one would ever recover from an experience like that. I don't mean myself. I mean the Coventry folk, their determination to get back to some sort of normality. What must it have been like the morning after the attack to see how all the familiar landmarks had disappeared, whole streets, your home maybe...? What do you do?'

'You get through,' said Harry. 'You hold on and you get through.'

Violet never paid the proposed visit to Linden Hill. Ella's aunt and uncle had been thrilled to discover that the young man with whom Ella spent most of her spare time had a connection with the place, and insisted she take him there to meet them at the earliest opportunity. After a long period of more than three years, since before Mrs Buckley's death, it was strangely unnerving for Harry to step once more inside the house which had played such a prominent part in his childhood. Ella's aunt insisted she call him Doris – 'Mrs Killingsworth is so formal' – and led him from room to room, while Harry related his memories of going there with Ron to play, or going alone to have piano lessons or do his practice. It was unsettling to see the corner where the piano had once stood empty apart from a rather forlorn standard lamp. What Harry wanted most was to be allowed to explore the house once more by himself, to view the rooms again with the eyes of a child, when the exciting prospect of discovery made the spaces seem vast and inviting, so different from the cosy and familiar rooms of his home. When they went upstairs, Harry longed to climb the hidden flight to the attic, where the view of Mr Jennings working in the garden below had first prompted his longing to become part of the secret, almost indiscernible life of trees and plants. But Mrs Killingsworth – Doris – led him from one end of the landing to the other without a detour, showing him only one or two bedrooms which were now completely empty.

'We don't have that much furniture,' she joked.

Harry told her about Noah's ark and the games Mrs Buckley had invented to entertain them. 'It was a magical house for us as children.'

'Yes, it would be nice to have some children here again,' said Doris.

'Perhaps we could bring the evacuees. They'd love it.'

'What a good idea. And please bring your mother. I'd so like to meet her.'

A date was suggested when Harry might take Violet to meet Doris and Jim. If the weather was good, it was proposed, they could sit in the garden. Two or three days before the visit was to take place, Violet told Harry before he left for work that she was feeling unwell. He settled her down in her armchair with a blanket over her knees. He prepared some food and left it on the table next to her chair so she could eat if she felt like it. When he came home that evening, he found her still sitting there, her head leaning against one of the wings, her arms flopped onto her lap with the palms upward. Her knitting was still on her lap except that the ball of wool had tumbled off and unrolled itself over the rug leaving a thin blue strand loosely festooned across the floor. The food was untouched. For a moment, Harry thought the worst had happened.

'Mother,' he said, shaking her very gently by the shoulder. 'Mother, are you alright?'

She gave a slight jerk and lifted her head heavily from its awkward position. She looked at him for a few seconds without speaking, as if trying to work out who he was.

'Oh Harry, it's you. I must have fallen asleep.'

Harry tried not to show his relief.

'How are you feeling, Ma? Can I get you something? You don't look very comfortable.'

'I think I'd better go to bed. Will you make me some tea?'

He helped her up the stairs and left her to get undressed. When he came back with the tea, she looked at him sadly. 'I think you'd better let Ella's aunt and uncle know I won't be able to go after all. I'm not well enough.'

'You might be better in a day or two. We could wait and see.'

'No. Tell them I'm sorry but it's not possible.'

And from that Harry surmised that, illness or no illness, Violet wanted to remember Linden Hill as it had been when Mrs Buckley was alive, that she had no appetite for adjusting to the changing times but felt safer with the memory of a past which had disappeared.

By November, Violet was very poorly indeed although the doctor seemed reluctant, or maybe unable, to diagnose the cause. He told Violet she needed to go into hospital for some tests, but she was resistant. It was exasperating, her unwillingness to deal with her health problems, her refusal to eat more than a few mouthfuls of anything Harry put in front of her. She started to complain of abdominal discomfort, and the doctor gave her some painkillers. Once more, he urged her unsuccessfully to go and have tests done.

'I don't need tests, I need rest,' she retorted.

'I'm sorry, Harry,' said the doctor when he left the house. 'I don't know what more I can do if she refuses to go to hospital.'

'What should I do?' said Harry.

'Just keep her comfortable.'

From this point, Violet hardly got up at all. She spent much of her day sleeping, Harry listening outside the half open door from time to time for the sound of her breathing. Ella came when she could to check on her and help her wash, and sometimes, with Ella helping her down the stairs, Violet would get up for an hour or so to sit in the armchair by the fire, always in her dressing gown. Harry tried to entice her with an evening at Edith's. 'You haven't been down there for weeks. That's not like you. I can come with you if you'd like to go.'

'No thank you. It's alright, Harry. I don't need to go anymore.'

Harry was too busy and probably a little too tired to puzzle over her enigmatic remark. Her decision not to go out was enough to tell him that Violet had given up on life and there was nothing he could do about it. Meanwhile, when the evacuees were at school and Harry was at work, Edith would come and sit with her friend. Amid the noise of the factory, Harry imagined them talking in hushed voices of their shared history as the afternoon light grew red and golden before fading from Violet's bedroom window.

Christmas approached, and Harry asked Violet whether she would like Ron and Ivy to come again. The previous year, despite, or possibly because of the Blitz, they had saved their petrol ration in the hope they could manage the journey from Essex to Berkshire if they came on the motorbike, to which Ron had attached a sidecar for Ivy. They had made a heartwarming sight when they arrived on Christmas Eve, just before darkness started to fall, looking like visitors from another world in their layers of thick clothing and goggles. Ivy could barely move in the sidecar, where she was packed in with luggage and presents, and an extra thick blanket. Violet bustled them both inside the house to get warm. It was a long time since Harry had seen her so animated. She had been looking forward to their visit for weeks and had cleaned the house as if she had been expecting royalty.

'Ron, you look tired,' she had said, once they were inside and had removed their outdoor clothes, giving Violet the opportunity to inspect her youngest son. 'Don't you think he looks tired, Harry?'

'Then we must make sure he has a good rest,' said Harry. Sit yourselves down and I'll put the kettle on.'

'I am a bit tired out,' Ron said to Harry, after Violet and Ivy had gone to bed, 'but I've been so busy at Rippers lately, you know how it is. But I feel fine. We're both fine. It's Mother who looks worn out.'

'She worries so much, that's why. She's convinced Fred's house is going to be bombed. She thinks he should have evacuated the children. And she worries about being left on her own here.'

'Is that likely to happen?' Ron and Ivy knew about Ella.

'No it isn't. But I don't think she believes me.'

'It's good of you, Harry, to look after Mother.'

'Well, I didn't volunteer to. It's just worked out that way. She hasn't needed much looking after until now. Since the war started, she's been so nervous of everything. I wish Father was still alive. He would have known what to do.'

'Yes, he would. I think the hardest thing for him when he was dying was the thought of leaving her alone.'

Harry thought about this conversation as he sat now by Violet's bed. Maybe she had had enough of being alone. One evening, she had confided in him how much she had always missed George. 'And so much more since the war began. He's never truly gone away, you see. He's always been with me, always here.'

Violet never gave Harry an answer about Christmas. She slipped into a phase of prolonged but shallow sleep. When she was awake, she was lucid, but feeble. The doctor told Harry to expect the worst, there was nothing more he could do. Harry wrote to Fred and Ron so that they could come and see her before it was too late. Ron came a few days later, staying overnight and sitting with Violet whether she was awake or not. After he had gone, Harry, granted compassionate leave, took over his vigil. There was nothing to do while he sat with Violet so he took out *The Jungle Book* and re-read it. Its familiarity made this possible. He had little concentration for anything new. One afternoon, having skimmed the newspaper, he picked up a book of poetry which Violet had always kept by her bedside. He opened it where she had left her bookmark, and read:

> *The curfew tolls the knell of parting day,*
> *The lowing herd wind slowly o'er the lea,*
> *The ploughman homeward plods his weary way,*
> *And leaves the world to darkness, and to me.*

By the time Harry had finished the poem, Violet was awake. She saw he was reading her book, but made no comment about it. Instead, she said: 'You will marry Ella, won't you? I know you'd like to. I know you've waited and I'm grateful. But don't wait any longer.'

'Don't worry, Mother. I'll do as you say.'

'Good,' she said, and closed her eyes.

What Harry never told his mother was that he had already asked Ella to marry him some months earlier. It was fundraising day, and she had volunteered to sell flags in town. Harry said he would bring Sidney and Victor, who had acquired some old bikes and were keen to cycle anywhere he suggested. Edith and Violet each gave them some money. They spotted Ella in the high street outside Woolworth's. She was with a St John's nurse, their affiliations distinguished by the crosses on their uniforms. There was a small crowd gathered around them, talking and buying flags. Ella waved when she spotted Harry and the boys on the other side of the road. They crossed over and Harry waited while the boys sorted out the loose change in their pockets. Ella held out her collecting tin to receive their money.

'Thank you, Sidney. Thank you, Victor. This is Nurse Armstrong. She'll give you your flags.'

While the evacuees were having their flags pinned to their jackets, Ella turned her attention to Harry.

'Would you like to buy a flag?' she said, shaking her tin at him and laughing.

'Only if you'll marry me,' was his unpremeditated response.

271

*

Violet died three weeks before Christmas. After the funeral service, Harry and Ron led the little procession behind her coffin down the church path and across the road into the graveyard where she would once more lie beside her husband. Fred followed them with his two sons. Fred's wife walked with Ivy, and Ella with Edith. It was a dreary day, and Harry felt his grief would have been almost unbearable had he not known the comforting presence of the woman a few paces behind him who could now become his wife. They stood around the open grave as the vicar committed Violet for burial, but as the coffin was lowered into the ground, his words were drowned out by the convoy of tanks which thundered eastwards along the nearby Bath Road towards London.

That first Christmas following his mother's death Harry spent with Ron and Ivy. Ella was on duty at Hall Place, and after that she intended to visit her parents in Coventry. She hadn't seen them since the bombing in November. Although their letters and occasional telephone calls assured her they were fine staying with their friends, she wanted to satisfy herself that they were comfortable and in good spirits. Besides, she wanted to tell them about her wedding plans. Although Harry and Ella were impatient to be married, they were aware of an impropriety in holding the ceremony too soon after Violet's death, even though the pressing demands of war had given couples leave to foreshorten their engagements. 'We'll wait, and not be tired by waiting,' said Ella, making Harry laugh. So they agreed to wait patiently until June, when the weather would be warmer and they could accept Doris and Jim's invitation to hold a small reception in the garden at Linden Hill. While he was in Essex, Harry was going to invite Ron to be his best man, something he had always hoped to do should the opportunity ever arise.

In the weeks succeeding the funeral, it was hard to believe Violet no longer inhabited the house she had lived in for over forty years, for the whole of her married life and her even longer widowhood. On his return from work,

Harry expected to find her in one of the usual places, drinking tea at the kitchen table while she tut-tutted over the newspaper, or sitting in her armchair by the fire with her knitting. In the last years of her life, she had stopped playing the piano. She had lost the heart for it. 'How can I play when Hitler is knocking on our door?' she had said to Harry. Nevertheless, sometimes as he neared the house on his way home, he believed he could hear her playing *Love's Old Sweet Song* or some other favourite, the muffled ghostly notes of the old familiar tunes coming to him through the chill of the wintry air. When he was inside, he would go up to the piano expecting to detect the vibrations of strings lately touched or the briefest echo of the piano lid being gently closed.

Violet's bedroom he left undisturbed, keeping the door firmly shut and abandoning its nightly blackout. In Violet's final weeks, he had spent many hours here, sitting by the bed to keep her company whether she was awake or asleep, more often the latter. Now he reverted to his former mode, a reluctance to enter the bedroom out of respect for her privacy. When the initial grief of her death receded, it occurred to him that when he and Ella married it would be sensible to move into his parents' room. It was by far the largest of the three bedrooms and contained the most suitable furniture. He proposed this idea to Ella.

'It would be practical,' she said, after thinking it over. 'And besides, your mother was happy in this house. I don't mind sleeping in her bedroom. It'd feel like a family tradition. I'd like that.' Harry was relieved Ella felt this way, but also glad that some months would elapse between Violet being obliged to vacate the room and Harry and his new wife taking possession. It will give Mother time to move out, he thought to himself, time to absent herself from the room which she had slept in virtually every night of her married life and then as a widow, lying alone in the bed and missing the warmth emanating from George as he slept beside her. The room where she had given birth to three sons and where she had finally done with this world in favour of the next, finally done with war by stealing a march on Hitler, Churchill and the rest to enter into an early unconditional peace of her own.

When the time seemed right, Harry asked Ella if she would help him sort through Violet's personal possessions. He was surprised to discover how little she owned. Her clothes and shoes, too small to be of use to Ella, were given to the Red Cross for the homeless victims of the Blitz, something Violet would undoubtedly have approved of. Some months before her death, she had made Harry write down how her few items of jewellery were to be distributed among her daughters-in-law. To Ella, she left her pearl brooch, the one she always wore when she went to Edith's for the evening, and a necklace her father had given her when she married. In the top drawer of the dresser, they found the leather clutch bag that Violet used to take with her to church, the contents placed in readiness for her next visit. Harry took out these few items and laid them neatly on the bed: a leather purse, a miniature version of the bag itself, containing the coins she would put in the collection tray; a clean pocket handkerchief, pressed and folded; and a tiny New Testament, its cover starting to come loose from the binding. Harry opened it carefully. The frontispiece was a coloured print depicting 'Dwellers in the Desert', a carefully assembled group of five nomadic men and their two camels, strikingly incongruous with the quiet village church where it was an aid to Violet's worship.

The final item was Violet's pocket diary for 1941. Harry had never realised she used a diary. Her memory was always so good and, besides, her life was relatively uneventful. There didn't seem much she would need to remember. Idly, he leafed through the pages and found the occasional appointment with the doctor or a family birthday, but essentially the diary reflected a life in which little out of the ordinary took place. Then he noticed a date that had been marked simply 'G.E.' and nothing else. Flicking backwards and forwards, he found more such initials, placed at two, three or four week intervals. His father's initials. The dates, perhaps, when Violet had visited George's grave, irregularly after she had stopped attending church or being well enough to go to the graveyard every week. He knew she sometimes went while he was at work. He couldn't recall how frequently this happened. One set of initials was in mid-September, a date Harry remembered because it was Sidney's seventh birthday and the boys had come to see Harry in the evening while Violet visited Edith. Had Violet visited the grave that day while he was at work? He couldn't remember. Maybe she forgot to mention it. Flicking through the last few months of the year, it became apparent that the September visit was the last one she had marked in. He was sure there had been subsequent visits. It made him sad to think that after that she quickly became too ill to go, aware perhaps that soon she would lie there herself, side by side with George once again. Harry returned the four small objects to the bag and snapped it shut. Her book of poetry he left on the bedside table.

Doris and Jim had found some spare wallpaper and curtains stored away in the attic at Linden Hill and, presuming he would prefer to redecorate the room before the wedding, offered them to Harry on the basis that there was little available in the shops. 'I hope you don't mind, Mother,' Harry said when he next visited her grave. 'I know how you liked it the way it was.' Then he went home and, in a mood that was a strange mixture of sadness and excitement, stripped the walls bare of the faded floral paper which Violet had chosen shortly before her own wedding. So pale columbine was replaced with brightly coloured roses, but apart from that, he made very few changes to the house.

Much as he missed Violet, Harry found himself frequently thankful that she had been spared so many of the shocks, some domestic, most of them global, which the war continued to inflict. That winter, tea and sugar, the staples of Violet's daily life, became even scarcer and there was a general shortage of just about everything. But this appeared as a mere inconvenience on the home front in the light of the news coming from Europe and beyond, from Africa, the United States, and the Far East. Harry dug out his old school atlas and acquainted or reacquainted himself with the countries and cities he read about in the newspaper, Manila, Bataan, Kharkov, Timor, and the islands of the Philippines. He stared at the world map and tried to take in the extent of the war raging in all directions of the compass. The RAF launched an attack on Lübeck, and the Luftwaffe retaliated with raids on Exeter and Bath, Norwich and York. Looking across the room at Ella writing a letter to her parents and feeling the surge of happiness he always experienced when he caught sight of her, his little cottage felt like the only peaceful and secret haven in the world. In February, the nation was left incredulous at the news that Singapore, supposedly unassailable, had fallen to the Japanese. He peered down at the tiny pink colony and wondered how much more of the region would fall to Japanese domination before the war came to an end, and what colours and what distribution the children of the future would see when they opened the pages of their atlases. When Victor asked Harry to explain what was happening, he found it increasingly difficult to believe in an allied victory and to project their future with any optimism.

His approaching marriage to Ella was at least something certain he could look forward to. The months were passing quickly now and the plans for their modest celebration were in place. Some weeks prior to the wedding, Ella had mentioned to Harry a piano piece she had heard on the wireless, and how much she liked it. He managed to get hold of the music and determined that he would play it to her on their first evening together as a married couple. It would be his wedding gift to her. He knew the piece a little and suspected it would be difficult to perfect in such a short time. He was right: the fingering, the rhythm, the arpeggios, it was technically beyond him but he would do his best. His days were so full with his shifts at the factory, his hours given to the Red Cross and to seeing Ella that he often found himself practising late into the night or first thing in the morning. To avoid the practical problems of page-turning, he was determined to learn the piece by heart. He had just enough time, and the performance would be better without that distraction. It was easier than he had expected to commit the music to memory, something he had seldom done in the past. For weeks he played almost nothing else. When Ella was coming to the house, he hid the music inside the piano, making sure that the items on top of the instrument were always put back in the same place. As he practised, he imagined her delight when she heard the music. He would lead her into the sitting room, he had already visualised the scene. A warm evening, the room filled with flowers from the garden, her armchair in the best position to feel the soft breeze from the open window, a glass of sherry poured ready for her on the side table, and Ella herself radiant with delight when she discovered the trouble he had gone to. He could barely wait to see the expression on her face.

There was one aspect of his forthcoming wedding which was less appealing to Harry and that was the inevitability of being the centre of attention for the first time in his life. He had mentioned this to Ron at Christmas.

'It's not so bad,' said Ron, who understood his brother's shyness. 'In any case, the bride always gets far more attention than the groom. Something to do with wearing a frock and looking more attractive, I suppose. Everyone'll be far more interested in Ella than in you.'

'Thanks very much,' said Harry, but he was reassured.

If Harry and Ella had married in peacetime, supposing they had met at all under those very different circumstances, the wedding would almost certainly have taken place at her parish church in Coventry. But since she had been stationed at Hall Place, she had adopted Harry's village church as her own and this was where she wanted the wedding ceremony to take place. It was hard that some of her friends and relatives would be unable to come, but her parents would be there, and anyway, they only wanted a quiet occasion, no fuss.

Ivy and Ron stayed with Harry the night before the wedding. Harry heard their motorbike pulling up outside not long after he got home from the factory and he went outside to meet them, aware that the occasion of their last visit was for Violet's funeral.

'I can't tell you how much I'm looking forward to this,' said Ivy.

'It's good to be here under happier circumstances,' said Ron, shaking Harry by the hand.

Now that some time had elapsed since Violet's death, it had become easier for Harry and Ron to talk about her. They spent the evening reminiscing about the last war, nothing Ivy hadn't heard several times already, but she enjoyed hearing the brothers talk.

'Do you remember the evening before we went away to school?' said Harry.

'Do I? It was one of the most miserable evenings of my life,' said Ron.

'Me too,' said Harry. 'I was determined not to cry but I really felt like it.'

'What about the day Fred joined the army? What a rumpus that caused. I'd never seen Mother so angry.'

'Not even when I managed to get Ivy drunk on my homemade wine? She was pretty annoyed about that.'

'Talking of wine...' said Ivy, who disappeared into the kitchen for a few moments and returned with a bottle of homemade wine given to her by a neighbour. They toasted Harry's future happiness before Ron and Harry resumed their conversation, Ivy interjecting with items for the next day which she was worried Ron had overlooked. 'Have you finished your speech, Ron?' 'Are you sure you've got the ring?' 'You did pack your best shoes, didn't you?'

Ron took all this in good part, joking to Harry that this was what he could look forward to. Harry rather enjoyed Ivy's fussing, which was indirectly on his own behalf. He didn't think Ella would fuss in the same way, although he rather liked the prospect of someone watching over him like this. Harry showed Ron the letter he had received from

281

Frank Chandler, wishing him well. 'I'm so very sorry I can't be at the wedding,' Frank had written. 'It would have meant a great deal to me to be there. I send you both my very best wishes for your future happiness, and hope you will bring Ella to meet me just as soon as the war is over.'

'Perhaps we could go together, the four of us,' Ron suggested.

'That sounds like a very pleasant idea. Roll on the end of hostilities.'

So the three of them drank once more to the future happiness of Harry and his bride, and then to the prosperity of Farningham School.

Harry had turned his old bedroom into a guest room, which is where Ron and Ivy were to sleep that night. Violet's room was ready for Harry and Ella to occupy and he wondered whether he should sleep in it now. But somehow he felt he should leave it vacant one last night, whether on account of his mother or his future wife, he wasn't quite sure, and he spent the night in the tiniest of rooms which had been Fred's all those years ago. He was reluctant to sleep, preferring instead to lie in the narrow little bed listening to the night sounds and savouring the promise of the following day.

There were many things about that sunny June day which Harry would remember for the rest of his life and they would come to him frequently and randomly long after the war had ended and his life had taken a new and unexpected direction. The smell of the garden and the expanse of the fields beyond as he and Ron stood talking and smoking a last cigarette just minutes before they left the house for the church. The drive back from Linden Hill to the house as dusk was falling, with Jim as chauffeur, and his car decorated with ribbons and flowers. Sidney and Victor chasing each other around the garden at Linden Hill, large crumbs dropping from the hunks of wedding cake in their hands.

Then there were all the images of Ella herself, the rightful centre of attention that day. Her 'make do and mend' wedding dress, perfect in every way, even though she later confessed that it was her mother's. The way she walked up the aisle towards him, purposeful, assured. The private smile she gave him after he had placed the wedding ring on her finger. The more public smile she beamed at the camera for the formal photograph by the church porch and which he glimpsed as he turned to check all was well before the button clicked. And the tear he saw her wipe away as he played *Blumenlied*, almost note perfect, when they were finally alone together.

Harry had never had a stronger sense of his world being in a state of equilibrium than he had that day. Never had he had a stronger sense of being here, alive, in this world or, less consciously, of George and Violet reaching out to him from their unknown region. When he set off for church that morning with Ron he believed that if he had just turned round, just glanced back, he would have seen his parents looking down at their sons from their bedroom window, George with his arm around Violet, waving goodbye and good luck.

If there was any dark corner in Harry's mind that day, it was so remote as to be almost imperceptible, the faintest awareness that there was still a possibility he might be called up, that the war was not yet half over and that he had not yet fulfilled the obligations that others already had in abundance. He remembered what Fred used to say when he came home from scout meetings: 'Country first, self second,' he would quote at them, and Harry wondered, if and when the time came, whether he would be willing to prioritise so categorically. It was a principle he might have espoused when Violet was alive. With Ella, it was so much harder to put duty first. But for today at least, the tuneless background interference of war was hushed and in its place was nothing but the tranquillity of music or silence.

June 1942 to Christmas 1944

To Harry, who had grown up with brothers, who had spent his school life and working life predominantly in the company of boys or men, whose female influences – Violet, Mrs Buckley, Mrs Shepherd – were essentially maternal, the experience of being married to Ella was like pushing open a door which had been left invitingly ajar and stepping forward into a newly decorated, brightly-lit room, the sunlight from the west casting its afternoon warmth upon a vase of freshly-cut roses, which released their scent to fill the air with unanticipated promise. His happiness was multifarious, and so all-pervading that he hardly knew where one source of delight ended and the next began.

It was remarkable, after several months of living alone, for Harry to find himself once more sharing his home with a woman. It was as if he had fallen asleep and woken up into the same life but with a new companion. Materially, very little had changed, but the feelings he experienced were of a different quality. For one thing, he felt a pride of possession in relation to Ella, his senses quickening whenever he introduced her as his wife. Often, when she was unaware of him watching her, perhaps when she was sitting in the garden, or at Hall Place when she was tending a patient, he would gaze at her and marvel anew that at last he had found his life's partner. For once, and in all humility, he wondered if the recuperating soldiers at Hall Place who were yet unmarried were jealous of his good fortune just as he had been secretly envious of Ron when he met and married Ivy or secretly envious of the patients themselves when he had first met Ella. His life was, he felt, extraordinary. As the war-torn world became more and more fractured, so his own existence became complete, coherent.

Harry often found himself scrutinising a postcard of Coventry which Ella's mother had sent her and which she kept propped up on a shelf in the kitchen. It was a painting of the cathedral which the artist John Piper had hastily completed just after the bombing raid nearly two years before. Unlike the photograph in the newspaper, it positioned the observer outside the ruined structure, looking towards the east end. The artist's touch had enhanced the fragility of the tracery with its glass blown away. As if it had been an illusion as to which element supported the other, the delicate stone pattern designed to brace the glass was itself starting to collapse now that the glass had gone, as if its purpose had been torn away. The cathedral walls – what was left of them - appeared vulnerable, exposed, and yet there was still a dignity about them which spoke of a refusal to collapse any further, to resist the reduction to a pile of rubble from which the chance visitor could no longer imagine the glory of the edifice before the bombing. What Harry liked most about the painting was the effect of light. The stone walls, the ground, the sky had all been painted in sad, muted colours, but from behind the eastern apse, a shaft of radiant white light shone up from the altar or down from heaven: it was impossible to say which, and equally possible to imagine both. A bright beam of hope, saying that the ruins were not the end, but there would be a rebuilding, a reconstruction to follow the devastation.

To give the newly-weds time to settle in, Edith had told Sidney and Victor that they were not to call for a fortnight or so. Eventually, she relented, and said they could go up the lane to see if Harry and Ella were at home. They dashed up the path and banged on the door, showing each other their crossed fingers as they waited on the front step. After a few moments, Ella answered the door, and laughed with delight when she saw the lads standing there.

'How lovely to see you both.'

'Please can we come in?' said Sidney.

'But Mrs Kenton said you weren't to feel obliged if you don't want us to,' said his brother.

'Of course you can. We've missed you.' She called to the interior of the house, 'Harry, come and see who's here.' Harry came into the hallway from the kitchen, pleased as his wife to discover who the unexpected visitors were.

'Come and have something to drink. How are you both? Would you like to go into the garden?' He led the boys through the house and back outside. Now they were a little older, he had been showing them the rudiments of gardening, and had allocated them a tiny patch of the vegetable plot. They ran over to inspect their little square of carrots, potatoes and leeks. In the spring they had helped

Harry to plant runner beans which Harry had now strung up with a wigwam of canes. They were amazed to see how much everything had grown in the few weeks since they had last been there, and their uncomplicated responses reminded Harry of his own childlike delight in growing things.

Ella came out with some lemonade and biscuits for the boys. She put the tray on the grass and they plonked themselves down in front of Harry and Ella, who sat on the bench.

'What have you been up to, anyway?' said Harry.

'Oh nothing much. You know, school, homework. Helping Mrs Kenton. We've had another ride on Captain. And we helped the land girls do some clearing.'

'No, I helped,' said Victor. 'You just loafed about.'

'No I didn't,' said his brother. 'Someone had to keep watch for enemy aircraft.'

They bickered on for a few more turns, biffed each other more or less playfully, then Victor whispered in Sidney's ear. 'Go on, ask them.'

'No, you ask them. You're the eldest.'

'No, you ask them. It was your idea.'

'Ask us what?' Harry wanted to know.

'You say.'

'No, you say.'

'Victor, you ask us,' said Ella.

'Well, the other night we were wondering, now you've got married, and when the war ends, you know, our mum might not want us back in London and we were wondering,

288

if we promised not to fight, if we could come and live here with you?' He turned away in embarrassment and gave his brother a thump. Harry and Ella looked at each other and smiled.

'Can we? Please?' asked Sidney. 'We promise to be good.'

'I think your mother will be delighted to have you back. Don't you remember how much you missed her when you first came here? Don't you want to go home?'

'I suppose so, but we can't remember what it's like. And we're having fun here. Mr Bartlett has told us we can go and ride Captain every week as long as we do a few jobs for him.'

Ella said they couldn't make any promises about what would happen at the end of the war, but she and Harry would think about another treat for the boys, maybe to the cinema, a suggestion which was met with whoops of excitement. She had already taken them several times, and *Dumbo* had now become a central character in some of their made-up stories of Mowgli. Harry wasn't sure about the liberty they had taken with Kipling, but Ella thought the writer would have been rather amused by it.

Having grown up in a city, it had always been very easy for Ella to get to the cinema and she went as often as possible. She had an eclectic taste, had enjoyed *The Wizard of Oz* as much as *Gone with the Wind* and *The Maltese Falcon*, but lately she had developed an enthusiasm for Hitchcock thrillers, especially *Rebecca*, which was one of her favourite novels. She was a huge fan of Celia Johnson, whom she had seen perform the role of the second Mrs de Winter at the theatre in London. When she explained the plot to Harry, he pulled a bemused face.

'So, this young woman can't understand why Mr de Winter has married her because he was clearly so besotted with his beautiful first wife?'

'That's what she's led to think. But later she discovers the truth, that Mr de Winter hated the first wife and it's his new wife he really loves.'

'Why didn't he tell her that in the first place?'

'If I try to explain, I'll give too much of the story away.'

'Well, I'm more than happy with my first wife, and I hope she knows it.'

Ella laughed and pointed to the local newspaper. 'Look, *Bambi*'s on soon. We could take the boys to that.'

So they took the boys to see *Bambi*. Although Victor pretended that he was getting a bit old for such stories, they noticed him wipe away a tear or two at the death of Bambi's mother, while Sidney wept openly. Maybe it hadn't been such a good choice for two young evacuees, but by the end of the film they had cheered up and were back to taunting each other.

'I saw you wipe your eyes,' said Sidney.

'Did not.'

'Did so.'

'But did you enjoy it?' said Harry.

'Yes, we did. Thank you for taking us.'

The next time Ella and Harry went to the cinema was a few weeks later. Celia Johnson was appearing in a film about the Royal Navy, playing the wife of a sea captain based on Lord Mountbatten. It was the first full-length film in which she had starred, and Ella persuaded Harry to go with her. 'Come on,' she said, 'you'll enjoy the music if nothing else.' They managed to get to a matinée one Saturday afternoon.

Harry, not expecting to enjoy a film about the war, especially when it portrayed events that had occurred so recently, was pleasantly surprised. He did enjoy the music, but most of all he found himself involved in the personal stories of the shipwrecked sailors of HMS Torrin and the rescued men of the Dunkirk evacuation. Yet the blending of fact and fiction troubled him, that complete, tidy packaging of facts into a tale that in reality was still being played out, and for who knew how much longer? Again, Harry had an uncomfortable feeling that for him the war had not really started, even though he had relinquished so much in order to devote the long tedious hours of his daily employment to the national cause. The film had reawakened his fear that soon more would be demanded of him, some requirement that he give up the life he knew and loved in Bottle Green, a presentiment he preferred to keep to himself.

On the way home from the matinee, Ella was very quiet.

'So how was Celia Johnson? Did she come up to expectations?'

'Yes, I think so. Except the way she played that part...'

'Go on.'

'Well, I don't think I could be like that if I were in her place. You know... forbearing, brave about her husband being away so much, and in danger. I'd be in pieces from the worry.'

Her fears touched his thoughts so closely, that all Harry could do was take her hand and squeeze it tight.

One thing Harry liked enormously about Ella was her cheerfulness, her refusal to be worn down by the war. The only time he had ever seen her go to pieces was that day when she heard about the bombing of Coventry. Even then, she had quickly found the strength to hold herself together. Otherwise, she seemed indomitable, despite her remarks about the wife of Captain Kinross. It was only the severe headaches she sometimes suffered which made her weak and vulnerable. She would come home from Hall Place looking pale and drawn, and sink into the armchair, leaning forward and holding her temples between her thumb and forefinger as if to release the pressure. Harry got to know the pattern of these attacks. He would take off her shoes and fetch her some tea. Then he would help her up to bed, drawing the curtains no matter what time of day it was. When she awoke from her deep sleep, the headache had invariably gone and, apart from looking a little washed out, she was back to her normal self.

'Do you think you should see the doctor?' Harry asked when this had happened several times in as many months.

'Maybe,' she said. 'I've always been prone to headaches, though. I did see a specialist in Coventry but he couldn't find anything the matter.'

Harry didn't like to press her although he would have felt happier if she'd gone to see Dr Roberts. 'Perhaps you could have a word with one of the doctors at Hall Place?' And then, not wanting to appear pushy, he let the matter drop.

By 1943, it felt as if the war might go on forever. Harry, whose life was now defined by his marriage to Ella, found it hard to recall the peacetime world he had known before he met her or to imagine what their future might be like when peace finally, somehow, was restored. It seemed better to live in the present. They had settled into a routine, and they were happy. When Harry wasn't working at the factory, he spent a considerable number of hours volunteering for the Red Cross, much of it at Hall Place. He and Ella spent most of their free time at home. If they were alone, they often sat in the garden talking, filling in the spaces of the years before they had met, moulding their separate lives into a shared history. They made a point of keeping an eye on Edith, who was less robust than she had been at the outbreak of war and was finding it an increasing struggle to look after the evacuees. Mr Kenton, who was working long hours at the farm, complained he had no energy for anything else. Whenever possible, Harry and Ella looked after Victor and Sidney or went down to visit them all at Edith's house, where Harry would help tidy the garden, and Ella helped with the housework. On Sundays, shifts permitting, they went to church. Mr Leonard, also feeling the strain of the passing years, had now relented and let Harry start playing again for some of the services. So if Harry had time to sit at his piano, he devoted it to practising hymns and voluntaries, promising Ella that one day soon he would start learning her latest request, Liszt's *Liebestraum*. He just needed to get hold of the sheet music.

On their first wedding anniversary, they walked to Warren Woods, taking a picnic with them.

'Can you believe a year has passed so quickly?' Ella wanted to know.

'Much too quickly,' said Harry. 'I don't want it to go so fast. Do you?'

'Only so that the war will end. Imagine what peacetime will be like. You can go back to gardening. The boys can go home to their mother. Who knows, I might finally get to meet Frank...'

They found a spot in the shade to sit and eat, and remind themselves of what they had been doing this time last year. For a while, it was possible to forget that they were nearly four years into a war that had the whole world in its grip, or so it seemed. Harry wondered how many more anniversaries they would celebrate with the papers dominated by news of victories and defeats in all corners of the globe.

By the time of their second wedding anniversary in 1944, something exciting was in the air. For days, rumours had been spreading through the village that the armed forces were on the move. Camps in the area were reported to be empty, and everyone had noticed the increased military traffic along the Bath Road. It was a Red Cross flag day and Ella had agreed to take up what she called 'her lucky pitch' on the spot where Harry had proposed to her. He had set off early to catch the works bus to his factory. When he arrived home later that day, Ella was already there, along with Sidney and Victor, who were waiting for him at the gate. Harry laughed when he saw them.

'I know why you're waiting there,' he said.

'Have you heard the news then – about the landings?'

'I have indeed.'

Inside, they took it in turns to reveal how they had learnt about the allied invasion of France. Sidney and Victor had been told at school. The headmaster had called a special assembly and made the announcement to the children, who then stood and sang the national anthem, waving Union Jacks that had been distributed by one of the teachers. Ella had suspected something was going on when, late that morning, she had become particularly busy with her flag sale. People started putting large donations in her collecting tin, florins and half crowns rather than pennies and sixpences. Eventually, a passer-by who stopped to buy a flag told Ella what she had heard on the wireless just after 10 o'clock. Harry had heard the news at lunchtime. An enterprising member of staff had arranged a small concert for everyone in the canteen. When it was due to begin, the manager came in and addressed the workforce, his voice shaking with emotion. 'I am sure you will all wish to know,' he said, 'that this morning the allied forces have landed in France.' The news was met with silence, and then, after a few moments, someone at the back had started singing 'Land of hope and glory', the whole crowd of workers joining in, many with tears running down their faces, Harry included.

'How does it go?' Victor wanted to know. Harry went into the sitting room, opened the piano and sang it for them.

'Play it again please,' said Victor. They were quick to pick up the words and the melody, and made Harry play it a third time. Victor put his arm round his brother and they swayed from side to side as they sang 'God who made thee mighty, make thee mightier yet'.

'We came to see if you want to come to church,' said Sidney when they had finished. The vicar had decided to hold a special service at 6 o'clock to pray for the success of the invasion. Before they left school, they had been asked to invite their neighbours to attend.

'It'll be an unusual way of celebrating our anniversary,' Harry said to Ella.

'Well, it'll certainly be one to remember when we're old and grey,' she said, linking her arm through his.

The weeks succeeding the Normandy landings were especially busy at Hall Place as the wounded of Omaha, Sword and Juno beaches began to take the places once occupied by the wounded of Dunkirk. Ella was working long hours and often came home feeling exhausted, her head thumping with tiredness. Harry would insist she put her feet up and take a nap while he made her some soup. She always seemed a little better after she had eaten, and she would smile as she listened to him play the repertoire she enjoyed so much, the old songs his mother had loved, the hymns they had had at their wedding, and the *Liebestraum* he had almost finished learning. If she was half asleep, he would practise the hymns for Sunday service, his foot on the pedal to soften the volume and not disturb her. Then, when Harry had finished playing, they would turn on the wireless and listen to the news, as day by day the allied forces gained ground over the Germans in northern Europe.

By December it really did seem as if the end of the war might not be too far away. Paris had been liberated some months before and by and large the allied onslaught was proving successful. But times were still hard: V2 rockets rained down on south-east England, rationing was tightened, and cold weather set in for the duration. A letter arrived from Frank Chandler, reporting from 'fly-bomb alley', somewhat deserted since the younger boys had been evacuated to Somerset. 'But life goes on more or less as normal for the older lads,' he wrote, 'and the barrage balloons will make unusual Christmas decorations.' Harry passed the letter to Ella to read.

'You know your mother often talked to me about the time you took her to Farningham, not long before the war started. Frank must have made a lasting impression on her.'

'Well, he certainly made a lasting impression on me.'

'I know. That's why I'm so keen to meet him. In the meantime, I'll have to rely on you for information,' she said, hoping to draw him out and surprised that for once he remained silent.

And so Christmas came, the sixth Christmas of the war, the third of Harry and Ella's marriage, and they would both be on duty at Hall Place for most of it. It was still bitterly cold, so it was a relief on Christmas Eve to enjoy a few hours by themselves at home in the warm. And that afternoon, Harry led the conversation back to Frank, telling Ella far more than he had told her so far. She knew about the English lessons, and the way Frank had encouraged Harry to read and to enjoy poetry. She knew about Frank's sense of humour, and his kindness to the boys when they were new and feeling somewhat bewildered. She could imagine the cottage where he lived on the edge of the school grounds, its study with the two friendly armchairs by the fire and the increasingly crowded shelves of books. But now Harry added more, about remembered conversations with Frank and about a quality he possessed which quietly fostered Harry's belief, first settling on him gently, like mist, as he sat in the school chapel with Frank at dusk, that there need not be silence between this world and the world which we cannot see but involuntarily gather towards us.

'I think that's what drew me to him in the first place,' said Harry, 'that spiritual quality.'

'Not to mention that he introduced you to your favourite poem.'

'That too. But he was alone and yet never quite alone. That's how I've always felt even when I was too young to realise it.'

Ella smiled. 'You'll never be alone now, Harry. Not now.' She picked up Harry's sheet music from the table. 'Will you play for me?' she said, handing him her selection.

'Shall I draw the curtains?' he asked, getting up and switching on a table lamp.

'No, not just yet. There's still some light in the sky. Can you see?'

So the curtains were left open a little longer and an unexpected visitor, hurrying to call and get home before the blackout, would have been glad of the soft light coming from Harry and Ella's sitting room, but, glancing inside, might have hesitated to knock and disturb the peaceful scene within.

V
2009

25 July 2009

Today, I am distracted by thoughts of another Harry, Harry Patch, the longest surviving veteran soldier of the Great War, who has died at the extraordinary age of 111. Almost obsessively, I have watched the news reports which have run throughout the day, and found myself calculating what the Elston brothers were doing at the time of the events which marked out Harry Patch's early life. He was born in 1898, the year Violet married George and nearly nine years before my Harry was born. Fred, a year younger than Harry Patch and still officially underage for posting abroad, was serving at the Somme when Patch turned eighteen and became liable for conscription. While Harry and Ron were settling into their new school in September 1917, Harry Patch was already in France, fighting in the Battle of Ypres, where he took a shrapnel wound, demonstrating more luck than the three companions from his Lewis gun team who died in the same blast and were mourned by Patch for the rest of his life. By the time my Harry was reading *The Jungle Book* for the first time, his namesake, having been sent back to England, was recovering from his wound and preparing to return to France. As Harry and Ron sat in their Kent classrooms on that chilly morning in November 1918 watching the hour hand of the clock move towards eleven, Harry Patch waited with his fellow soldiers

303

on the Isle of Wight for a rocket to be sent up from camp headquarters, a signal that a ceasefire had been agreed and an armistice signed.

The nation has fallen in love with Harry Patch. This is clear from the media coverage of his death. But this emotion takes many forms, not least the unfaltering tenderness towards a survivor who can connect us to those we have lost. How precious was the last Englishman living to have experienced the horrors of the trenches, a man who, in the treacherous mud of Passchendaele, can have had no idea that he would live for more than a century, more cherished, more esteemed the older he became, the embodiment of Kipling's fighting Tommy, the subject of many books and of a poem by the poet laureate, the recipient of an honorary degree, the freedom of a city, the gratitude of a nation.

If I am honest, Harry Patch's life is only tangential to the life of the man I have been writing about. Almost ten years older than my Harry, his early experiences of the Great War were dramatically different. Yet there is something I am trying to tease out of Patch's life which will bring me closer to the subject of my own private narrative. What is it that draws me so strongly to the life of the celebrated veteran? I am clearly not alone in my interest. I scroll down the extensive collection of messages that have been left about him on the BBC website, messages from people of all ages who have found something in Patch's life that has touched their own. He helped the young to understand more about history, more about the waste and futility of war. For others, he epitomised a generation that is owed a nation's ransom, his modesty, dignity and consideration for others making him a worthy vessel for that indebtedness. What can I add about Harry Patch that has not already been said? All I can say is that somehow, through Harry Patch, who was already alive when Harry Elston was born, and who drew his last breath and slipped away only a few hours ago as I sat at my desk peering into the lost decades of the past, I have a channel by which I can reach back to the younger man to whom this is dedicated.

I am fascinated by the attention afforded to Harry Patch, feted by the nation. Online, I watch again the BBC obituary. I see Harry, obliged to depend on a wheelchair, being brought onto the stage during the Festival of Remembrance at the Royal Albert Hall. Even the Queen is standing to show her respect. I see him with a well-known historian, his biographer, who has taken him back to the battlefields, now peaceful rolling farmland, where Harry is still able to discern in its gentle contours the brutal set of his horrific theatre of war. I see him sitting beside the poet laureate, who reads in his sonorous voice his poem, 'The Five Acts of Harry Patch'. 'Patch, Harry Patch, that's a good name,' it goes. 'Shakespearean.' It is a good name. Perhaps it is the name that attracts me even more than the life. Henry. Henry Elston. Harry to his family and friends. A very good name. A name that stretches down the years, redolent of a distant generation, that lasts the test of time. The poet laureate finishes reading and the camera zooms in on Harry Patch. 'Thank you,' he mouths as the poet shakes his hand. Harry Patch. I zoom in on your life. I can watch its scenes with the press of a computer key but all I have for my Harry is a tiny collection of faded photographs and tattered documents, the faint traces of a life lived in what is now Jennie's house and in another house which was demolished over twenty years ago. From these meagre gatherings, I have tried to reconstruct the unnumbered acts of Harry Elston and now I have him waiting in the wings for one more defining scene.

For eighty years, Harry Patch never spoke about the war, not even to his wife. Not until he was one hundred years old and found himself in the gaze of the media did he realise that speaking the unspeakable might do some good. My Harry, who died when Harry Patch still had more than thirty years to live, also spoke very little about his early life. So much of what I have written has been surmise, deduction, invention. But I am in little doubt how much the years at Farningham School meant to him since throughout the sixties and seventies, when I knew him, he would make the annual pilgrimage to Kent for the Old Boys' Reunion. Sometimes I would go with Harry - with him, and with Ron and Ivy, my grandparents. On a summer's afternoon, we would assemble in the school chapel for a short service, after which Ron would show me the choir stalls he helped to carve and construct, while the rest of the Old Boys, some alone, some with their wives, would mill around on the grass outside, shaking hands and remarking how another year had flown past. Usually we took a stroll through the grounds of what was now a peaceful retirement village. Among the bungalows, the schoolhouse still remained, but it had been converted into dwellings, this place where Harry first heard Frank Chandler, grieving for the loss of his nephew, declaiming Kipling's 'If'. Tea was served in the primary school down the hill, opposite the parish church where Mrs Shepherd was buried. And then later, before heading home, a pint or two in the pub as the long shadows of the viaduct arches stretched out along the river and across the valley.

Something else about Harry Patch emerges as significant. The poet noticed it, gave intimations of it, describing Harry, late in life in his nursing home, still whispering with his long dead companions on the Lewis team. Patch himself alludes to it, recalling a wounded soldier who died in his presence, certain to his last breath that his mother was waiting in the next world to welcome him home. What did he learn from the Great War, a journalist asks Harry. 'I shall always remember,' rasps the veteran, 'that death is not the end.'

It is nearly a year since I first knocked on the door of Jennie's house, almost as long since I started to reconstruct the story of Harry's life. Now the story is almost told, I still find myself disinclined to write about the events which took place in February 1945. I have avoided them once, by leapfrogging not only the war itself but with it those terrible weeks towards its conclusion, and taking Harry instead to the other side of the world already carrying his desolation with him. I took him to Singapore, filled his head with thoughts of the distant past in the hope this would spare me (and him, I suppose) the pain of confronting his more recent history. I brought him back to England and got him settled once more not, as I might have hoped, far away from Bottle Green and close to Ron, who could keep a brotherly eye on him, but less than three miles from his former home and less than a mile from the spot where Ella is buried. Even now, I might avoid telling this most painful part of the story were it not for the fact that it is at the heart of everything I have come to understand about Harry. But I cannot make Harry an actor in these scenes. I cannot inflict his pain anew. Instead, I will leave him for now playing the piano that Christmas Eve at dusk, the curtains open to catch the last light of the day, with Ella sitting in the armchair humming along to the Londonderry Air and feeling grateful to be free for once of the headaches that seem to have plagued her more frequently in recent weeks.

When the new Coventry Cathedral was consecrated in May 1962, Harry mentioned how much he would like to go and see it. This is one of my earliest memories of him, several years later, on a family outing to Coventry. It was summer, but grey and overcast. We picked Harry up in Knowl Hill and cut across country to the start of the M1, the first time any of us had travelled on the new motorway, this celebrated road of the future. But it was the sense of expectation in the car, Harry's quiet excitement about seeing the resurrected city for himself, that redeemed what, to a child, was a long and sometimes tedious journey.

Only one photograph has survived of that day, taken as it happens from the same angle – standing within the ruins and looking down the nave towards the altar - as the newspaper image which Harry showed to Violet the week after the bombing. Without the piles of rubble, the space seems much larger, and many people, locals and visitors, stroll around the area, their fashions showing that this is the sixties, when hemlines were creeping up and young men wanted to look and dress like the Beatles. To the left of the photograph, the new cathedral rises like a miracle above the ruined north wall of the original building. The stumps of the medieval columns punctuate the open space of the nave, and are being used as seats. There is no sign of Harry, who has maybe wandered off by himself. Only now, so many decades later, do I have any notion of what he must have been thinking about that day, what he must have been feeling as he wandered around the old and new churches, the old one still whispering of shocking devastation, the new proclaiming that life can, phoenix-like, begin again.

That evening, we returned late to Knowl Hill to drop Harry home. He insisted we stop and have some supper. While the adults talked in the kitchen, I perched on the faded and musty sofa and stared at a curious painting on the wall depicting a darkened room where people sat around a table without communicating with each other. In the spaces behind them hovered half-seen preternatural figures who somehow completed the ensemble, as if the seated people, although apparently oblivious to them, were comfortable in the knowledge they were there. I had never seen a picture quite like it but even as a child I believe I had an inkling of what it meant. Harry came in and saw me gazing at his painting. 'Have you seen this?' he asked, taking another smaller frame from its hook on the wall, revealing an unfaded rectangle in the wallpaper. 'You like poetry, don't you?' The item he handed me filled my lap. I held it carefully, avoiding putting my fingers on the glass, as I read Kipling's poem for the first time while Harry sat beside me. When I had finished reading, I handed it back and watched as he returned the beloved object, his totem, to the place where it had hung for nearly twenty years.

After supper, Harry played the piano for a while. I had seen a piano being played at school, but the teachers only played hymns as we filed in and out of assembly or sang between the reading and the prayer. This was something different altogether, the elaborate arm movements of Liszt or the tremulous hand movements of Harry's party piece, 'The Lost Chord'. Every now and then, a note would sound wrong, even to my untrained ear, and I crept over to the piano to watch Harry's arthritic fingers searching for the right position.

'Thumbs are bad today,' he muttered to himself, as he closed the piano lid and reached for his cigarettes.

I sometimes wonder what Harry, who never learned to drive, never travelled abroad after his army service in the

Far East, who hardly ever watched the television unless there was a gardening programme, would have thought of the world in the twenty-first century, the world which Harry Patch lived to see. What would he have made of modern warfare, so extensively televised, its every development so immediately available for reporting? These days, I often think of him when I switch on the news channel to watch the repatriation ceremonies of the fallen soldiers of Afghanistan. I imagine him sitting beside me, in awe at the huge Globemaster aircraft, its belly heavy with coffins, circling the airfield before landing at RAF Lyneham. A pause ensues, followed by the dread moment when the underbelly lowers its ramp and the first group of pallbearers, tiny from a distance, emerges to bring out the flag-draped coffin, their legs appearing first, like a curious insect moving tentatively onto a bleak concrete terrain. The last post is played as the coffin is carried across to the waiting hearse. Then some while later, the scene switches to nearby Wootton Bassett, its high street lined with onlookers waiting to pay their respects. Harry and I watch, along with thousands of others, as eventually the funeral cortege approaches. The waiting crowd falls silent, and the only sound is the steady tolling of the church bell. The hearses come slowly towards the camera, passing a row of standard bearers, who gently dip their flags out of respect for those who have given their lives. Flowers are thrown onto the black limousines which carry the precious burden of the dead. Applause breaks out among the crowd. After the procession has passed, people start to disperse. One or two are interviewed by the BBC commentator. Some have no direct connection with today's dead, but have come because they too have lost loved ones, perhaps in an earlier war, and with no hope of repatriation. They quickly wipe their eyes and clear their throats. Beside me, I wonder if Harry still feels the diminishing shock of death and weeps again for Kipling's son, for Albert Kenton, Reginald Chandler, William Holloway – maybe now standing shoulder to shoulder with the fallen of Afghanistan – and I see his tears merge with the tears of all those who weep today, and with those who wept for Harry Patch and his generation. So many tears, they flow together and rise into a flood.

I have left Harry at his piano, playing to Ella on a wintry but sunny afternoon during that last Christmas of the second world war, but time moves inexorably on, and soon it is January, February, and Harry has applied to join the Royal Army Medical Corps. Ella continues to work as a nurse at Hall Place. The newspapers continue to report allied successes as the troops advance across northern Europe. One evening, Ella comes home more exhausted than usual, pressing her hand against her forehead as if to hold back the pain. She staggers through the front door and asks Harry to help her to bed. Upstairs, he pulls off her shoes as she collapses, still dressed, onto the eiderdown, and buries her head in the pillow. When, after an hour, she is no better, Harry rushes down the road on his bicycle to fetch the doctor, who comes at once and quickly decides an ambulance is needed. By midnight Ella is lying in a hospital bed with Harry by her side, holding her hand. In Germany, the allied forces are bombing Dresden, unleashing a firestorm many times worse than the one which devastated Coventry.

Harry outlived Ella by nearly forty years. After his return from the Far East, his life slipped into a simple routine and he had no wish for diversion or excitement. Apart from his annual trip to Kent and occasional family events such as a visit to Ron and Ivy or our own expedition to Coventry, he was content to spend his days quietly in Knowl Hill, tending the garden at Hall Place, and playing the organ at church on Sunday mornings. He visited the graveyard at least once a week, sometimes more, to tend the graves of his loved ones. Change happened only gradually. He saw Joe and Norman from time to time, but eventually their contact with each other dwindled to a Christmas card and an occasional telephone call. Ella's aunt and uncle at Linden Hill became too old and frail for such a large house and moved away to a cottage by the sea, not far from Doris's younger sister. Harry was sad to see them go. He never visited Linden Hill again, although he often walked past the house to peer over the hedge and remember the happy times of his childhood and, later, his courtship and marriage to Ella. When Edith Kenton died in 1950, Jessie stayed on in the family home in Bottle Green and the meetings with Mrs Leath continued for a while until she decided to retire or, as she put it, 'to stop asking the spirits to come to me and wait patiently until it's my time to go to them'.

Victor and Sidney, the evacuees, had gone back to their mother in Clapham in the summer of 1945, while Harry was in India. They kept in touch but did not see Harry again until they were grown men working in the city. They arrived one Saturday afternoon in Victor's car, a Morgan, top down, hooting the horn excitedly as they pulled up outside Harry's house. They leapt out without bothering to open the doors and ran up the path together as if they were still small boys. Harry was overjoyed to see them.

'You haven't changed at all,' they told him, meaning it.

'You have,' said Harry, wiping away his tears.

He showed them round his house and they piled the presents they had brought him onto the kitchen table, flowers, beer, chocolate from their mother, some cigarettes and two huge cigars. Harry was overwhelmed. They carried the tea tray out into the garden where they told Harry all about their lives in London, their jobs, their parents, and the cycling holiday they had just returned from in Scotland. They were both car mad and had argued that morning whether they would come in Victor's Morgan or Sidney's Vauxhall. The Morgan had won on account of the weather.

'Come on, Harry, we're going to take you out for a spin,'

'In a two-seater?'

'That's no problem. You sit next to Victor and I'll follow up the rear on your bicycle. Where shall we go?'

Harry decided, with this arrangement, it was best not to take them too far. He suggested they could see the gardens at Hall Place and then go for a drink at The Old House at Home. Victor made sure Harry was comfortable in the car before getting in himself. Harry grinned at Sidney who was wheeling Harry's old bike into the road.

'Better than a carthorse, eh?' said Sidney as he set off in front of them at breakneck speed.

When they arrived at Hall Place, Harry showed Victor where to park, round the back by the kitchen entrance.

'You sure your employer doesn't mind us being here?' Victor asked. It was the first time he and Sidney had visited the grounds.

'No, but try not to shout your heads off.'

Harry showed them the flower beds and his most recent project, a rockery down in a damp sunken area beyond the formal part of the garden. From there, they could get a good view of the best side of the house.

'This is where Ella worked during the war, isn't it?' said Victor, the first time she had been mentioned since their arrival.

'That's right,' said Harry. 'That's how we met.'

Victor was quiet. 'Isn't it difficult working here now that... after what happened?'

'Not at all,' said Harry. 'I like it.'

'We were so sorry when we heard. We liked her so much, you know. Both of you. Do you remember when we came and asked you to adopt us?'

315

'Of course. We were very flattered. Not sure we could have put up with all your fighting though.'

'Oh we stopped fighting when... when you went away,' said Victor. 'Lost the heart for it, I suppose.'

'Well, I'm glad you're good chums now,' said Harry. 'I'm pleased. And very pleased to see you.'

After that, Victor and Sidney visited Harry every few months, taking it in turns with their cars. Sometimes, they would bring flowers for Ella's grave and they would walk with Harry to the graveyard, chatting as they went along the lane, but falling silent as they stepped through the gate. Harry liked them being there and believed Ella did too. It never felt like an intrusion. On the contrary, it was as if he was being accompanied by the sons they never had.

And so Harry's life went on, year by year, no disasters, no calamities. After Mrs Leath stopped making private visits, he started attending a weekly spiritualist meeting instead, at which he made some new and lasting friends. When he retired from Hall Place, he lavished all his attention on his own garden, a source of increasing delight in his later years. And when the wind was in the right direction, he still opened the piano lid to tackle the pieces that had presented such a challenge when he first learnt them thirty years earlier.

Harry died one fine day of spring when the air suddenly contained that hint of freshness which only comes when winter is well and truly finished. He had spent the morning doing some chores in the kitchen, listening to the radio and thinking about what he would plant in the garden that year but unable to muster the energy to begin the task that day. At lunchtime, he made himself a sandwich and, deciding it wasn't quite warm enough outside, took it into the sitting room with the newspaper and sat down in his armchair. He didn't eat his sandwich but fell instead into a light doze which turned into a deep sleep from which he did not wake. One of his friends, calling early that evening as arranged to go with him to the spiritualist meeting, was concerned when there was no answer. Looking through the window, he saw Harry asleep in his chair, the newspaper on the floor, and the uneaten sandwich on the table beside him.

I wonder what Harry thought about as he slipped into his final sleep that afternoon. In that disorientated state, I hope he did not relive the awful memory of Ella's last days, when she lay in hospital, barely knowing him or responding to what went on around her. Or that terrible moment, in the days following her death when he hardly knew what had happened or how to go on, when the doctor who had looked after Ella called him in to discuss the post mortem and to ask Harry if he knew his wife was expecting a baby.

In his final minutes, I hope Harry dreamed of happy times, playing with his brothers in Warren Woods, travelling home with Ron after their first year away at school, tending the gardens at Hall Place, sitting with Ella in the afternoon sun in the first weeks of their married life in the house at Bottle Green. This is how I want to leave him, in his favourite armchair, a faint smile on his lips, drifting away to the *Blumenlied*, thinking of Ella, no longer anticipating their long-awaited reunion.